K. R. QUILL

The Century Soldier

Contents

Content Warnings

This book openly portrays struggles with mental health, specifically PTSD, depression, and suicidality. If you or someone you love is struggling with mental health, please connect them or yourself to a mental health professional.

There is a scene briefly depicting child SA on page 142, should you need to skip it.

There will also be scenes briefly depicting violence. Should you need to skip those scenes, please do so.

Additionally, there is a mature, X-rated scene at the end of Chapter 15.

Dedication

To those who never get to recover, those in the healing process, and the healed.
I see you. You're strong when you may not want to be.
You're valued in this world.

May we push for a better future.

Chapter 1

W hy does my brain feel fuzzy? My thoughts aren't...where...
immense pain...
Cold. It's *freezing cold.*

Wait, my name, what's my name? *I... I...*

I concentrated until I felt my brain hurt. No name. But I must have a name, I've got to have a name...

There was a woman's voice, calling a name. It sounded familiar, too familiar to be coincidence.

"Eryn, Eryn, wake up. Wake *up!*" said the voice, rising in pitch as she continued.

I forced my eyelids open. I immediately regretted the decision as a harsh white light blinded me, and I could suddenly feel a scratchy piece of fabric that covered my body.

"You're awake!" the lady squealed, making me flinch at the sudden sound. I squinted through the light, trying to solidify the blurry person beside me.

She seemed sweet. Spiky blond hair stuck up from her head like icicles growing the wrong way, and her ice-blue eyes had large, dark bags underneath. From the way she held herself, I doubted they were natural dark bags. She held her thin, skeletal frame as tall as she could, but it was clear that if she hadn't been leaning on nearby surfaces, she probably would've fallen over.

My eyes finally focused. I could make out a symbol on the right side of her chest. I wasn't given time to figure it out before the lady started speaking.

"Hi, my name is Celestina! Don't worry, you're peachy! You'll probs feel a bit fatigued, but that'll shoo in no time. Can you sit up for me?" And she smiled at me.

Her quick speaking gave me a small headache, but on a groan, I sat up on the metal table I was lying on and took a look around the room. There was nothing special about it. Metal walls, door, table, and no windows. I turned slowly to the girl, careful not to make myself dizzy or sick, but I had a metallic taste in my mouth that gave me a sense of unease.

"Where am I?" I asked, the words coming out disjointed and monotone. My voice was weak and scratchy as if I was on my deathbed. I coughed, and the girl smiled again.

"This is Vue Institute, the world's leading SMC! And outside of that, you're in Lorinia City!" She moved to a wall and pressed a small depression. "This place was founded by Theo Vue and his partner, Selena Vue. They're Hawkings, for sure. Mr. Vue was known for his atomic research. Dr. Vue is more G&E based. Their work still lives on. Dr. Vue still works here occasionally, but she's getting really old. Mr. Vue died before we had the chance to use the Elder Treatment."

Wait, what? This seemed so wrong.

"Hold on," I said, my voice still sounding scratchy. "Why are you talking funny? What's an SMC? G&E? It sounds like you're speaking a different language. And, while you're answering my questions, why am I in a… hospital? Am I still on Earth?"

She stared at me for a moment, letting my questions hang in the air.

"Eryn, I don't know how to say this so you won't freak, but… um… We think you've been in medically caused stasis for… one hundred years. There was a vault and a file… we just discovered you, or else you'd have been awake sooner," she said, snapping her mouth closed at the end of the sentence.

I processed this information, biting my lip as my fingers tapped a quick rhythm on the hospital bed. That could explain why I couldn't remember jack squat. Would being frozen for one hundred years cause memory loss?

"As for the other things, an SMC is a Science and Medical Center, G&E is Genetics and Engineering. Yes, you're technically in a hospital, if you want to call it that. And yes, you're still on Earth," Celestina provided, giving me a weak smile.

"I can't remember anything. Well, no memories or anything like that," I said. "Is that normal?"

"Given that you were in a cryolab, potentially. There's some wack things that being cryogenically frozen can cause, most of which haven't been figured out. Well, except for some organ and muscle damage. But it makes sense to me that you could've lost memories from that," she responded, nodding thoughtfully.

I moved around uncomfortably as I felt the hospital gown begin to catch on my skin in weird ways, making me feel itchy and very annoyed.

"Do you have anything else for me to wear?" I said, the words coming out a little harsher than I meant them to.

"Not yet. I have to run some tests."

I stopped scratching my back and looked up to glare at Celestina. "This thing is very itchy, I'll have you know. Can't I do this in more... comfortable clothes?"

She crossed her arms and shook her head. "No. Lie down."

With a groan, I did as asked, fidgeting constantly from the itchy fabric.

She had me move all my muscles in different directions until she declared they were completely fine, which was accompanied by a surprised shake of the head. Then she did some sort of scan to see my organs, according to her. Apparently, if nothing was wrong with my muscles, something had to be wrong with my organs. However, the scan came up clean.

"Weird, this is so *weird*," Celestina muttered, looking at pictures of my insides up on the little screen, leaning heavily on the desk in front of her.

To lighten the mood, I said, "Well, I mean, you are looking at my guts."

She gave a half-smile in my direction, then went back to studying the picture.

With a sigh, I looked around the room again and noticed a pile of clothes. "Wait, are those for me?" I asked Celestina.

She glanced at where I was pointing and nodded. "You can change now. I'm all done."

Growling at the fact there had been other clothes, I slid off the table, wobbled a bit, and blinked until I regained my balance and stopped seeing floating silver dots. I carefully went to the pile of clothes to unfold them. They looked comfortable, so I shrugged out of the hospital gown I had on and pulled on the set. My brain was insanely happy about the fact that my pants were cargo pants and had a plethora of pockets, and the fabric was also decorated with a light, brown-green camo pattern. I slipped on the black tee, then examined the last item.

It was a red leather jacket, plain except for an embroidered patch. A black dragon, curled around a miniature Earth, rested on the sleeve. I put it on, loving the worn, familiar feel, even if I couldn't place it. Last, I sat on the floor to pull on a pair of black combat boots, which fit me perfectly.

I pushed myself back up to my feet, feeling comfortable and ready for anything. I sank into a position that felt natural, but I couldn't remember what it was for. My right foot was back, feet a little wider than shoulder-width. My elbows were pulled into my sides, fingers loose. I bounced on my feet.

My stomach then saw fit to growl, and I shot it an exasperated look, my hair falling over my face. I took a moment to grab a strand and examine it. Loose curls, and it was a reddish-gold color that looked like actual gold when the white hospital lights hit it the right way.

Turning to Celestina, I saw her still looking intently at the picture, holding it way too close to her face. "Celestina?" I asked, trying to get her attention.

"Yeppers?" she replied, bringing the picture down from her face.

"Is there any chance I could get something to eat?" I prodded, my question complemented by another hungry rumble from my abdomen.

She stared at me for a second, swayed, and then started collapsing toward the ground.

I lunged forward, getting there just in time to prevent her from hitting the floor. Lifting some of her weight, I got her onto the hospital bed.

"I'm so sorry!" she said, tears forming in her eyes.

I held her hand, feeling strangely at home in this situation. "It's okay. You look pretty exhausted."

She nodded. "That, and…"

I waited for her to finish her sentence, but her lips were sealed.

"And what?" I said gently, grateful that my voice was sounding somewhat kind.

"Well, I usually have… my supports. They help me. But the guard at the front of the SMC took them from me this morning. Said he'd seen me walk and that I didn't need it," she explained, folding into herself. "Usually, it isn't a problem, but this guy is just a jerk and knows I won't do anything about it."

"Is there a wheelchair or cane near here that you can use in the meantime?" I glanced around the room once more, seeing nothing.

"There's a closet right outside the room." Celestina nodded toward a gray door set in the wall on the other side of the room. Then, she started to get up from the bed, but her legs buckled, and I had to catch her again.

"Why don't I help you walk out there? Take some of the weight off your feet."

Celestina looked at me with a smile. "I would gratefully like that, thank you."

We arranged her arm over my shoulders so it was comfortable, then began walking toward the door. Somehow, I managed to get the door open while still supporting her weight.

At least doors hadn't changed. Yet.

She directed us to a door right beside the one we came out of. The hallway we had stepped into was relatively empty, except for a person dressed similarly to Celestina way down the hall.

Celestina opened the door to the closet and pointed to a folded contraption in the corner.

She leaned against a wall while I pulled and, managed to open the wheelchair in one try.

I set it near Celestina, and she sank into the seat.

"That's much better, thank you. Now, let's go get you something to eat. I've let you take care of me for too long already."

"I *am* starving. I haven't eaten in a hundred years," I quipped, grinning to make sure she knew it was a joke.

She chuckled. "That's true. Also, what pronouns do you use? I forgot to ask earlier. I use they/them pronouns!"

"Oh, um, she and her!" I said, caught off guard. "And they works, too."

As we ambled down the hallway, Celestina began to tell me about themself, after I asked a few questions. By the time we reached an elevator, I had learned that they had five older brothers, loved cats, and had wanted to be a medical professional ever since they were ten.

I listened to their stories with interest, absorbing all the information they gave me about themself. The elevator doors opened, the compartment empty. We stepped in, and Celestina continued their insatiable chatter on the ride down. Every so often they would use a word or a phrase that I didn't know, and I stopped them to ask them to explain it. After a few of these, Celestina told me I was just as bad as their grandmother.

The elevator beeped as we came to a stop, and the doors opened. What I assumed was the main floor was laid out before me. Gargantuan, filled with people. The majority were in some sort of lab coat or scrubs. The others were dressed in different styles; some I recognized, many I didn't. The ones I recognized, like togas and chitons, seemed out of place, and there were many styles from other countries that I didn't have names for.

Celestina took me to the cafeteria, an equally large affair as the lobby had been. Tables were scattered around the area, filled with people eating and chatting. Many people sped by us with plates, like they had somewhere to be five minutes ago. Everything was digitized, too. There wasn't a single person at the counter taking orders, just giant, neon menus sitting over a row of five rectangular boxes, all different colors. People pressed buttons above the rectangles, and after a few seconds, a tray slid into place in front of them with food on it.

"What are those?" I asked, pointing at the rectangle things.

"Food replicators. You put in your order, and it cooks your food."

They led me over to a deli on the far side. "This is the best place; it's totally rad. They have amazing soups and sandwiches." They pointed out several menu items that were their personal favorites. I decided to go with one of their suggestions, and they let out a loud "Yes!" when I told them, drawing a few curious looks from people close to us.

I pressed the buttons after Celestina put in their order, quickly getting the hang of how it worked. Celestina swiped their I.D., which had been in the pocket of their white stretch suit, through the card reader. Soon, our order was ready, and we took our food to a relatively empty table.

I took one bite, and I was in heaven. The food was extremely rich, and after a few bites, I forced myself to drink a small amount of water between each mouthful. Controlling myself, I ate slowly, letting myself adjust to eating again and savoring each delicious piece.

Halfway through our sandwiches, a boy approached our table. Celestina froze, mid bite, as the guy took the seat next to them. He seemed about our age, with chestnut brown hair and green eyes and a smile that screamed *playboy*. He was wearing a black uniform, similar to mine, except he had a metallic-looking vest and a gun holster instead of a leather jacket.

"Theo," Celestina said with venom. I felt my eyes go wide at their unfriendly tone, then turned again to look at the boy sitting beside them.

"Hi, blushy-boo. How's your day been?" he asked them with a cocky grin.

I made a noise of disapproval at his attitude. Then he turned his eyes on me, and I felt my stomach clench.

"And who is *this*, blushy-boo? A friend?" he asked Celestina, never taking his eyes off me. They glittered with mischief, and I felt like throwing up, possibly in his lap. He surveyed me like a piece of high-quality meat, which made me want to slap that cocky grin off his face.

I was about to reply, but Celestina finally found their voice. "Get the fucking flippers away, Theo. I'm not in the mood. Yerick took my supports this morning, so I'm a *little* grouchy. You understand. We don't want you here."

I nodded in a silent moment of respect at the firmness in their voice.

Theo simply laughed. "Oh, blushy-boo, I would, but I can't." Then he leaned over and grabbed a chip from Celestina's plate. They glared at him so hard, I almost thought he would catch on fire.

This time, I spoke.

"Apologize." I said, softly, layering cold steel into my voice. "And go get them their supports."

Theo huffed. "Why should I? That's a lot of work."

I glanced around the room, then leaned forward and motioned for him to lean in.

He quickly leaned in, and I grabbed the front of his shirt and twisted it, pulling him a few inches across the table. But not enough so anyone else would notice.

"Because," I started, whispering in his ear. "I've been asleep for a hundred years, and my patience is a bit thin. I would also guess that your buddy could get in trouble for taking away Celestina's supports. Get them and apologize. I won't give you another chance."

I let him go, and he landed on his seat, frozen for a brief moment. Without a word, he got up and walked quickly away.

"Oh, my shitnugget what? How... why... what... what question am I even supposed to ask here?" Celestina sputtered, eyes wide in shock. "He doesn't listen to anyone. And I've worked with him enough to know that not even his bosses can make him move like that."

I shrugged. "I don't know. I guess I can be scary?"

"You guess? I would be terrified if you had done that to me." Celestina shook their head. "Jeez, who are you? Or who were you? Before, I mean. Cause you have balls."

"Thanks, I think?" I asked, not sure what else to say. Looking back up, I saw Theo walking over with a pair of silver braces in his hands.

"Here, it won't happen again," Theo said, handing the silver braces off to Celestina. "I'm sorry."

They blinked a few times, then gave Theo a half smile. "Thanks, Theo."

Celestina leaned over to put on the braces. Getting a closer look, they were more mechanical than I thought. They strapped them on around their thigh and calf, leaving a gap where the knee bent. Once the supports were on both legs, Celestina moved them around experimentally.

"Good, they're okay. Need a little grease, but they needed it anyway. Moving on, why are you still here Theo?" Celestina asked. "You're not assigned security detail, are you?"

"I am. You know where they found..." Theo looked at me and gestured his hand.

"Eryn," I supplied.

"Eryn, right?"

Celestina shook their head. "No, my supervisor just said she had an interesting case for me since I specialize in memory loss and cryostasis degeneration. I got here this morning, they immediately brought in the cryotube, and I went to work. Boss told me to call in extra help if Eryn wasn't adjusting well."

"I'm right here," I muttered, mentally shying away from the idea of a bunch of medical professionals all in the room with me at once. That would've been too much.

Ignoring my mutterings, Theo continued, "They found her capsule in the basement of an abandoned CI facility that we were cleaning out. They've found other capsules before, but this one was the only one that seemed to have escaped the other rounds of clean out several years ago."

"CI?" I asked, looking at Celestina.

"Core Intel," they explained, glancing at me, then back at Theo. "Could they be CI?"

Theo shrugged. "Maybe. Or her capsule was just stashed down there. We don't know. We'd cleaned out that facility before, but this was the first time we found a capsule in the basement in this particular facility. The bosses thought it was odd, but they had more pressing things to worry about."

I let out a large, dramatic sigh. "Well, I suppose I might as well go. It appears as though this is a private conversation."

"You can't," Celestina said, shaking their head. "I have to stay with you. I'm a reorientation nurse. It's one of my specialties. We're a little more involved than other nurses. Especially since I have specialties in cryostasis degeneration, I'll be useful to have on hand if you start having any symptoms."

"And him?" I asked, nodding at Theo. "Why is he here?"

"Standard procedures for new wakeups. I'm your security, just in case, for the first couple of days," Theo explained.

"And what are you protecting me from?" I asked, scrunching my eyebrows.

Theo opened his mouth, then closed it and looked at Celestina.

I nodded. "Less to protect me, more to protect them from me?"

"We don't know what you might be capable of, and there's been a history of irritability and uh… outlashes." Celestina gave me a half-smile. "This is my specialty, but it doesn't come without risks. There's a reason there are very few nurses like me."

"Understandable. None of us know what I'm capable of, least of all me at this point," I said, nodding. "So, do I have to stay here, or is there a facility or something…?"

"You'll be staying with me. This is the way I do my practice. Not very many choose to do so, but I feel as though it aids with reintegration. All my patients have made a full recovery and are living successfully in society now." Celestina swung their legs out from under the table and they stood to fold up the wheelchair. "That said, let's start with our first step outside, shall we?"

I silently followed, copying Celestina as they put their trash into an incinerator. I thought that was a bit dangerous to have inside an SMC, but I suppose it worked.

Walking beside Celestina, with Theo following close behind, we stepped out into the lobby again. Celestina set the wheelchair against a wall, where it was quickly picked up by someone carrying more wheelchairs. It was still busy, bustling with people moving through the building. I stood in place for a moment to watch. Observe.

One person, who wore a toga and was talking to a man in a white lab coat, appeared to be pregnant. She gestured animatedly as the lab coat shook his head. I watched as a woman in flats that were slightly too big for her tripped over her own shoe and barely caught herself from falling before running off to her destination. There was an elderly woman in a wheel-less wheelchair, which glided forward, hovering inches above the ground. Headed straight for us.

Though the woman was older, she still held a glimmer of her youth. Her form was slight but toned in the upper half. Her laugh lines showed around her mouth, and her wrinkles were there, but only as fine lines.

Without stopping to consider why, I pulled Celestina over to her.

The woman noticed me first, looking startled for a split second, then regaining her composure.

"Hello," she said softly, cocking her head to the side, and looking as though she were studying me. "And who might you be?"

"This is Eryn, Dr. Vue." Celestina looked at me. "Sorry to interrupt you, we were just headed outside for our first look."

"Oh, no, never a problem, my dear nurse. It's nice to meet you, Eryn. I assume you're dealing with some memory loss? Very common after cryostasis, I'm afraid."

"Yes," I said, studying her. "You look familiar to me though."

"I imagine I look like how your grandmother might have looked." Dr. Vue laughed. "I do also have one of those faces."

"Mm," I grunted, still looking at her.

"Well, we better go," Celestina said, tugging at my arm. "And leave you to your work."

"Yes, of course. It was nice to meet you, Eryn. I hope you recover your memories soon." Dr. Vue smiled.

We started walking away, but we turned back around when Dr. Vue called for Celestina.

"Where are you taking her first?" Dr. Vue asked, stopping her hoverchair.

"I was planning on first look, and then the shopping district to get her some clothes," they answered, turning us both to face Dr. Vue.

"Tell them to put it on my tab." Dr. Vue said, her tone firm.

Celestina blinked a few times. "Dr. Vue?"

"Let me help this patient, Celestina. I heard from your supervisor that she's been out of it for a very long time." Dr. Vue's voice softened. "I'm not hurting for money by any means. And I trust you won't take advantage of my kindness."

Celestina shook their head vigorously. "We would never, Dr. Vue. Thank you."

Dr. Vue nodded her head at me. "Well, then have fun, my dears. I'm off to work on another project."

Without another word, she turned and zipped away.

Chapter 2

We all stood in stunned silence for a few moments, until Celestina shook their head.

"Well, that was incredibly surprising and kind of her, and we have a schedule to keep. Eryn, are you ready for first look?"

I blinked. "Uh, sure."

They took my arm and walked me forward, with Theo trailing behind. When we reached the doors, they slid open, and we stepped out into bright sunlight.

It took a few seconds for my eyes to adjust, but when they did, I... Well, I don't even have words for it.

Silver and white skyscrapers stretched toward the sky, glinting like scales on a dragon's hide. Pretty much every single building I saw looked like that, save one. A giant blue tower rose in the distance, standing out like a peacock among pigeons. Every tower, including the blue one, had plants climbing up the building or contained in small, fenced landings at different levels. I could see the glint of solar panels on every building. Cobblestone streets extended out in every direction. Bicycles zoomed by, gliding over the ground like Dr. Vue's hoverchair had done. Trees grew everywhere at ground level, and I could hear running water tinkling somewhere off to my left.

"What's the blue one?" I asked, unsure where to start.

"That tower is owned by Clevand Corporation, which is headed by Mr. Apollo Clevand. The top five floors are his home and personal workshop, while the rest belong to the corporation employees. He pays them very well, and it's very prestigious to work there," Celestina replied, smiling. "I've only met him once. He was really nice from what I could tell."

"We're not allowed anywhere near that tower," Theo commented from behind us. "Rumor has it that Mr. Clevand doesn't like the CI. He has an agreement that no CI members are allowed to go in the building without his permission."

"That's just a rumor. Besides, we won't be going there today. What else do you have questions about, Eryn?"

"The plants." I waved in the general direction of a tree.

"We grow those for oxygen. If you go out beyond the city… well, I'm just going to say it. There's only desert out past the city edges," Celestina said, grimacing. "That bit is usually a shock for you folks who have come out of cryo. Well, those who have been in for fifty years or more."

I took in a deep breath. "So this… this is only here."

"Yes, we're the only place left that can support plants. And they're important for us to survive, too. They give us enough oxygen to breathe."

Theo grunted.

Celestina turned around to glare at him but didn't say a word. Theo rolled his eyes.

I looked between the two, aware that there was some kind of argument brewing.

Grabbing Celestina's arm, I gently shook it. Their gaze came back to me.

"Shops. You said we were going to shops," I said, smiling at them. "What shop are we going to first?"

That got a smile. They wrapped their arm around mine. "This way!"

We turned to our left and began walking, passing several people on the way. I saw a small stream off to my left—I assumed that was the running water I'd heard earlier. Even though the streets seemed full of people, it felt calm. There was the murmur of people talking to each other as they went along, water running beside me, and the rustling of the leaves. I felt at peace.

Soon we arrived at a smaller white building, and by smaller, I mean four stories instead of ten.

"Here we are. I have a friend who works here. She'll size you and make you some new wear," Celestina said, walking us toward the doors.

I glanced back to see if Theo was still following us. I caught him staring thoughtfully at me before he noticed and put on a pair of wraparound shades.

Once we were inside, Celestina walked up to the receptionist. "I'm here for Kimi Vandyke."

"Do you have an appointment?" the receptionist asked, raising her eyebrows.

"I'm a friend. Could you just call her down?"

The receptionist pressed her lips together but touched a microphone piece on her ear. "Kimi, you have two customers in the lobby. One says they know you."

The lady listened for a second.

"She'll be right down. Take a seat, please, and tell your security he can wait outside. This is a safety-assured facility, I promise."

I turned and saw Theo stood behind us with a hand on his pistol. Weird, I hadn't noticed it before.

"Go outside, Theo. We'll be fine," Celestina said over their shoulder.

We watched him silently walk over to a bench in the lobby and sit. Celestina shrugged, then dragged me to a pair of seats near the front desk.

Not too long after, a tall, willowy, dark-skinned girl with blond hair that faded to blue came out. "Celestina!" she cried, running over and giving them a hug. Celestina laughed and hugged her back.

"Hey, Kimi. I wanted to introduce you to Eryn. She/they pronouns. She just came out of cryo, and she needs sizing and new wear," Celestina said, gesturing toward me.

Kimi let go of Celestina and turned to look at me. After looking me up and down, she nodded. "All right. Follow me."

We followed her up two flights of stairs, down a hall, and finally to a room that said *Vandyke.*

"Right in here!" Kimi said, holding open the door for us.

We stepped inside, and I glanced around the room. There was a little circular stage-looking thing in the middle of the room, some rolling carts on the far side, and what looked like a regular changing room to my right.

"Okay, now that we're up here, it's nice to meet you, Eryn. How have you been adjusting?" Kimi asked, as Celestina took a seat on a chair I hadn't noticed by the door.

"Pretty well, I think. I don't really have any memories of my past, so there isn't too much that's a large shock right now."

Celestina chimed in. "They're in perfect physical health, too! Don't know how."

I side-eyed them, and they just shrugged. "It's true."

"Okay, good to know that you won't be passing out on me. What type of clothes do you want? I assume you need a new wardrobe but may only be able to afford one or two pieces," she said, glancing at Celestina.

They shook their head. "Nope, Eryn's getting a basic closet. Courtesy of Dr. Vue."

Kimi's eyes went wide with shock. "You're joking me."

"Nope," Celestina said, shaking their head again. "Dr. Vue very kindly offered to pay for Eryn's new clothes."

Kimi looked me up and down again. "Who are you?"

"That's what I've been wondering," I said dryly, snorting.

She sighed. "Well, then, let's get started. Step up here."

Kimi pointed at the circular stage in the middle of the room. I walked over and stepped up carefully, trying to place myself in the center.

"Okay, this doesn't do anything crazy, but it does make a weird noise. Just a warning. It's going to scan you to take measurements, and then we can work on a list for a basic closet based on what you're currently wearing."

I nodded in understanding and stood still while she pressed some buttons and made the machine whir.

Soon, the thing was done, and Kimi asked me to step off the platform.

"Okay, so it looks like you're wearing a leather jacket, a cotton-blend T-shirt, and cotton cargo pants. And combat boots? I like your style," Kimi said, nodding. "So, we could start with several T-shirts, another pair of cargo pants, maybe a couple pair of loose linen pants? You might like those. And it looks like this jacket is falling apart, so how about a new one?" Kimi rattled off.

I fish mouthed for a second before a word came out. "Um, sounds good. I could try on the linen pants. I wouldn't mind maybe some tank tops? And maybe one dress, I suppose. I don't know how many fancy things there are to go to, but it seems right," I said, letting the last word hang in the air as I looked first at Kimi, then at Celestina.

"It's always good to have something nice on hand. Are you sure you would be comfortable in a dress though? You could always get a suit set," Celestina said, smiling.

"I could?" I asked, looking between Kimi and Celestina.

Kimi nodded. "You could if you wanted one."

"Then yeah, a suit would be great," I said, smiling at Kimi. "Thanks."

She smiled. "No problem. Let me get a pair of linen pants and a tank top for you to change into while I input your order. No telling how long it's been since those clothes have been washed."

Kimi disappeared into another room, and then came back quickly with clothes draped over her left arm. "Here you go. Go in there and try these on."

I took them from her and stepped into one of the changing rooms. It was a big room, with a couch, clothes racks, and several mirrors. There was even a bathroom in the corner. I took off my jacket and set it carefully on the couch. Then I stripped off my black combat clothes and threw them onto the same couch, on the other end.

Pulling on the linen pants and tank top, the fit felt just right. The fabric was soft enough not to be irritating and lay close enough to my body that the pressure just felt… right.

After checking the outfit a bit in the mirror, I went over to my jacket. It had pockets, and so did the cargo pants. I emptied them out. Maybe they had clues to who I was. I found a set of keys, a multipurpose pocket tool, and a golden chain that held a heart-shaped locket. After stuffing the keys and tool into a random pocket, I opened the heart. On one side was a dog; on the other, a little girl that was not me. She was smiling up at the camera, a blond, brown-eyed, gap-tooth child no more than five.

To my surprise, a name came to mind when I saw the picture of the dog. "Hera," I whispered. Then, I felt the sudden urge to cut my hair.

I walked out of the changing room to see Kimi and Celestina chatting.

"Hey, how do the clothes fit?" Kimi asked. Celestina was also looking, but they got up within a few moments.

"You remembered something."

I nodded as they came to stand beside me. Kimi went to my other side to look at the locket in my hand.

"The dog's name is Hera. And I also have a *very* strong need to cut my hair," I said, reaching up with a free hand to grab a few strands.

"Oh, I can take care of that here. Follow me," Kimi said, turning to walk to a corner of the room behind the changing room.

"Who's the girl?" Celestina asked, pointing at the other side of the locket while we followed Kimi.

I shrugged. "I don't remember."

Celestina tilted their head to one side. "Could be a sister or a daughter." They studied the picture. "She bears a very close resemblance to you."

I looked at the picture again, trying to imagine myself with a daughter.

"Sit down over here," Kimi called out, pointing at a chair.

I did as I was told, sitting in the chair and putting my feet up on the footrest.

"Okay, how short do you want it?" she asked, grabbing tools and putting them all in one place.

"Shave it on the sides and back." I brought my hands up and ran them along the sides of my head. "Cut it short on the top. Like, make it only a couple inches long up there."

Kimi raised her eyebrows. "You want it short short."

"Yes," I said firmly, my discomfort growing by the minute as my hair brushed against my skin.

Kimi nodded and went to work. While she did that, Celestina leaned against the wall and studied me.

"You haven't had a child," they declared, nodding. "Your body didn't show any of the signs when I was checking on you. So that must be a sister."

I felt my head get lighter as chunks of hair went drifting down to the floor. "That's good, right? So, we know I had a little sister and a dog."

"It's a good place for you to start regaining your memories. The picture must've triggered the memory of the dog. That was really fast though. Even with a picture," Celestina pondered, taking in a deep breath. "I don't know. To be honest, I've never had someone in this good of condition or have their memories start coming back so quickly. Even if it is just the name of a dog."

"Done," Kimi said, and I looked up to see myself in the mirror.

The tension in my shoulders left. I felt so much better.

"Thank you." I smiled wide. "This feels way better."

Kimi smiled back. "Of course, I…"

She was cut off as a scream sounded out through the building. We all paused, and time seemed to freeze for a moment.

"What was that?" Celestina asked nervously.

Several more screams sounded out.

Without another word, I hopped out of my seat and moved toward the door before I knew what I was doing. I ran out the door, quickly fastening the locket on as I did so.

"Eryn, wait! Where are you going?" Celestina yelled, but I was already far enough ahead they couldn't grab me.

What are you doing? I asked myself as my body moved as though it was on autopilot.

Hearing another scream from downstairs, I turned onto the stairs and took them two at a time, trying to move as quickly as possible. When I reached the first floor, I heard what sounded like someone begging in a frantic voice. Hanging a right, I stopped in front of a room that said *McWren* and heard whimpering.

Kimi and Celestina caught up moments later.

"What are you *doing?*" Celestina hissed through their teeth. "People are screaming, and you run toward it?"

"I have to help," I said, internally surprised by the cold tone of my voice. "Stay behind me."

With a gape from Celestina and confusion from Kimi, I turned and silently opened the door.

Inside were two guys in all black. One hung on to a small girl who was struggling, and the other pointed a gun at a family of three.

"Hand over the money," the guy with the gun said. Another young girl about four years old handed the guy the money, with her hand shaking.

There was a hole in the wall, which I was assuming was some improvised construction these two had decided to complete.

Before I could put together another thought, I was attacking them.

It was like I was moving without fully thinking, like I wasn't entirely in control. Like I had done this so many times that it was natural for me.

I quickly walked, soft-footed, into the room. Coming up behind the one with the gun, I grabbed his arm in one hand and the gun in the other and yanked the gun out of his grasp. Before he could even turn, I socked him in the jaw.

He fell backward and passed out, surprising me. How strong was I?

Turning my attention to the next guy, I saw the eyes of little girl he was holding go wide. She looked at me, then opened her mouth and chomped down on his arm.

With a yelp of pain, he let her go, and I slid the gun toward the door and moved into the opening the little girl had created.

I avoided one swing, then punched upward into the guy's stomach. When he leaned down, I came up with my elbow to break his nose.

Groaning, the guy stumbled back, holding his nose. I moved in again, wrapping an arm around his neck and going behind him. He gasped for air as I choked him and eventually passed out in my arms.

I carefully lowered him to the floor.

"Is he alive?" I heard, and I looked up.

Kimi and Celestina were standing in the doorway, and Kimi held the gun I had tossed away. Celestina seemed to be frozen in shock.

Then I looked past her and nearly started laughing.

Theo was in the doorway, gun ready, but the gun was pointed at the floor, and an astonished expression animated his face.

I turned to the family, then bent back down and took the money from the boy's pocket. "Here," I said, handing the mother the money. "I think it would be best if you left."

They didn't argue, but simply ran out the door with their money.

I turned to Theo. "Got any handcuffs?"

Theo nodded, unclipping them from his belt. He tossed a pair to me, and I put it on the second guy's wrists. After I was done, I pried Kimi's frozen hands from the gun and unloaded the magazine and handed the gun to Theo.

"You have military training, don't you?" Theo asked, breaking the silence with sharp words.

I whirled to face him. "What do you mean, *military training*?"

"I mean, you ran down here and seemed perfectly fine taking out two guys by yourself. And one had a gun," Theo said, pointing at the two guys laying on the ground. "No one with any sense runs toward screaming."

I gestured with my hands. "Okay, so… what does that mean?"

"You're dangerous," he said, earning noises of disagreement from Celestina and Kimi.

"You all saw what Eryn just did." Theo pointed at the guys again. "Celestina, I think we need to take her in. She seems dangerous. Probably a CI agent. Maybe worse."

Celestina shook her head. "No. Eryn doesn't have her memory. Until we know who she is, she's staying with me. It's the safest option."

"She could…" Theo started, then glanced at me. "…you know!"

Celestina turned to me. "Eryn, do you have any desire to hurt me? Do you feel so angry that you want to hurt me?"

"No," I said, shaking my head. "I would never hurt you. And I feel in control of myself."

Now, whispered a voice in my head, but I firmly told it to shut up.

"Twenty-five," I said, the words falling out of my mouth.

Freezing, I held Celestina's gaze as everyone else stared at me.

"I'm… twenty-five?" I said, dragging the uncertain words out of my mouth. "I don't know where that came from."

"Your memory. Pieces of it are coming back. Sometimes memories are tied to the things we do. The fighting must have let you remember something else," Celestina said, coming to stand next to me. "Are you feeling light-headed or dizzy?"

I shook my head. "No. Just hungry."

"Again?" Celestina snorted, shaking her head. "You must really need to catch up on your meals. Let's get you back to my house for some food."

"We have to deal with those guys first," I said, gesturing at the two people tied up on the floor. One of whom was starting to move.

"Let's see what else you can do," Theo declared, looking at me. "Interrogate him."

I looked uncertainly between Celestina and Theo. Celestina nodded encouragingly.

"Why are you letting me interrogate them?" I squinted at Theo.

He sighed. "Celestina won't let me take you in. You clearly have some training. I want to see how much. And it seems to be helping you regain your memories. The sooner you remember who you are, the sooner I can take you in."

"Comforting," I said sarcastically, glaring at him. "But fine."

"What happened?" The guy who had awakened moaned.

Before he could move, I was down beside him, holding him by the collar of his shirt.

His eyes shot open and stared at me, and then shifted to Theo and Celestina. "Look, we didn't mean to hurt anyone! Me and my brother see…we don't have nobody else, and our jobs don't pay near enough to keep us from starving! Please, don't put us in containment! My brother wouldn't last more than a minute…"

"Shut up," I said.

His mouth snapped shut.

I looked at Theo, then back to the guy. "I need both of your names, and nothing more, understand?"

He nodded. "I'm Marc. Me brother's called Marl."

I let go of Marc's shirt, and he slumped down.

"Thank you, ma'am," Marc said, crawling over to his brother. "Me brother is mute. Hasn't ever been able to speak a word."

After checking his brother, Marc scooted back a little bit, looking at me. "Ma'am, what's your name?"

"Why do you want to know?" I asked, crossing my arms.

He coughed. "Is it Eryn?"

The surprise must've shown on my face because he simply nodded. "It is. Ya know, there's a museum that has a statue that looks exactly like ya, same name and everythin'."

I stared at him in shock.

"What museum, Marc?" I asked, pulling him to a standing position.

"CI Museum, miss," he said. "Would you mind loosening yer grip?"

Muttering an apology, I let him go, then uncuffed his brother. Theo made a sound of protest, but I glared at him, which effectively shut him up.

Then a flash of memory.

I was ten. In a bland gray gym, facing off against another little girl my age. And again, older this time. As a teen?

Shaking my head, I looked over at Theo. "We should let them go."

"No. Protocol dictates we take them in," Theo said, crossing his arms. "Maybe you didn't have military training if you can't remember that."

"Look at them, Theo," I replied, pointing at Marc. "I can see his ribs. And his brother's. They're starving. Who would lock them up for starving?"

Theo opened his mouth to say something, then closed it with an annoyed look on his face. "No one's arresting anyone for starving. But they held a family at gunpoint to rob them."

"To get money they don't have, for food they don't have," I pointed out, noticing that Marc's brother was starting to wake up. "Plus, your job right now is to protect Celestina from me, not to arrest them."

Theo looked over at Marc as he helped his brother Marl up from the floor.

Come on, Theo, I thought. *Have a heart.*

"Fine. But they do it again, they're gonna get arrested. Anyone else would arrest them," Theo finally said, and I let out a sigh of relief.

"Go." I fixed my gaze on the brothers. "Get out of here."

Marc nodded and Marl signed "Thank you" to me as they both scrambled out the hole they had made in the side of the building.

Chapter 3

Turning to talk to Celestina, I saw that they were gone. Kimi had vanished, too.

"Where did they go?" I asked, glancing at Theo.

He shrugged. "I don't know, I didn't see them leave."

I walked out of the room, looking down the hallway to either side. No one.

Theo followed me out into the hallway and shadowed me as I made my way back upstairs to Kimi's dressing room. Thankfully, both were there.

Kimi was sitting on the ground, head between her legs, as Celestina rubbed her back and murmured at her. They both looked up whenever I shut the door. Kimi immediately put her head back between her knees.

"Is everything okay?" I asked, looking between Kimi's back and Celestina.

"Just a little shock from what happened downstairs. Nothing to worry too much about," Celestina said, continuing to rub Kimi's back. "Come sit down with us."

I walked over to them and sat down, feeling awkward.

"Have you remembered anything else?" Celestina asked, removing her hand from Kimi's back and shifting position to sit cross-legged on the floor.

I shrugged. "A bit. I had this memory of being young and being in some kind of gym, fighting another girl my age. And then another one like that, but the girl and I were teenagers that time."

"Wait, how young were you in the first one?" Celestina asked, leaning forward.

"Ten, I think."

"Ten? No way." Celestina gasped, and even Kimi looked up when I said that.

I brought my shoulders up and dropped them. "I don't know."

"Hmmm," they said, looking me up and down.

"I do have a question though." I made eye contact with Celestina. "What's the CI Museum? And what, exactly, does the CI do?"

Celestina looked at Kimi, then came back to me. "That's a topic for later. Why don't we head back to my house, and we can discuss it when we've gotten you some food."

I nodded and stood, holding a hand out for Kimi and Celestina to take. Celestina took it immediately, and I hauled them to their feet.

Kimi took a little longer, slowly unfolding from her position like a flower opening to the sun. Eventually, she took my hand, and I pulled her to her feet.

"Thanks," she said, smiling. "I'm going to head home after this. My girlfriend will be worried. But first, let me get you your new closet."

Kimi went to the back of the room and pulled out a rack from the wall, on which hung three garment bags. She pulled a cord at the top of each one, and they shrank to halve the original size. After taking them off the rack, Kimi brought them over and gave them to me.

"Here's your clothes." Kimi gave me a half-smile. "I hope I'll see you again, all right?"

I smiled back. "Definitely."

She hugged us both, then waved as we left her room. We made our way back to the lobby, where Theo waited for us. I guess he had stopped following me whenever I walked through the lobby. Wasn't paying attention.

"Ready?" Theo asked, standing from his seat.

"Yes," Celestina responded for us.

We walked out of the store, Celestina and I side by side with Theo trailing behind.

After crossing the street, we wove our way between multiple buildings before stepping out onto a relatively flat platform.

I stopped, staring at the sight before me. A row of what looked like turnstiles blocked the walk, but beyond that, at the place where you would normally see a train, there were no tracks. Just an open overhang. But underneath… a train waited.

Twelve egg-shaped compartments connected with something that looked a lot like silver snakeskin. Each compartment had a pair of sleek sliding doors, and small, oval-shaped windows. It floated, making no noise, waiting.

"How…?" I asked, the only word I was able to get out.

Celestina chuckled. "Come on, and you'll see."

I followed them through the turnstile, where we stopped for a moment as they explained to the guard they were my reorientation nurse.

When he cleared us to go, we all went through and stepped into a compartment.

"The legendary floating trains. Developed and went on their first test run in 2097. Completely free of natural gasses, powered by a small amount of electricity and a lot of water. Don't ask me how that works, I just know it does," Celestina told me as I walked around, touching the seats in the car.

After I investigated the seats, I sank into a cushion, sighing in relief. Finally able to relax.

"Hey, I'm going to go into the nap compartment. I'm a little tired. Are you two okay in here?" Celestina glanced between Theo and me.

"We won't hurt each other," I said, waving a hand. "Go take a nap."

"Okay." They took a step away before turning back. "We're getting off at Hydra Street, by the way."

"Got it. Go," I said, shooing her with my hands.

They threw their hands up in surrender and went into what I assumed was the nap compartment off to our right.

That left me alone with Theo. I looked at him and decided he would probably be annoyed with me if I talked. Instead, I stared out the window as the train began to slide away from the station and out into another part of the city. Buildings and their plants passed me by as we went along.

Then I heard Theo speak from behind me. "Eryn?"

"Yes?" I raised my eyebrows as I turned to face him.

He cleared his throat, then met my gaze. "I wanted to apologize. I… I realize I have… Well, I've been an asshole."

I stared at him.

"Listen, I don't apologize very often. Celestina can tell you." Theo ran a hand through his hair. "But I shouldn't treat you that way. My therapist says…"

He was cut off when my body, again, acted without thinking, and leapt across the compartment to slap a hand over his mouth.

"What are you doing? I'm trying to…"

"Shhh!" I clamped my hand firmly over his mouth and pointed to my ear with the other one.

There was a faint rattling from the compartment on the other side of the compartment, the one Celestina hadn't gone into. I removed my hand from Theo's mouth and gave him a warning look.

I leaned back, appearing to look casual, but every fiber of my being was alive and buzzing with warning.

The door clicked, and four bulky men filed into the compartment. They all wore masks and black clothing, hiding their identities.

Instead of feeling unnerved, like any *normal* person, I felt an excited buzzing in my body.

"Looky here, fellas. A sweet little couple, and one's CI standard issue," said the biggest of the men, as the rest pulled guns on us.

My mind was working overtime. Assessing, calculating.

I met Theo's eyes, seeing the fear there that was absent in me.

I had to protect.

To buy me some time, I curled in closer to Theo. "Please d-d-don't hurt us. We'll give you… anything… please leave us alone," I stuttered, trying to look the part of a naive girl.

Aha. Idea.

The big guy responded, "This little one's got manners. I might keep her, boys. But we'll have to get rid of her boyfriend."

I let my gaze slide behind the men and on a window.

Knowing I wouldn't get another chance, I focused on that spot and let out an unearthly scream that made everyone else jump and follow my line of sight.

In an instant, I was out of my seat and knocking guns out of my target's hands, throwing them to the far side of the cabin.

Theo caught on quick and went for the other two.

My first target, I headbutted in the nose, then drove an elbow into his midsection hard enough to bruise organs. He went down, nose bleeding, whining and crying in pain.

I quickly turned to the other one, who was ready for me. He charged at me like a bull, and I jumped to the side, catching an arm around his neck.

Leaping, I hooked my legs around his waist and locked my first arm with my second. Soon, the guy was gasping for breath, and a few seconds later, he passed out.

I turned to check on Theo when a loud voice yelled, "Stop, or I'll shoot!"

Pausing, I swiveled my head. The leader had Theo in a headlock with one meaty arm, and the other held a pistol to Theo's head.

I stood there, breathing deeply, looking for a way out. Then I heard a low-pitched humming in the ceiling. And it definitely wasn't the train.

Hoping it was what I thought it was, I started talking.

"You really don't want to do that. I mean, two of your buddies have already been beaten by a girl. You saw what I did. I know how to kill a man. Torture, even." I grinned evilly, going for the gusto. "Once, I castrated a man because he was rude and called me a bitch. What do you think your punishment will be?" I cracked my knuckles and smiled again, and at this point, both the thug and Theo looked shocked and very uncomfortable.

Thankfully, I didn't have to vamp more, because a piece of ceiling fell and hit the thug on the head, knocking him out. Released, Theo scrambled away and stood, coming over to me.

Looking up at the hole, I yelled, "Come on, we won't hurt you!"

To my surprise, Marc and Marl dropped in through the hole.

"Marc? Marl? What are you doing here?" I asked, taking in their grimy appearance.

"We saw you get on the train with that other person, and then saw these beauties climb on. Recognized them. Nasty guys; they're part of a gang. We figured they weren't up to any good, so we followed. Marl noticed they went into your compartment, so we climbed on top and got in," Marc said, Marl nodding in agreement.

I couldn't help smiling. "Thank you," I said, glancing at the fallen leader, then at the hole in the ceiling.

"That should probably be fixed," I quipped mildly, letting my gaze rest on Marc and Marl.

"No problem," Marc said. Marl pulled out a small spray canister, shook it, then signed at Marc.

"Got it." Marc grabbed one side of the ceiling piece. He glanced at us. "Care to help?"

Theo grabbed the other side of the ceiling piece. I hovered, unsure what to do. Marl signed to me, but I shook my head.

"I'm sorry, I never learned sign language," I apologized, feeling a twang of guilt.

Marl smiled and nodded, then signed to Marc.

Marc translated, "Can I get on your shoulders to use the canister?"

I turned to Marl and nodded. Squatting down, I used my hands to balance until Marl was securely on my shoulders. Finding a good stance, I straightened, feeling for my center of balance. To my surprise, he wasn't very heavy. It only took about a minute to fix the ceiling, and when Marl was done, the ceiling looked like new.

"What is that stuff?" I asked Marl, nodding at the canister.

He signed rapidly to Marc, who said, "It's Quick-Fix Cement. Marl invented it himself."

I looked back at Marl with new curiosity. "That's amazing, Marl."

He signed, and this time I needed no translation. He touched the fingers of his hand to his chin, then brought them down. *Thank you.*

I heard one of the four thugs moan and easily knocked him back out. "Theo, do you think there's any sort of security on this train? Someone who might have handcuffs," I asked, holding out a hand for his pairs.

He tossed them to me. "I have no idea, but I can go check."

I nodded my thanks and snapped the handcuffs on two of the four men.

Theo took off for the front of the train, and I was left with Marc, Marl, and the four unconscious thugs. "So, is that what you like to do? Invent things?" I asked both of them.

Marc smiled, and I took his hesitation to study him.

It was obvious that Marc and Marl were identical twins. Both had ragged black hair, a soft, oval-shaped face, warm brown eyes, and slim, lean builds. Their clothes consisted of torn jeans, grubby T-shirts, and patchy leather jackets. They were far from clean; it looked like they had been living in a garbage heap. But it was easy to see kind, warm-hearted boys under the grime.

"Yeah, Marl likes to invent things. He's real good at that. Got a real brain for it. Me, I like computers. When we were forced to go to public school, I used to hack into the teacher's pages and change lesson plans. It was really fun. No one ever caught me," Marc said, half-heartedly kicking one of the thugs when he tried to wake up.

Theo then chose that moment to come back into the compartment, along with another guy in tow. The unknown guy looked at the four thugs, and then at Marc and Marl.

"What about those two? They don't look real honest," he said, pointing at them.

I stepped across the carriage to stand between the guy and the twins. "They're fine as they are," I warned, voice soft and firm.

He shrugged and snapped the handcuffs on another thug. "Got it. Why don't you guys move to another carriage, and we'll let this one be for these beauties, huh?"

Nodding, I gestured for Marc and Marl to follow me, and I went the same direction Celestina had earlier. We stepped into the other compartment, which was filled with beds with little curtains that could be pulled around for privacy.

I sat down heavily on the closest bed, and the twins did the same. Setting my head in my hands, I immediately fell asleep.

Chapter 4

What seemed like a few seconds later, Celestina was shaking me awake. "We're here."

I looked at them through sleepy eyes, giving a jaw-cracking yawn.

"Come on," Celestina coaxed.

I forced myself to stand and followed them off the train.

I wobbled a bit as I stepped onto the platform, and Celestina grabbed my arm to steady me. "Are you okay? Theo told me what happened, and then I saw you passed out in the nap compartment. I think you've probably expended too much energy for one day. I'm going to get you some food once we get to my house."

"I'm okay," I said, yawning again. "Just tired. And hungry. Where's Theo? And Marc and Marl?"

Celestina sighed. "They're coming with us. Theo was already going to stay at my house, because it's his job and all, but Marc and Marl… They begged me, and made puppy-dog eyes, and I couldn't refuse. Theo also vouched for them, and I'm too soft-hearted to leave them. So, they're coming with us."

I nodded and leaned on Celestina for support as we began walking down the street.

As the street came into view, all sorts of houses lining the street bombarded my vision. I spotted a mound of dirt, which I suspected was some sort of underground house. There was another shaped like a strawberry, leaves and all. Some were normal, some were distinctly abnormal. But there were too many for me to process them all right now.

"Ow, my eyes," I said, squinting at the buildings.

Celestina glanced at me and chuckled. "Yeah, some of these houses are strange. Gotta show their uniqueness. You should see the inside of some of these normal-looking ones."

We stopped in front of a two-story silver house with a caduceus carved over the doorway. Looking at it made me glad that the sun was setting, so that I wasn't blinded by the glare.

"My house. C'mon, you'll love her." Celestina dragged me up the steps. They pressed their hand to a small pad next to the door, and I heard a whirring noise and a *click*.

"Welcome to my house!" Celestina declared, opening the door.

I leaned on Celestina as we walked in and followed a short hallway into a combined dining room and kitchen. The dining room was spacious, with white marble floors and elegant gray walls. A shimmering gray table floated in the middle of the room like a giant silver plate. Smaller silver plates lay stacked against the wall.

The kitchen was separated from the dining room by a waist-height marble countertop. I looked closer and noticed, rectangular, black screens on the edge, spaced about three inches apart. The kitchen itself was a marvel. Marble counters rested beneath dull, grey, metal cabinets. A small plate sat atop what appeared to be the dishwasher, which had no noticeable way of opening. The fridge was a cool blue, the only splash of color in the room. The items inside hung suspended, with no real organization.

The stove was a bunch of floating black plate things, hovering over a piece of metal countertop.

Finally, all I could get out was, "Wow."

Celestina beamed at me, then snapped their fingers. "AIHNA, are the rooms ready?" they asked into the air.

I considered for a moment that they were crazy, then quickly dismissed the thought when a mellow voice rang out from the walls.

"Two rooms are ready, Celestina."

I looked up to see speakers higher up on the walls, then looked back at Celestina.

Looking immensely proud of themself, Celestina said, "That was AIHNA, Artificial Intelligence House of the New Age. She's a prototype, but a friend made her and wanted to see how well she worked."

"Hmm, creepy," Theo said.

I jumped when I heard his voice. I hadn't seen him come in behind us.

Glancing past him, I saw Marc and Marl bringing up the end, staring at the house in amazement.

Celestina snapped their fingers twice, and two of the plates leaning against the wall slowly came off the stack and floated toward us.

When they arrived at the table, Celestina helped me to one. "Sit here, don't move. I'll be back."

They gestured at the three others to follow her, and they did. Celestina led them out of the room, and suddenly, all was quiet.

Exhausted, and feeling a headache coming on, I set my head down on my hands.

"You appear to be hungry and dehydrated. Allow me to care for you."

I brought my head back up, slowly processing that the voice had, once again, come from the speakers in the walls.

"AIHNA?" I asked, feeling a little foolish for speaking to a house.

"I am here."

Before I could say anything else, a hovering tray floated and set itself down in front of me.

The tray was nothing special and held a small bowl of soup and a glass of water. But the fact that the AI knew I was hungry and thirsty, and had given me food, was the hard part to believe.

"Thank you, AIHNA," I said, slowly bringing the glass of water to my lips.

"Please drink the water slowly to rehydrate your body at a good pace. Drinking quickly could make you nauseous, and you could…"

"Thank you for the reminder, AIHNA," I interrupted, taking a sip of my water after I did so. "Can I ask you a question?"

"You can ask me a question."

"How did you know? That I was hungry and thirsty."

"Your body reported that you were low on energy, and your hydration levels were very low."

I mumbled to myself. That didn't answer my question, but I was too tired to ask anything else. Turning my attention instead to the soup, I began slowly eating, spoonful by spoonful, taking my time.

When the soup was about halfway done, Celestina came back. "I thought I told you to stay in your seat? Why'd you get up?"

"I didn't," I said, after swallowing a mouthful of soup. "AIHNA got it for me."

Celestina stared at me like I was crazy. "What?"

"Isn't that part of what she does? She said that she knew I was hungry and thirsty, and then brought me this food. I didn't move an inch."

"No, that's not what she's supposed to do. Yes, she can cook, but only when you ask her to." Celestina pursed their lips in thought.

I shrugged. Not my issue.

Celestina shook their head. "I'll worry about that later. Finish your food and let's get you to sleep."

We sat in silence as I finished my meal, barely able to lift the last couple of mouthfuls into my mouth.

"Also, I put the garment bags from Kimi in your room already, so no need to worry about that," Celestina said, taking my dishes as I let out another yawn.

"Thank you for that" I forced myself onto my feet. "Thank you for being so kind, and for opening your home. I'm very grateful for all of your help, and I promise I'll get out of your hair as soon as I can."

Celestina put my dishes on a plate over what I earlier assumed was the dishwasher, and the dishes sank into the counter. Once they had disappeared, Celestina came over to me and put one of my arms over their shoulder.

"You're not out of my hair until I say you are, Eryn," they said, smiling. "I need to make sure you've got most of your memories back before that happens."

I walked with them as we crossed the room to a small hallway, and then turned into the first door on the left.

Inside was a small bedroom, which looked relatively normal, thank goodness. No sleep pods or whatever else kind of technologically advanced sleeping things they could come up with.

"Could we go…" I started, interrupting myself with another yawn. "Could we go to the museum tomorrow? Check out that statue?"

"We'll see. You expended a lot of energy today, and you seem pretty danger-prone."

"Like Daphne?" I asked, grinning.

Celestina squinted at me, then let out a big sigh. "You know how much my grandma references that show? What's it called, *Shaggy-Doo*?"

"*Scooby-Doo*," I corrected, grimacing. "Do I talk like a grandma?"

"A little," Celestina said, helping me sit down on the bed instead of just falling onto it. "You're catching on pretty quick though, so I don't imagine it'll be too noticeable."

"Good," I muttered, attempting to yank the sheets from where they were tucked at the head of the bed.

"Sleep well. I'll be down the hall, second door on the right, if you need me," Celestina backed out of the room, waving before they shut the door.

I nodded and mumbled something, and then, deciding that the sheet was too much effort, laid my head on the pillow and passed out.

Chapter 5

I *was young. Ten.*

My parents stared at me, blurry figures, as I was put into a black suburban and the door was slammed in my face.

With a quick blur, I was suddenly in a gym. We were doing a drill with punching bags, the dull thud of gloves the only sound in the room.

"Gloves up!" a voice called out, and we all stopped and pulled off our gloves.

"Eryn versus Kaila! In the ring, now!"

Shaking, I stepped into the boxing ring, wanting to lean against the flexible railings for support. But that would make me look weak, so I didn't.

Kaila faced me, just as young and scared and determined as I was.

Taking a deep breath, I raised my fists to fight.

I woke up panting, sweat pouring down my forehead. That was a memory, I knew it. A memory of me when I was younger… in some kind of training. Training to fight.

"Eryn, are you fine? Do you need me to call Celestina?" AIHNA's voice said softly.

"No, don't call them. I'm fine," I whispered, wiping the sweat off my forehead. I glanced around and saw a cracked door that looked like it led to a bathroom.

Getting out of bed, I winced as I put my weight on my legs. Oh, was I sore.

I hobbled over to the door and pushed it open, then let out a sigh of relief when I confirmed that it was a bathroom.

After stepping in and shutting the door, I tugged off my clothes and spent a couple of minutes figuring out the shower buttons before I could work it properly.

Lukewarm water sprayed out of the nozzle, and I scrubbed myself off and thoroughly washed my short hair. The water and the bathing felt good, and I was beginning to feel better. Less like a scared ten-year-old.

Once I stepped out of the shower, I grabbed a towel I found in a cabinet and searched for my clothes with the towel wrapped around me.

I found them sitting in the little closet inside the room. After doing some rummaging, I found another set of linen pants and a tank top. I threw them on and rubbed my hair until it was mostly dry. Then I crawled back into the bed.

I grabbed the other pillow and hugged it close to my body, squeezing my eyes tight until I fell back into the dream.

I was older now. Maybe sixteen. Fighting another girl, twice my size. She was fearsome—her height alone should have given me pause.

It didn't.

When the trainer sounded the start bell, I dashed forward, sliding between her legs, then using my momentum to swing around and kick the back of her knee.

She shortened a couple inches for a second, but that was all the time I needed to jump on her back and wrap an arm around her throat. Attempting to pull my arm off her throat, she scrabbled at my forearm, leaving scratches all over it before she finally passed out.

A moment of silence, and then a cheer rang out from the watching group. I stared at each one of them, numb inside, until I met the eyes of the trainer.

He was bald, and muscular, and looked like he ate rocks for breakfast. But he smiled at me. "You'll do just fine."

The gym blurred, and suddenly, I was running full speed at a group of armed men.

I pushed off the ground and bounced off the wall to kick my first target in the head, landing my heel right on his nose.

As his hands covered his face, I landed and kicked his knee backward. He screamed in pain as ligaments tore and bones cracked.

The fighting was a haze, and soon I stood, covered in blood, over ten dead or injured men.

My eyes shot open, and I took several deep breaths, controlling myself. What at first was fear from my ten-year-old self had quickly become excitement as I had ripped into that unit of men.

What was I? A killing machine? I'd go to jail for sure.

But that wasn't what I was worried about. This sense of heaviness had come with the memories. I felt drained, like I had nothing left to give anything.

I had killed people. Their blood had been on my hands.

Sitting up, I scooted back against the headboard and pulled my knees to my chest, rocking myself back and forth, back and forth.

The memory of one of those men's dead faces flashed in my mind, and I mentally cringed.

Burying my face between my knees, I felt first one tear, then another, then a whole torrent pour from my eyes.

I didn't want to. I didn't want to.

The thought kept cycling over and over in my mind. My body was shivering, making the bed rattle a bit, and I clutched my knees even tighter, hoping the pressure might help calm me down.

Getting my breathing under control, I took deep, controlled breaths until the shivering had stopped.

"AIHNA?" I croaked, my voice sounding more nasal after crying.

"I am here."

"Can you bring me a glass of water? And some tissues."

"There are tissues to your right. I will get the glass of water."

Looking to my right, I saw that there were, in fact, tissues there. I grabbed a few and spent the next minute or so clearing out my nose.

Soon, the door creaked open, and a small tray came floating in, supporting a glass of water.

I accepted it gratefully and drank it slowly, taking a couple moments here and there to blow my nose once again.

Once the glass was empty, I set it down on the nightstand and lay back down, falling right to sleep.

This time, with no dreams.

When I woke up again, a window behind the headboard, which I hadn't noticed the night before, was open, and light shined through.

Groaning, I turned onto my side and covered my face with the sheets.

Then there were three neat knocks at my door.

"Yes?" I called out, voice muffled by the sheets.

"It's Celestina!" they called through the door. "Breakfast is ready if you're hungry!"

I tossed the covers off at that. "Coming!"

After digging through my clothes, I changed into a pair of black jeans and a black tee, trying to at least look presentable.

I checked in the mirror and grimaced at the way my hair was sticking everywhere and the dried tear tracks running down my face.

Dipping my face into the sink, I washed off all signs that I had cried during the night. I didn't want any of them to see me like that. I had to be strong. Couldn't look weak.

After doing that and half-heartedly ruffling my hair, I left the room and followed my nose to the kitchen.

Walking back into the room I had eaten soup in last night, I got a better look at it, now that I was awake and it was light outside.

It was nicer than I had seen last night. Windows lined the upper parts of the tall walls, letting in lots of light. There was a set of stairs in the corner, and how I had missed that last night, I don't know.

"Morn!" Celestina said cheerily, putting plates on the little bar that separated the kitchen from the dining room.

"Morning," I replied, much less enthusiastically. "What're these?"

Each plate sat behind a little black plate, and the one I was watching blinked with a green light until it settled as "EGGS."

"Dish Tellers! They tell you what dish is by it, and what ingredients are in it, in case you're allergic to anything and need to know."

"Hmm." I traced the outline of one. "I wonder if I have any allergies?"

Celestina set another dish on the bar and nodded. "You could. Again, that's why you have me. Any allergic reactions—I can treat you."

"Is there anything you can't do?" I reached for a plate at the end of the counter.

"Uh…" They trailed off, staring at the counter. "No? Wait, no, I can't do brain surgery. Or any kind of prolonged surgery."

Staring at them, I scooped eggs into my plate. "That's what you can't do? Brain surgery?"

Celestina's face turned red, and they looked off to the side. "Hey, reorientation nurses have to know a lot. We never know what might happen."

I grabbed one more spoonful of eggs, then started grabbing some waffles. "*Hey,* I was complimenting you. That's seriously impressive and a little terrifying."

They laughed, and I cracked a smile.

"Thanks, I appreciate it. It was a long eight years of training, but it was worth it."

"Eight years?" I asked, looking up at them. "How old are you?"

"Twenty-five," Celestina replied, coming around to grab a plate themself.

I quickly counted in my head. "You were seventeen when you started training?"

"Sixteen," Celestina corrected, putting some fruit on her plate. "We start college at sixteen. Isn't that what you did?"

"I don't think I ever went to college," I said quietly, taking my plate over to the table. "Where's Theo and the twins?"

"Wait, no, you don't get to just skip over that," Celestina said, coming to sit next to me. "Did you remember something?"

I looked over at her and nodded.

"What did you remember?" they asked eagerly. "And how much?"

Shaking my head, I ate a forkful of eggs before I answered. "Nothing that I think I wanted to remember. And a little bit."

"Oh." Celestina tilted their head. "I'm sorry. You don't have to talk about it unless you want to. Let me know if you need any help though. Trauma's a bitch."

I nodded again and dug into the eggs.

"As for Theo and the twins, they're still in bed upstairs. They didn't get up like you did."

Snorting, I continued to eat my breakfast. Who would miss out on food?

After eating for a bit in silence, I swallowed waffle and spoke. "So, what else do you have to show me in the city? I don't think I want to go to the museum just yet."

Celestina brightened. "There's so much to show you! We should definitely go get coffee, and then I'll take you to meet some of my friends!"

"Okay." I shoved another forkful into my mouth.

We finished off our breakfast, and Celestina ran upstairs to see if Theo and the twins were getting up, so they could come with.

Moments later, they came back down the stairs with three groggy men in tow.

"Awake yet?" I called out with a chuckle.

Theo glared at me while the twins shook their heads.

I stifled my laughter as they all grabbed breakfast and wolfed it down.

Theo wore the same outfit he had yesterday—he probably didn't have other clothes—as did Marc and Marl, although they definitely looked a lot cleaner than they had yesterday.

Once they had shoveled down some food, we all got up and left the house, and walked down the street to the train station.

Being more awake, I looked at the other houses more closely. They were all *very* different, as I had noted last night, but they all had one thing in common—plants.

They were everywhere. And they made everything look bright and *alive*. I loved it.

When we made it to the train station, we had to wait a couple minutes before the train showed up. While we waited, something nagged at me. Something was missing.

"Cars," I said, causing everyone to turn and look at me.

"What about them?" Celestina asked, tilting their head curiously to the side.

I gestured around. "There aren't any cars."

"Of course not," Theo said, pushing his sunglasses up his nose. "They're loud and a pollutant and have been gone for at least fifty years now."

I pursed my lips. "Hmm."

At that point, the train started pulling into the station, so we turned our attention to the doors and all got on.

"We'll go to a coffee shop on Water Street," Celestina said, making Marc and Theo groan. Marl gave Celestina a very harsh glare.

"Come on, Eryn hasn't lived here her whole life like you all have. This is a chance to introduce her to the joy *we* had as kids," they said, crossing their arms. "It's fun and you know that."

"What's so bad about Water Street?" I asked, looking between everyone's faces.

Theo glanced at Celestina. "It's a street that has a river running on it. Like, the street is a river. You have to canoe down the damn thing."

"Sounds fun," I said, nodding my head. "As long as we don't tip over."

Theo's face turned red, and Celestina busted out laughing. I stared at them with an eyebrow raised.

"Don't you..." Theo started, but whatever he was going to say, he didn't finish.

"Theo's done that before," Celestina said, laughing. "And got his suit *drenched.*"

I didn't think Theo could get any redder, but he did. He went from watermelon to tomato in a couple seconds.

"Why were you wearing a suit on a canoe?" I asked, letting out a snort.

"Listen, I... I was *trying* to be nice to someone who isn't doing the same for me right now!" Theo whipped his head toward Celestina.

Celestina smiled and sighed. "Yes, yes, Theo was nice enough to volunteer to be my date to a dinner when I had just broken up with my shitty ex. The suit did look very nice."

"There's the appreciation," Theo said, crossing his arms. "No wonder we didn't hang out after that."

"I said I was sorry! It is a funny story, you gotta admit," Celestina said, smiling.

"Hmph," Theo muttered, sitting back in his seat.

The space suddenly became very awkward as no one said anything more, and everyone chose to sit in silence until we got to Water Street.

When the train finally stopped, we got off onto the platform, and I got my first look at Water Street.

It was, in fact, a giant river running as far as I could see in front of me, to my right, and to my left. Boats were hooked up everywhere, and it seemed that they were kind of a free for all.

As I watched, a small family of three stepped up to a little podium and pressed something on it. A boat silently moved beside the platform, the family climbed on, and then they began rowing.

We got in line for the podium, and eventually got up there.

"You want to do the honors?" Celestina asked me, pointing at the button.

I smiled. "Absolutely, I do."

I pressed the button and watched as it flashed green, and then a boat pulled up to the platform.

"We'll take a boat, and they'll take a boat," Celestina said, nodding at the guys. They leaned over and held the end of the boat. "Get in!"

I carefully stepped off the platform and into the boat, then slowly lowered myself onto the bench. Seated, I braced my feet as wide as they could go to stabilize the boat. Celestina climbed in after me, making the boat rock a bit.

Looking down, I saw the oars next to me and pulled them up. Putting them in the oarlocks, I glanced up at Celestina. "Which way?"

They pointed, and I started rowing.

Chapter 6

We rowed to a little coffee shop down Water Street called The Burnt Bean. I was a little confused by the name, until Celestina explained that that was how you made coffee. I took her word for it, and we got in line.

Once we got up to the counter (which was manned by robots), Celestina made their order and then looked at me. "What do you want?"

"Um…" I trailed off, looking at the menu. "English breakfast tea?"

"What size?" the robot ground out.

"The smallest you have," I replied, creeped out by the voice that sounded much less friendly than AIHNA.

The robot rang up the order, and I followed Celestina off to the side to wait for our drinks.

"Do you not like coffee?" Celestina asked as we sat down on a bench.

I shook my head. "I don't think so. Also, I have a question I've been meaning to ask about the whole gang thing yesterday."

"Go for it," Celestina said, crossing their legs.

"Okay, so a hundred years in the future, there's still gangs? And poverty?" I gestured at Marc and Marl. "Call me crazy, but wouldn't that not be a thing?"

They shrugged. "That… wasn't a priority."

"What was?" I asked, staring at them.

Before they could respond, the robot called our names for our drinks.

We grabbed them and walked back outside of the cafe, and Celestina sighed. "Listen, there's a lot that happened. Good things, bad things. I couldn't tell you all of it, because history is *not* my strong suit, and rumor has it that there are a lot of secrets. But the gist is that the government values money more than life. We all kind of hate it, but we've just… accepted it. We don't have a way to fix it."

They looked pretty upset, so I stopped myself from asking any other questions. We sat in silence, listening to the lapping of the water against the walls of the street.

"Let's go to the library next," Celestina said, nodding their head. "That way, Raven can point you toward some good books. And we can get you a library card."

"Sounds good to me." I looked around for a trash can to throw my cup into.

Celestina got up, and I followed suit as they threw away their cup into what I could only describe as… well, there isn't another way to put it. A giant barrel full of water. It was a giant barrel of water.

They dropped their cup in, and I watched as a bunch of little swimming bugs came up and started tearing it apart.

I dropped my cup in, and the little buggers went to work on my cup as well.

Interesting.

Once we had gathered up the guys, we summoned another couple of canoes to row back to the train platform. As we went, Celestina pointed out different shops and restaurants along the street. I absorbed each one, thinking about how peaceful everything was. At least on this street.

Once we managed to get on the train, Celestina pulled me over to a map on the wall that I hadn't seen previously. It showed the train lines, but more importantly, it was a map of the entire city.

The city consisted of a bunch of concentric circles, spreading out bigger and bigger until the last ring, which denoted the end of city limits. Train lines ran like spokes on a wheel through the rings, connecting them. You could go anywhere using the rail line.

"This is amazing," I commented to Celestina, staring at the map. "And no cars makes it even better."

They nodded. "The train is free, too, for everyone. Saves me a lot of money. I remember my parents talking about how much less money they spent once all of these were installed."

"What's beyond the city limits?" I asked, tracing the outer ring with my finger.

"Nothing but desert." Celestina shook their head. "The rest of the world is very, very lifeless."

Studying the map, I thought about how small of an area it represented. We seemed so… small.

Celestina went on and pointed out where the SMC was, where the shop Kimi worked at was located, and the library we were headed to.

"It's called the Great Library," Celestina said, tapping on the map. "It has all of what remains of the earth's literary works. Anything we could get our hands on, there's a copy of."

"Like the Library of Alexandria," I commented, nodding.

"Library of what?" Celestina asked, tilting their head. "What's that?"

I stared at them in confusion. "You… don't know what the Library of Alexandria was?"

They shook their head. "Nope."

After recovering from that surprise, I went on to explain the Library of Alexandria to them, in as much detail as I could remember. Celestina was baffled that such a thing had existed and they had never known about it.

Their bafflement was tabled when the train stopped and announced that we were downtown.

We all got off the train and made our way into downtown, which was packed with plants, and streams, and had solar panels on every roof. The buildings, like the other ones near the SMC, were various shades of white.

Walking down the streets, I felt at peace. Everyone around us was just going about their business, talking with co-workers, hanging out with friends, going shopping.

Spotting a couple of larger, fancier buildings without solar panels, I tapped Celestina on the shoulder and pointed at them. "What buildings are those?"

They looked where I was pointing. "Those are… those are where all the

CEOs of all the companies are. Those are their headquarters."

"Wow," I said, nodding. "How many more like those are there?"

Celestina gave me a half-smile. "Only those two."

"What?"

"Oh, I can answer this one," Marc piped up, coming to stand with Celestina and me. "Those corporations, especially the people, own just about everythin' in this city. Includin' the government folks."

"Marc!" Celestina said in a hissed whisper. "Not so loud!"

"It's true," Marc whispered back. "We all know it!"

"Well, I don't," I whispered, looking between them expectantly.

Celestina pursed their lips. "We'll talk about it more in the library, come on."

Soon, we walked up to a giant building that looked like a bunch of white books on their edge.

"This is the Great Library," Celestina said, gesturing with their hand. "I want you to meet a friend of mine. She's the head librarian here. She can answer a lot more of your questions than I can."

We walked in the giant, heavy doors, and I was in awe. There were hundreds of shelves, filled to the brim with books. Librarians walked around in silver and white suits, wearing silver headsets, controlling little robots that zoomed around and carried books to and fro. The sheer amount of books was amazing.

Without realizing it, I had stopped to stare. Celestina tugged my arm, and I followed again, still in shock over the beauty. As we went, Marc and Marl peeled off from the group, making a beeline toward a shelf. Theo stayed with us, walking a few paces behind.

We approached a young woman who was chatting with a couple other people. They both left once Celestina and I got closer.

"Raven," Celestina said, doing a small bow. "How're you doing today?"

Raven bowed back. "Doing well, and you?"

"Good! I brought a patient with me today. Well, not just a patient," Celestina said, turning to look at me. "It kinda feels like we might be friends now."

"I'm good with that," I agreed, turning to Raven and executing a small bow like Celestina had done. "And it's nice to meet you."

Raven smiled. "Nice to meet you as well. My name is Raven, and I use they/she pronouns."

"Eryn. And she/they pronouns," I said, grinning. "Celestina told me you could point me in the direction of some history books so I can do some catching up."

"Of course. Let's get you a library card first," they said, walking me toward a desk. "This can also serve as a form of ID until you get a job. Free of cost. Paid for by your local government."

"Hmm." I filled out the spaces I knew.

Celestina walked up beside me. "You can fill in my address for now until you have your own place."

They repeated their address to me, and I copied it down. Once I had filled out everything I could, I handed it back to Raven.

She looked at it and frowned. "You don't know your last name?"

"No," I replied, shaking my head. "Can't remember it."

Raven looked at Celestina. "Nothing on their file?"

"Nope, just a first name," Celestina said. "I thought it was odd, too."

"In that case, let me be the head librarian I was hired to be and search the archives for your name." Raven moved behind the desk and typed rapidly.

"You still have mechanical keyboards?" I glanced at Celestina.

They chuckled. "Yeah. A lot easier to replace and less glitchy."

"How do you spell your name?" Raven asked, bringing their head up from the computer.

I spelled it for her, then they went back to typing. She soon wore another frown, and her eyebrows scrunched together.

"What?" Celestina and I asked at the same time.

"Your full name is redacted."

I blinked, unsure what to say, as Celestina sputtered. "Redacted?"

"Yep, redacted," Raven confirmed, looking at me. "I found your first name all right, but it's in an almost completely redacted file."

"Shouldn't they have released those files? They should be from a hundred years ago!" Celestina said, leaning on the desk.

"Yes. Typically, it's a fifty-year period before files become unredacted. But anything coming up in relation to your name, Eryn, is blacked out," Raven said, looking back at the computer. "Except for one other thing."

"What?" I asked, finally finding my voice.

"These redacted files…" Raven said, trailing off. "They all come from the CI archives."

I again lost my voice. We would have to go to the museum after all.

Feeling my throat begin to close, I felt the urge to just run and keep running. Make up some excuse that would keep us from going there.

But another part of me, the calm, steady part, had already accepted that this life, this peaceful one where I could just walk around the city and exist, was gone. I could still do that, of course, but if the rest of my memories were anything like the nightmares last night… I had a feeling there would be too many demons inside my head for me to be at peace completely.

"We need to go to the museum," I said firmly, looking over at Celestina. "That seems like the only way we'll get any answers with my memories."

"Are you sure?" Celestina asked, studying me. "That could be a lot for you."

"I know." I sighed. "Trust me, I'm aware of what could happen. But it does me no good to just keep avoiding it. Plus, that's what you're here for, right?"

Celestina smiled weakly. "Yeah, that's what I'm here for. If you're really sure…"

"I am."

"Then we can go right now. The CI Museum is only a couple of blocks away," Celestina finished, nodding.

We turned around to see Theo standing behind us, putting on his sunglasses.

"I'm coming with you two, of course. You might need help restraining her," Theo said, nodding at me.

"Hey," I said, sticking my tongue out at him. "Watch it. I could probably knock you on your ass."

He snorted but didn't say anything more, except to inform Celestina and I that Marc and Marl were going to stay at the museum for a while.

With that, we made our way out of the library and back onto the street, Celestina leading the way.

We passed another couple of buildings before we came upon a building that was slightly more gray than other buildings around it and had a long-ass line out front.

"What's going on? The museum's never this busy," Celestina said, stopping to stare at the line.

"I think it's the museum's 100th anniversary today." Theo cursed under his breath. "I should've remembered. They've been talking about it for weeks. They're putting on a bunch of cheesy events for the public."

"How are we going to get in?" I asked bluntly, studying the line. "Are we going to stand in this line?"

"We're not standing in any line. Follow me," Theo said, taking off.

Celestina and I followed him around the line and toward the side of the museum. It was a lot more empty over there, with the only people being two guards dressed similarly to Theo.

"Hey, Ronan, what's up?" one of the guards called, raising a hand. "You on patient duty again?"

"Flowers, good to see you, too." Theo grabbed the other person's arm in a friendly greeting. Flowers did the same, clutching Theo's arm at the same time.

"What brings you all over here?" Flowers turned to look at Celestina and me. "Hey, you must be Celestina! Theo talks about you all the time. Good to finally see your face."

Celestina said "What?"

At the same time, Theo frantically said, "No, I don't!"

I looked at Theo and had to swallow a laugh. He had turned as red as a tomato and glared daggers at his friend.

"I, for one, would like to know more about what's been said." Celestina glanced at Theo. "But we're here because Eryn, my patient and friend, needs their memory back. And all clues of who they were are pointing straight here."

"You know how crowded it is in there?" Flowers said, with the guard standing next to him, nodding his head in agreement. "Plus, not sure we're allowed to let y'all in."

To my surprise, Theo spoke up again. "C'mon, Flowers, do me a solid here. I'll owe you one."

I nodded. Theo was a lot nicer than I had originally thought.

Flowers seemed to consider, then leaned over to his buddy at the door and whispered in his ear. The other guard busted out laughing, and I glanced back and forth between them, waiting for one to say something.

"All right, Ed and I are agreed, you can come in. However, our deal is that we let you in, and you ask Celestina out on a nice date like you been saying you were going to do." Flowers smiled wickedly.

Celestina's eyebrows shot to the top of their forehead, and I'm sure I looked just as surprised as they did. Theo, on the other hand, was looking at Flowers in exasperation.

"Really, man? You really had to do that?" Theo groaned, dragging a hand across his face. "Fine, I'll do it, just let us in."

"Nuh uh, you gotta ask now, so we can see what their answer is," Ed said, matching Flowers' mischievous smile.

Theo took a big breath and stared daggers at them. When they didn't say anything else, he turned toward Celestina. He was, again, red as a tomato, and I thought it was hilarious.

"Celestina," he started, his voice cracking.

His buddies by the door broke out laughing, and he shot them a glare.

Clearing his throat, he tried again. "Celestina, would you go on a date with me? We could go to that little Greek place you like on Water Street for dinner."

I glanced at Celestina, and noticed that they were also a blazing red.

"Yeah, I'd like that," Celestina said softly, smiling at Theo.

He looked ready to melt into the ground.

I sat in silence as the two guards by the door hooted. I was happy to see Theo and Celestina looking at each other somewhat like a deer in headlights.

"All right, you folks can go in," Flowers said, turning to unlock the door. He opened the door, and I led the way this time, sure that if I didn't, the other two would never move.

Celestina came in right behind me, and Theo followed. The door slammed shut behind us, and we collected ourselves as we sat in the dimly lit hallway.

"This way," Theo said, clearing his throat.

We followed him down the hallway, and as we were walking, I felt Celestina grab my hand and squeeze it. I squeezed back, knowing exactly what they meant, and then let go.

Soon we were in the full light and were surrounded by people and exhibits.

"This is early CI," Theo said, leaning in so we could hear him. "Probably a little too far back for you. We're going to move into the next room. Follow me and stay close."

We did as he asked and stayed right behind him as we made our way through the packed room of people.

As we passed under the archway into the next room, Theo once again leaned in. "This is probably close in time to where you might have been, if you were in the CI. I know Marc mentioned a statue. There are a couple in here, and a couple in the next room, I think. Look around and see if there's anything you recognize. We'll follow you."

I nodded and started looking around.

There were so many people that I had to squeeze through a bunch of groups just to see an exhibit. I beelined for a couple of statues and photos, which were likenesses of older men.

Nope, nothing I recognized there.

I made my way around the room, checking every exhibit, even the ones that weren't people. Nothing even brought back a sliver of memory.

Moving on through the crowd again, I pushed my way into the next room, where I froze in my tracks.

There were exhibits all around the edges of the room, which I didn't look at, nor did I care to at the moment. My gaze was fixed on the statue taking up the center of the room.

The statue screamed confidence and control. She stood, tall and proud, shoulders down, arms crossed, wearing a T-shirt, camo pants, and a pair of combat boots. The feet stood a shoulder's width apart, in parade rest.

A gun rested in the holster on her hip. Her hair was cropped short. And her eyes... Her eyes were piercing, like she would rip you apart if given the chance.

"Oh, my shit," I heard Celestina breathe behind me as my eyes wandered down to the plaque below the feet of the statue. It read:

Eryn "The Dragon" Vue

Director of the CI

May you always protect us.

I felt my breathing pick up.

My mind wasn't entirely there, in the museum. It was earlier in my life.

Gun shots. Blood. The sound of knives cutting flesh.

Dead eyes.

"Eryn? Eryn? She's dissociating. Eryn, I need you to focus on me, can you do that?"

I saw Celestina in front of me, and I fought against my mind to think about them.

"Focus on the details," Celestina said calmly, while Theo kept people away from us.

I looked at Celestina's clothes. They were wearing a blue shirt, a teal color, with black shorts. The shorts had fake pockets. Why did they always put shitty pockets in clothing that is marketed to women?

That thought was just enough to bring me back to reality. I noticed that I, at some point, had made it to the floor, and was sitting with my knees up to my chest.

"Celestina?" I asked, my voice trembling, "Can we leave? I don't think I can be here anymore."

"Of course, let's get you up," they said, scooping an arm under me and helping me stand. "Theo, we're good, let's go."

Theo nodded and led the way out of the museum. Whereas the pack of people hadn't bothered me before, the noise grated on me now. I wanted and needed *out*.

Soon enough, we were in the fresh air, and I took in a deep breath.

"Let's go home," Celestina said, adjusting their arm under me to help stabilize me on our walk home.

Chapter 7

Once we got back to Celestina's place, everything was a blur. Celestina took me to my room and sat me down on the bed, saying that they were going to get me some food. I kept trying to focus on the little details of the furniture to stay grounded. Memories kept flooding back, and every time I thought I was done, more came.

Celestina returned to my room with a bowl. "Eat."

I woodenly took the bowl and spoon from them and started routinely putting spoonfuls of soup into my mouth.

Once the bowl was empty, Celestina took it from me and sat in silence with me.

They were the first one to break the silence. "You know, there is benefit in telling someone about the things you've gone through. Do you want to try telling me one of the memories right now?"

I gulped and nodded. Opening my mouth, a squeak came out first. Then I cleared my throat and spoke.

"I guess one… Well, the locket? You remember that?"

Celestina nodded.

"That's my sister. My little sister. And I see this memory of her… her… " I sniffed, tears rolling down my face, desperately trying to keep some composure. "She was run down by her old gymnastics instructor and his car. Every bone was broken. I still remember the sound and how much blood there was."

The tears came a lot quicker now, and snot was threatening to roll down my face as well. Celestina handed me a box of tissues, and I blew my nose.

"I'm sorry," they said, wrapping an arm around my shoulders.

I leaned in and cried, so very glad that they were there, and I wasn't dealing with this alone.

There was a tentative knock at the door, and I brought my head up and quietly said, "Come in."

The door opened, and in came Theo, then Marc and Marl. In any other circumstance, I would've been embarrassed for them to see me like this. But for now, I was just grateful they were here.

"How're you feeling?" Theo asked, coming to sit on the other side of me. "It seems like you've been through a lot of rough shit."

"I'm feeling shitty," I said, blowing my nose again. "But I'm also glad you all are here."

Theo tentatively put another arm around my shoulders, and Marc and Marl sat on the floor. Each put a hand on one of my calves. They all sat there with me as I cried myself out.

When I felt drained of all energy, I simply looked at Celestina. They understood immediately and told everyone it was time for me to get some rest.

They all cleared out pretty quickly, with one last reminder from Celestina that they were right down the hall if I needed them.

After I nodded in understanding, they closed the door, and I was left by myself. The emptiness in the room was palpable, but I was too tired to care at this point.

Dragging myself to the top of the bed, I didn't even bother to get under the covers before I fell asleep.

Alarms blaring. Something had gone wrong. Someone had raised the alarm.

We were running, Ryan and I. Sprinting as fast as we could with the package in our arms.

There were men behind us, and they were gaining.

Ryan knew I was the faster runner. He shoved the package into my arms. "Go!"

I grabbed the package and sprinted as fast as I could. The sound of gunfire echoed behind me, but I kept running, sure that Ryan would follow.

Bursting into the outside, I saw John in the getaway car. The door was open, and he was yelling at me to hurry. I jumped in and turned to check on Ryan, but he was nowhere to be found.

When I tried to go after him, I realized the doors were locked, and John pressed the gas, making the car squeal as we peeled out.

I kept yelling at him to go back, we had to save Ryan, but he kept saying Ryan was gone and staying would only get us killed, too.

We drove for several minutes, and I was sobbing into my hands, wrecked at the idea that Ryan was dead. I could picture his dead body, lifeless on the ground. At this point, I had seen too many dead bodies.

The car stopped, and John kept murmuring things at me.

Alarm bells went off in my head.

Looking up, I saw John's hand raised, preparing to jab a syringe into my body.

Screaming in fury, I grabbed his arm and twisted it so hard I broke it. I could hear the crunch. The syringe jabbed into his body, and I pressed down, delivering whatever was in it straight into his heart.

He was dead in moments, a look of shock and pain on his face.

I took in deep breaths, then stared in horror as I realized what had just happened. Two out of three people in my unit were dead.

Scrambling out of the car, I grabbed the package and ran.

When I made it back to base camp, I was breathing hard, and others started pouring out of the makeshift buildings to see what was going on.

Waking up, I cut off a scream that had been building in my throat.

Taking in deep breaths, I closed my eyes and paid attention to my heart. I waited until it was no longer racing, then opened my eyes.

Glancing at the clock, I noticed it was the middle of the night still. Everyone would be asleep.

"AIHNA?" I whispered, unsure if the AI would hear me.

"Yes. I am here."

Breathing a sigh of relief, I thought about what I needed at that moment. Now that my memories were mostly back, I did remember that working out had always made me feel better.

"Does Celestina have any workout equipment in this house?" I asked, still in a whisper.

"There is a small gym in this house, which Mx. Celestina typically uses for physical rehabilitation, although anyone in their home is welcome to use it."

"Where is it?" I asked, moving to stand from the bed.

AIHNA didn't reply, but then I just… knew. It was down the hallway and to the right, last door.

Shaking my head, I stood. Maybe Celestina had told me, and I had just forgotten?

Too stressed to think about it further, I cautiously opened the door, making sure it didn't squeak as I slid out of my room.

Going down the hallway, I found the door easily and slid inside the room. Small gym? AIHNA wasn't joking.

I was thinking Celestina had a small workout room with a couple pieces of equipment, but nope. Apparently, the height of the house wasn't all the second floor. And the building went back farther than I had thought.

Examining the room, I found all the regular gym equipment, but there were other things, too. A large mat in the center, under a hoop hanging from the ceiling. There were long pieces of fabric a few feet away, and a pole. Some small pieces of gymnastics equipment. A long rope also hung from the ceiling, and a small, one-lane track ran around the center of the room.

I pulled off my shoes, knowing the combat boots would be too clunky for what I wanted to do.

Walking to the center mat, I took my time stretching out the muscles in my body. It felt good to have that stretch.

Once I was warmed up, I went to the small track, which honestly wasn't that big, and started walking.

The steady rhythm of my footsteps calmed me, and before I knew it, I had increased my pace to a jog. I beat a steady rhythm into the ground, letting the vibrations of my jogging resonate up my body.

Once I got bored, I slowed down, stopped, and considered the other pieces of equipment. My body was itching to just *move*.

Unsure what I was capable of after a hundred-year nap, I took it easy at first. Light weights only. And when those were too easy, I upped the weight.

It seemed I could lift as much as I could before the cryo.

No muscle degeneration.

Celestina's comment floated back into my mind. I must not have lost any of my muscle in cryo.

Eyeing the gymnastics equipment, I briefly considered whether I should. I remembered being trained on those when I was young—at the tender age of ten—but I had used them less and less as I had gotten older.

What the hell.

Moving over to the bars, I jumped up to grab the first one. Swinging back and forth to gain momentum, I flipped myself over, around, and threw myself at the second bar.

My hands grabbed the bar easily, as if no time had passed at all between my young self and the person I was now.

After a few more rounds feeling the satisfying *thud* of the bar in my hands, I dismounted.

Barely breathing hard, I walked back over to the mat to stretch.

As I sat down, the door opened, revealing Celestina's worried face and Theo's grim one right behind.

"Here you are! I was worried sick when you weren't in your room!" Celestina said, letting the door close behind them.

Theo caught the door before it closed completely and let himself in.

"I'm okay, just need to move," I said, stretching. "What about him?"

"*Him* is here to make sure Celestina doesn't get hurt," Theo said, wiggling his nose.

I stuck my tongue out at him and continued stretching.

"What all have you done?" Celestina asked, sitting beside me on the mat.

"Jogged for a bit, did some weights, used the bars," I replied, leaning to my right, stretching my arm over my head.

They nodded. "And how do you feel? Any dizziness or fatigue?"

"Nope," I said, shaking my head. "I'm where I was before I was frozen."

"How did you get frozen? Do you remember?" Theo asked, standing at the edge of the mat.

I shook my head again. "The last thing I remember, I think—it's still all jumbled around in here—was sitting in my office at the CI, doing paperwork."

"Hmm." Celestina stared at me. "Could you fight Theo?"

"What?" I paused my stretch to look them in the eye.

"Fight Theo. So I can see how well your body is doing," Celestina explained, although I still didn't take it as much of an explanation.

I gestured at the equipment. "Why not have me do one of these things?"

"Because fighting was what you did before you got some of your memory back. It seems like the motions help trigger memories for you. And I want to see if you're still in good shape."

"That doesn't make sense," I argued, having completely given up on stretching. "I told you I am where I was before cryo. And you've seen me fight, in the clothes shop."

Celestina sighed. "Do you remember what I said about how you didn't have any muscle or organ degeneration?"

"Yes."

"Well, what I didn't tell you is that is *highly* unusual. And seeing you fight like you did… I have a theory, but I want to see how accurate it is," Celestina said, making a calming gesture.

"What theory?" I crossed my arms.

"I don't…" They started before looking at my face. "Fine. I think your mom gave you some kind of enhancement something or other."

"My mother? What?" I sputtered, confused. "How do you…?"

"Eryn, your last name is *Vue*. Who else do you know with that last name?" Celestina shook their head at me.

I opened my mouth for a moment, then snapped it shut. "*Oh.*"

"Dr. Vue is Eryn's mom," Theo said, nodding. "Now that I think about it, you two do look alike. And act alike, too."

I couldn't say anything, because as soon as Celestina said it, I remembered. And they were right.

"Holy shit. And she didn't say anything!" I spat out, making annoyed noises.

"Yes, now, will you please just fight Theo? I'm sure you've been wanting to do that since you met him."

"Hey! I resent that."

"You were a bit of a jerk, at first." Celestina turned to look at him. "And you're still not all that good at the sensitivity thing."

Theo muttered something under his breath but didn't say anything else.

"Fine," I said, standing. "I'll do it. But because I want to see if I've lost anything."

Celestina held up their hands. "Whatever you want."

They looked at Theo, and he let out a huge sigh. He leaned down to take off his boots and his holster and set them together off the mat.

Stepping on the mat, Theo joined me in the center.

"Don't go easy on me," I said, smiling.

"Don't worry, I won't," Theo replied, then swung his fist toward my face.

I leaned out of the path of the punch, and went low, jabbing him three times in the stomach.

Hearing the breath getting pushed out of his lungs, I hooked a foot around his knee and pushed him the same time I pulled his knee forward.

He went down, hitting the mat with a *smack.*

I let him get back up, but this time was different. My eyes were more focused, and it was like I was in hyperdrive.

Theo came at me more cautiously this time, faking a few punches before attempting to unbalance me by kicking at my ankles.

I easily dodged it. It was like every move he made was in slow motion, like he was moving through syrup.

Moving in with my attack, I hit him with a flurry of moves, feeling him block each move slower and slower each time.

Then, an opening.

I grabbed him and threw him over my shoulder. He landed on his back. Before he could get up, I straddled him and turned him over to where I had an arm around his neck and my legs wrapped around his body.

He tapped my arm three times, and I let him go.

I rolled to my feet and watched as Theo's chest heaved as he caught his breath.

I offered my hand. He took it, and I pulled him up.

"You're... strong..." Theo said, wheezing.

"I gathered that," I said wryly, smiling. Looking over at Celestina, I called, "Was that enough?"

"Plenty." Celestina nodded. "I definitely think your mom did something to enhance you to make sure you were okay. I wonder if she knew about the cryo?"

I shrugged. "I don't know. All I know is that I have questions for her, and I want to just be whoever I am now. Yeah, I'm a good fighter," I said, pointing at Theo. "But I have no desire to do that again. You have no idea how many dead bodies I saw when I slept."

"And I won't ask you to do it again," Celestina said, raising their hand. "On my honor."

Nodding, I walked over to help Celestina up. "Can I help you with lunch? After I take a shower, of course."

They smiled. "Sure. I'll see you in the kitchen in a bit."

Without another word, I left, grabbing my shoes as I headed out the door.

Once I was back in my room, I stepped into the bathroom to rinse off all the sweat, and my vision went fuzzy.

A blurry image swam in front of my eyes. Thinking I was about to pass out, I felt around for the bed and sat down.

But then I heard a garbled clicking noise.

"What the hell?" I muttered.

A blurry blue blob came into my vision, moved right, then left, and then I heard the clicking noise again.

Soon, it cleared up.

I sat in place for a moment, unsure as to what had just happened but decided not to worry about it.

After all, I was still getting flashbacks. Maybe this was one.

Chapter 8

Once I had showered off, I went to the kitchen. Celestina was there, waiting for me, as I went to stand next to them.

"What're we making?" I asked, rubbing my hands together.

"My special lasagna," Celestina said, smiling. "It has alfredo sauce!"

I laughed and helped them out with anything that they asked me to do. Chopped some onions, nearly cried, and then cooked some chicken.

Once we put the lasagna in the oven, Celestina turned on the little TV that was in the dining room. The screen popped on to show the daily news. We lazily watched some weather reports, just relaxing and not really talking.

Then *BREAKING NEWS* rolled across the center of the screen.

"Hello, Lorinians! This is breaking news! We have reports that the plants are beginning to wilt on the west side of the city. Anonymous reports say this has been going on for days now, with strict instructions not to tell citizens. This information is brought to us by a whistleblower, who will remain unnamed. Stay tuned for more."

The room took on an uncomfortable silence, with Celestina and I both staring in shock at the ad that had just come up on screen.

"No, no, no," Celestina said, shaking their head. "This can't be happening."

"What does it mean?" I turned to look at them.

Celestina ran a hand through their hair. "The plants are what keeps the city alive. If they're wilting… we're losing oxygen. We could die."

Standing up from my chair, I glanced at Celestina.

"What?" they asked.

"I've decided answers can't wait." I held out a hand. "You coming?"

"Now? The SMC is closed today," Celestina called out as I went over to yank on my shoes.

"I don't care. This is not happening when I finally have a chance at a life. And she's the only one I know who will see me. I don't even know if she'll be able to do anything, but I am not going to sit here and do nothing." I yanked the laces on my boots.

"I thought you said…"

"That was before they"—I pointed at the TV—"said the city might be dying, and I might not be able to live a life I want to live."

"Fine, I'm coming. But you better be safe about this" Celestina stood.

"Let's go. I don't need Theo tagging along," I commented, heading toward the front door.

We left the house and quickly sped toward the train station, hopping on as soon as we could.

Once the train was moving, I let out a sigh of relief.

Celestina sat next to me. "Are we actually doing this?"

"We are," I said, glancing at them. "Now, which stop do we get off at?"

"Asclepius Street." Celestina pointed at the map on the wall. "Three stops away from here."

I nodded, and with nothing else to say, sat in silence.

When we arrived at the correct station, we got out, and I followed Celestina to the SMC. The front doors were open (thankfully; I didn't want to have to remember how to pick a lock).

We walked in, and it was almost empty, with no one except the guard at the front desk.

Walking up to the guard, Celistina said, "Yerick."

He looked up at us. "Ah, tiny Tina! What're you doing here when the building's closed?"

"I told you not to call me that. We're here to see Dr. Vue," Celestina said through gritted teeth.

Yerick laughed. "Dr. Vue has said no visitors, sweet cheeks. So, I'm afraid you're out of luck."

I took a deep breath in, then leaned over the desk and grabbed the front of his shirt, like I had done to Theo.

"One, you call them *Celestina*. Not tiny Tina. Not sweet cheeks. Celestina. Second, you're going to call up to Dr. Vue and let her know that Celestina and Eryn want to meet with her. Got it?"

Yerick nodded as much as he could, wide-eyed. I let him go, and he punched buttons and spoke into a tiny microphone.

A couple of men in black suits showed up a few minutes later.

"They'll take you to her," Yerick said, eyeing me.

I nodded, but my gut was telling me something wasn't right. They started ushering Celestina and I toward a stairwell.

They took us down the stairs, and after going down a couple flights, I knew we were definitely going the wrong direction. One guy's hand kept hovering over the gun every so often. Every time he did so, his buddy kept turning his head to the side and coughing.

I looked over at Celestina, who met my eyes, and I saw fear for the first time.

Holding their gaze, I mouthed, "Drop."

They reacted quickly, immediately hitting the ground, and I went on the attack. Within seconds, the two men were down and unconscious.

"Come on," I said, offering Celestina my hand.

They grabbed it, and we went back up. When we reached ground level, I paused. Motioning for Celestina to stay still, I flattened myself against the stairs and peered over the top.

Yerick wasn't paying attention. He stared intently at his computer, one hand on the desk, the other underneath. From where I was laying, I could hear moans. Disgusted, I motioned for Celestina to get up, and I did as well, covering them as we moved up the next set of stairs.

Once we were out of view, I led them up one more flight.

"Here," I said, pushing open the door for the third floor. I stuck my head through, and immediately pulled back.

Watching the door, I glanced at Celestina. "Go up to the next landing. Hide. I'll call when I'm done."

Without protest or question, Celestina went up the stairs. Bracing myself for what I was about to do, I took a deep breath. Then the knob on the door started to turn.

Grabbing the knob, I opened the door quickly and slammed it into the guy coming to check out the disturbance. He was out immediately, and I rolled into the hallway, staying low as I heard the hum of bullets.

I knew I had five more guys to take out. Zig-zagging across the hallway, I dodged gunfire. The guards missed me, except for one that got me in my left arm.

Ignoring the flash of pain, I jumped the nearest guy and wrangled the gun from him and knocked him out. By chance, this guy also had a standard issue stunner. Using the guy as a shield, I grabbed it, dropped the gun, and took down the rest of the guys in quick succession. I dropped the stunner, ran back to the stairwell, and called for Celestina.

They came down the stairwell, unharmed, and followed me into the hall and to the unguarded door. I looked back at them and noticed they seemed unnerved.

"They're not dead, just knocked out. I don't want to kill any more people," I said, grimacing.

Celestina shook their head and purposefully ignored the bodies. Assuming that they were still recovering from their fear, I opened the door, and saw Dr. Vue in her wheelchair, pointing a gun at me

"How many guards does it take to protect my mom?" I asked, glancing back at the hallway. "You really think six is enough?"

She dropped the nose of the gun. "Eryn. You remember."

"I do, and I have some questions for you," I said, taking the gun from her and setting on a nearby counter.

Her office was cluttered, to say the least. Papers everywhere, awards and certificates on every possible surface.

"Why didn't you say it was you? The front desk called in a threat and everyone went into guard mode. If you had just told the guy to tell me it was you, none of my men would have to wake up with headaches," Dr. Vue… my mom… replied, her shoulders dropping.

The guard downstairs must've called us up as a threat on purpose then.

Nothing could really change the unconscious men outside though, so I wasn't going to worry about it. I stood there awkwardly for a few seconds, then cautiously went over to hug her.

"I may have scared the guy a little bit when I told him I wanted a meeting with you," I said, smiling.

Then tears started leaking out of my eyes.

"Mom," I said, my throat closed.

"Eryn," she replied, and I could tell that she was crying, too. We stayed like that until I heard a cough behind me. Awkwardly, I stood and moved to the side.

"Mom, uh… I brought Celestina with me. Obviously," I said, gesturing at Celestina.

"I see that. Thank you for helping my daughter get her memories back," my mom said, smiling.

Celestina grinned and reached a hand up to scratch their neck. "Not a problem at all, Dr. Vue. Just doing what I was hired to do."

My mom looked back at me, and then her gaze fell to my arm. "Honey, you have a bullet in your arm," she said nonchalantly.

I glanced at it. "Oh, yeah, one of the guards got me. Mind getting it out?" I shrugged quickly out of my jacket.

Pain rocketed up my arm as I pulled it out of the sleeve. Gritting my teeth, I kneeled in front of the desk and set my arm on top. Mom rolled up her sleeves, then rolled closer to the desk.

"It's minor, barely under the skin. Easy enough to get out. Care to assist, Celestina?"

Celestina stepped closer and rolled up their sleeves.

"What about anesthesia? Or a numbing salve?" Celestina asked.

An unearthly snort came out of me, and my Mom gave me a disapproving look.

"That's what I wanted to do every time this happened, but no, none of that," Mom said, sticking her tongue out at me.

Shaking their head, Celestina grabbed gloves from the top of a nearby cabinet and snapped them on. "I shouldn't be surprised."

"Here you go, dear." My mom passed Celestina a pair of tweezers, some alcohol, and a bandage.

They swabbed the area with alcohol, which stung a bit, then took the tweezers and grabbed the bullet. It felt weird, as always, to feel the bullet being pulled out, but it didn't hurt as much as it used to. I kept perfectly still until the metal was out of my flesh, then grimaced as Celestina pulled the bandage tight around the wound.

My mother watched, looking impressed. "You're very talented."

Taking off the gloves, Celestina looked up, and I could tell they were blushing. "Thank you, Dr. Vue. I appreciate the compliment."

Celestina threw the gloves into a biowaste bin, then turned to me. "We're here. There are several unconscious men in the corridor. I believe you wanted to ask some questions? Or should we do something about the men in the hallway?"

It was my turn to blush.

My mom replied for me. "They'll be fine. Physical is her... style. No need to worry about them. We're safe enough with Eryn in here."

I sighed. "You really had to go there?"

"I'm your mother, dear. My job is to embarrass you," she said, grinning at me.

Shaking my head, I turned to Celestina. "Sorry about her."

Celestina just smiled and said, "It's okay."

Turning back to my mom, I looked around the room. "Can we speak somewhere a little more private?"

Mom rolled out from behind the desk and toward a door with a mop sign on it.

"Supply closet?" Celestina asked, looking confused.

I shook my head and grabbed her hand, pulling her along as I followed my mother. Mom put her biometrics into a pad on the side, and the door moved over to reveal what I assumed was her lab.

We silently followed her inside. It still looked the same, but it was... updated. The walls were pure white, and the benchtop was a bright silver. Her wall of parts for her bioengineering projects was organized the same, but all the parts were newer, shinier. Her big equipment was organized by type, and was all clean.

"Lab looks great, Mom," I quipped.

"They keep me updated," she replied curtly. She stopped by a bench and turned to face me. "So, what are these questions you have?"

"First, do you know why I was frozen?" I asked, figuring I would get the most nerve-wracking question out of the way first.

She shook her head. "No. I thought you were dead."

"That's comforting," I said sarcastically, letting out a breath I had been holding. "Second question, have you seen the news?"

My mom gestured in frustration. "Which news? You'll have to be more specific."

"The plants wilting," I shot back, crossing my arms. "You do bioengineering, right? Can you fix it?"

She let out a short bark of laughter. "I do bioengineering with humans. Different cellular structures. I can't do shit with plants."

I blew air out of my nose, feeling my anger start to rise. Taking a couple of deep breaths, I pulled myself together. "So, what's going to happen? Is it fixable? I kinda like the idea of not being a soldier."

"It's probably not fixable, given that the only person who *could* fix it was found dead in their apartment two years ago," Mom said, sighing. "In my own opinion, they were murdered."

"You think Dr. Burns was murdered?" Celestina asked, eyes wide.

She nodded. "The timing was too suspicious. They'd talked with me about how the government wanted full rights to their research, and Dr. Burns was afraid they would do something bad with it. So, they burned their notes. A week later, they were dead."

"That seems weird," I said, shaking my head. "Why would they kill someone that they needed information from? And also, what the fuck kind of government do we have now?"

"For your first question, if they had someone else who had the information they needed, and they didn't want Dr. Burns blabbing. For your second, not a very good one."

"Okay…" I trailed off. "So, you can't do anything, and the only person who could is dead. Brilliant."

"Chances are, the plants will continue wilting. They don't give a shit. And they think I'm old and senile and don't pay attention, but I do. I heard they were building a spaceship," Mom said, raising her hand to keep me from speaking. "I know it sounds far-fetched to you, but Celestina would know as well as I do on this. It's entirely possible they would let the city die."

"Why?" I asked, looking between the two of them.

"Profit," Celestina whispered, looking at my mom.

She nodded. "Profit. People in a panic will do anything to save themselves and their families, including paying everything they have. Especially if it looks like the only chance to survive."

"So how—" I stopped when my mother fixed her gaze on me. Taking a deep breath in, I shook my head. "No."

"You were made for this," she said, reaching out and taking my hand.

"No," I said, shaking my head more rapidly.

"Eryn…"

"It always has to be me, doesn't it?" I yelled, making both of them take a step back. "Can't you see I'm tired and fucking traumatized?"

"Eryn, please. You can do this," Mom said gently, as if talking to an animal about to run. "No one else has the freedom."

I growled and looked at my mom, then over at Celestina.

They looked scared but were looking at me with sympathy.

Breathing deeply and trying to keep myself under control, I turned back to my mom. "What do I need to do to have a chance at a normal life?"

She turned away from me and rolled over to a storage cabinet. After unlocking it, she grabbed a box from inside and rolled to the benchtop. "This is what will keep you safe." She moved aside the latch and opened the lid.

Celestina and I moved closer to see what she had in the box.

They looked like little flesh-colored pills, with a scaled pattern down the body. They sat there, ten in a row, nestled inside a soft foam.

"What are these?" Celestina asked, eyes wide with wonder.

"A bioengineered pill, that, when it touches human skin, sinks into the body. After a week, all parts of the body are infused with micro strengtheners that make the body stronger and impervious to disease or any type of sickness. That's what'll get you where you need to go," Mom said as we studied the little pills.

"Where is so dangerous that I need one of these?" I asked, tracing the outside of the box with one finger.

"The desert. But you already have one. After Ryan died, when you came home, I put one on you while you were taking a nap." Mom placed a hand on the counter. "I know I should've asked permission, but you weren't who you used to be. You were self-destructive, impulsive, and had temper issues. Neither your father, myself, nor Apollo knew what to do."

"Who's Apollo?" Celestina asked, looking up at me.

I took in a breath. "Apollo was part of my unit when I used to do field missions as part of the CI. He was the only one who didn't die when we were sent on a mission to retrieve a package from a warehouse. He and I got closer when I stopped doing field missions and became the director of the CI."

"Oh, I'm sorry," Celestina said, placing a hand on my arm. "I'm sorry you lost your unit like that."

"Hazard of the job," I said, shrugging. "But I appreciate it."

And then, to my everlasting embarrassment, I broke into tears. You can only hold your emotions in to a point.

I leaned down and hugged my mother, who held me and murmured words of comfort in my ear.

Forcing myself to stop, I took some deep breaths and wiped away my tears, pulling away from my mom to do so. And as I looked at the pills through blurry eyes, a thought came to me. "Mom, how many of those pills do you have?"

She grimaced. "Only those ten. Two of the parts involved are extremely rare; one no longer exists. Those are the only ones left."

She shut the case and latched it, then handed it to me. "Use them wisely. To get to where you need to go, you're going to need a team. Here, let me see them again real quick."

Mom took the box back and set it on the benchtop. She rolled to a low cabinet, pulled out gloves, and pulled them on swiftly. "Celestina, sit down, sweetheart," Mom ordered, her tone sweet but her words brooked no argument.

I grabbed a chair from a corner and set it down for them. Celestina sat and rolled up her sleeve so that the fabric was bunched above the shoulder. Mom opened the box and carefully pulled out a pill with a pair of tweezers.

"It shouldn't react with gloves, but you can never be too safe," Mom commented, carefully lowering the pill until it touched Celestina's shoulder.

It immediately shot out these little spindly legs, as fine as spiderwebs. They latched onto Celestina's skin, and the pill melted into their flesh, leaving no trace. Celestina sat, tense, bracing herself for pain that would never come.

I examined the area. "You said it takes a week to completely affect the body?"

My mom nodded. "Yes. I originally made twelve of these. I used one on you. You should know the other was used on Apollo. I would go visit him. He may be of some help."

My head snapped around. "Apollo's still alive?"

Mom smiled.

"Yes, he is. In fact, he was one of the first that I used the Elder Treatment on. I imagine he was probably mentioned to you as Mr. Clevand." Mom rolled back the way we had originally come, discarding her gloves near the door, and holding the box on her lap. "Your destination in the desert is one you should know well. Do you remember a year after you became director?"

"Yes," I said, my heart beating faster.

"The base?"

"That one? It's abandoned!"

"And it will have what you need."

"And that will be?"

"You'll know when you see it."

Then it hit me again. Apollo was alive.

"I need to go see him." I declared, heading toward the door.

"Slow down!" My mom yelled, hands on her hips. "I have more to tell you."

Pausing, I turned back around and walked back to her. "Yes?" My hand twitched, betraying my newfound energy.

"Remember what I was working on just before you went on… well, the mission where Ryan didn't come back?" Mom asked, handing me the box and rolling to another door.

"Yeah. You said that particular project would never work." I raised an eyebrow.

"And you told me I could do anything, and the only obstacle was myself. Turns out you were right." Mom pushed the sliding door to one side. Inside the little closet rested a large pair of wings, a shining, metallic ebony.

"How…?" I asked, reverently stepping forward to stroke the feathers, which felt like thin pieces of metal.

"The inspiration came from the little pills. The skin adhesion bit, not the rest. Fortunately, the skin adhesives were very reproducible, and I was able to transfer that onto the Sky Fliers. Once put on, they will never come off. But they can disappear when you want them to. Completely disappear. That, your father actually took care of. I have no clue how he did it, hence the only pair of wings I have is this one. Take them." Mom urged.

Without hesitation, I stepped forward and took them out. "They're beautiful," I said, stroking the feathers again.

I turned to Celestina. "Would you do me the honor of putting these on me?"

She smiled in bewilderment and gently took the wings from me. "I would be honored. This is nothing like what I expected this trip to be."

I stripped off my shirt and crouched. My legs trembled as they held me up, waiting for the wings.

The first thing I felt was a sensation like an ice cube on my upper back, between my shoulder blades. Then sharp, piercing heat, like a burning itch. I gritted my teeth, and it passed. There was now an unfamiliar weight on my back, but I could feel the muscles, and the strength, and the urge to fly.

I grabbed my shirt and put it back on, surprised when the material passed right through the wings, and then created slits where my wings protruded.

I rolled my shoulders, stretching the new muscles. And then I willed the wings to disappear, and the weight was gone.

"This is amazing, Mom. Thank you." I gave her another hug.

She hugged me back, and when we finally released, she gave me a sad smile. "Go, save us. I'm sorry."

On impulse, I hugged her again. "I love you," I whispered into her ear, and squeezed her tight.

"I love you, too, and I always was and will be proud of you."

Mom gently pushed me away, then rolled behind her desk. "Go," she urged, making a shooing motion with her hands and accompanying it with a smile.

I made myself leave the room, glancing at her one more time. What was so wrecked about my life that I couldn't even have a proper reunion with my own mother?

But, like a true soldier, I continued forward and didn't look back.

Chapter 9

As Celestina and I walked through the hall and back down the stairs, I handed her the box of micro-strengtheners. "Here, take these, and make your way back home. Make sure Theo, Marc, and Marl get one. I'm going to see Apollo," I told her, rolling my shoulders.

Celestina gave me a confused glance, and went to speak, but I shushed her before they could. We had reached the bottom of the stairwell, and Yerick was still… distracted. His face was illuminated by the glow of his holoscreen, but if we made a wrong move, he would definitely notice us. And I didn't want him to call security again.

Running through the options in my head, I grimaced as I realized I only had two.

"Did you ever learn to army crawl?" I asked, speaking low into her ear.

They shook their head.

Letting out an exasperated sigh, I whispered, "Stay here."

Dropping to the ground, I began to inch forward, slowly, not wanting to draw attention until the last second. I paused as the guy glanced toward the stairwell. Holding still, I waited until his attention was back on the holoscreen.

When his eyes refocused on the pixels, I inched the last few feet, then lunged and grabbed his ankle.

He yelped in terror, jumping up from his seat and backing away. I rolled to my right and jumped into a crouch, then moved forward, hooking him under the jaw. His head whipped backward, and his eyes rolled back, and I lunged to catch him before he hit the ground.

Awkwardly holding him up, I maneuvered until he was seated in the chair. My eyes caught the image on the holoscreen, and before I could remind myself not to look, I glanced that way.

Immediately regretting my decision as the video burned into my eyeballs, I motioned Celestina out from the stairwell. They crossed the room, and I came out from behind the desk to join them.

"Are you really going to see Apollo?" Celestina asked, pushing open the door.

"Yeah. I need to see him."

"Was he there when…" They trailed off, gesturing in the air.

Nodding, I ran my hand through my hair. "I had a unit that I worked with in the field when I started. Ryan was a weapons specialist, like me, and we on and off dated for a lot of our time together. John was an explosives expert, and Apollo was our tech expert. My last mission in the field, John backstabbed our unit. I'm fairly certain he got Ryan killed, and he nearly managed to kill me as well. I managed to… take care of him before he could kill me. Apollo was there for me after all of that happened. I came back pretty traumatized. In fact… for about half a year, I was suicidal."

Celestina just nodded, so I continued.

"Apollo was there for all of it. Never judged me. Made sure I was safe. Thanks to him, I never made an attempt."

They took my hand and squeezed it. "I'm grateful they made sure you were safe. Go see them. I'll take care of Theo and the others."

"Thank you," I said, pulling them in for a quick hug. We walked out the doors, and I turned to look around me.

Spotting a fire escape, I jumped and grabbed hold of the first rung.

"Be safe!" Celestina called out, drawing several curious looks from people on the street. None cared enough to make a comment though.

"I will," I called down, then started climbing.

Easily getting to the roof, I looked at the ground several stories below. It looked pretty damn far. I would probably splat if this didn't work.

Flapping my wings, I backed away from the edge, and without a second thought, ran and jumped.

My wings responded as if I'd had them all my life. They snapped open, and I glided, and with a couple flaps, gained altitude. I felt no difference in my breathing, which I'm sure was due to Mom's micro-strengtheners.

Tucking my wings in close, I dove, hearing and feeling the wind whistle by my face. When I came low enough, I snapped my wings open and soared back up into the sky.

Feeling like I had the hang of it, I started flying toward the tall tower where Apollo was.

It wasn't too windy, thank goodness, or I'm sure I would have struggled more. I climbed a bit higher, now level with what looked like the eighty-ninth floor out of ninety. As I flew closer, I saw a little bit of movement through a window on the ninetieth floor. I flew by it, catching only a glimpse, but that glimpse made my heart jump for joy.

Apollo was there. And it was like he hadn't aged a day.

Wheeling out, I targeted a window two down from the one Apollo was in front of, then gained altitude so I could dive and break the window.

Why I decided to do that instead of using the door… I had no idea. Maybe I was just too excited.

With a deep breath, I dove, aiming for the window. I hit it with my full body at the last second, and it shattered into a million mini plastic pieces.

I was in luck. Wasn't bulletproof glass.

Still made a lot of noise, though. As I stood from the dust that now littered the floor of what looked like a secretary's office, the light switched on.

"Who the hell are you? That was a window of my own design, it should have been indestructible!"

Grinning underneath the shadow of my wings, which were currently covering my face, I delayed the moment.

He always was cute when he got angry.

"Sorry, I do tend to make a mess," I said, lifting my head and folding back my wings to get a better look. He was just as I remembered, except… Was he taller? And when, exactly, did he get so attractive? His once slightly round jaw had become sharper, and he seemed like he was more sure of himself too.

His face was worth the wait.

"That's the first fish I've seen since I got out of the cryolab," I commented, reaching forward to close his mouth with two fingers under the chin.

"Eryn," he said, my name a sob on his lips.

He stepped forward and hugged me fiercely. I wrapped my arms around his neck, rising up on tiptoe to reach. To my surprise, tears leaked out of my eyes, and I felt the tremors of Apollo's body as he cried into my shoulder.

"It's okay, it's okay, I'm here." My voice was choked with emotion, occasionally crooning a nonsense word or two.

Finally, we pulled apart, and... suddenly, I was... cold. I wanted to have his arms around me again. My body leaned forward, but my mind pulled me back. I had never liked Apollo that way. So why did I want to press my body against his? And my mind was whispering, *maybe a bit closer next time...*

Shaking that train of thought, I used the end of my sleeve to wipe away the tears on my face.

"You look tired," I said, noticing the dark circles under his eyes. His emerald eyes, which were piercingly beautiful as he stared at me. Grabbing his hand, I pulled him into his own office and sat him down in the first chair I found.

He sat down, then yelped and leaped back up, holding his ass.

"Damn prank chair." Apollo muttered, looking sheepish. He moved to a hovering chair in a circle of ten holoscreens.

"How have you been?" I asked, not sure what else to say.

"I haven't slept in two or three days... or maybe four? I've been using energy packs to keep going. But never mind that, how are you *alive*? We all thought you were dead!" Apollo said, almost sounding like he was scolding me.

"Wasn't dead. I was frozen."

"Frozen, like cryo frozen?"

Nodding, I grabbed another chair. "They found me in a cryostasis tube in an old CI base. I don't know which one, but since it was shut down, I'm guessing it was one of the old war bases."

"Those all shut down ages ago," Apollo said, shaking his head. "How did they not find you earlier?"

"I don't know. That's all I was told."

Still shaking his head, Apollo stared at me. I could see the tears welling in his eyes, which he wiped away with a sleeve.

Then, to my surprise, he held his hand out to me. His fingers had calluses that had been missing a hundred years ago.

I glanced from his hand to his eyes, and he was still staring. Didn't say a word.

Not needing anything else, I took his hand. He squeezed it and held on to it, and I could feel a comfortable connection between us. My shoulders dropped, and I realized that this was the first time in a while that I didn't feel scared.

"Are you okay?" Apollo whispered, almost so quietly that I had to lean in to hear him.

I shook my head as tears began to drop from my eyes. "No."

"I'm here."

That was all I needed to move into his arms. I sobbed disjointed words into his shoulder about all the memories and the nightmares.

Apollo held me as I cried. He murmured nonsensically to help calm me down, like he used to do. I felt so safe I was a little bit terrified.

When I was able to bring my head up from his shoulder, he handed me a box of tissues.

"Sorry about your shirt," I said, nose stuffy, as I saw the large tearstain on his shirt.

Apollo chuckled. "Perfectly fine. It'll dry."

"Okay," I replied, nodding. Since I was calming down, I felt a little bit of embarrassment creep in, especially knowing that I was here to ask for his help. And there was no easy way to go from crying into his shoulder to saying, *Hey, you wanna help me with this really dangerous thing?*

So I started easily. "There was something else I came here to talk to you about that might be pretty dangerous."

Subtle.

"What's wrong?" Apollo asked, straightening in his chair.

"I'm assuming you're aware of the plants wilting?"

"Yeah, but there's not too much I can do about that. I know tech, not plants."

"I'm going to Base 24."

Apollo stared at me. "Why would you go to Base 24? That place was shut down for a reason."

"My mom suggested it."

"Since when do you *listen* to her?"

"Since I am currently not part of the CI and have no desire to jump back in with them."

"Why do you have to do this?"

"Because I feel like I have to!" I yelled, making Apollo lean away from me. Silence.

I took deep breaths, aware Apollo was staring at me with what I assumed was concern.

"I have abilities. Because I have abilities, I have responsibilities. Even if I wanted to not do anything, I couldn't, so I have to do something."

Apollo nodded. "Okay. I'll help. I want you to see something, too."

"What?"

"Look for yourself. This came in on my personal satellite, and I can't make head or tails of it."

I ducked under the holoscreens and looked at the one he was pointing at. It was a fuzzy image, like a very shaky, shoddy quality camera, and you could only tell that it was a blob of color.

"There's audio," Apollo added, tapping the screen. It played, and something about the video was familiar to me.

"Play it again?" I asked, and he obliged.

Then it clicked. "I saw this." I stared at the blurry image, wishing I could just put on glasses and it would resolve itself.

"What? Where?"

"In my head." I grimaced as I heard how crazy it sounded. However, the weirdness of the statement didn't seem to register with Apollo. He yawned and mumbled.

"Come again?" I asked, wary of the way his eyes were drooping.

"Do you still have your thing that can control tech?" he repeated, right hand idly tapping numbers into a blank screen.

"Yeah, I think so."

"Try controlling this holoscreen. I think I might've… Well, we'll see." Apollo finished, eyelids drooping a little farther.

I turned my attention to the holoscreen and saw the numbers he had written there. Focusing, I pushed the numbers into a picture. The lines flowed together as the image formed in my mind. The one in my brain barely finished before the holoscreen did, and I panicked.

"Fuck," I muttered to myself, focusing to erase the image or create something else, but the image didn't move.

Apollo yawned again and turned his gaze to the screen. His eyes went wide. "That's sweet."

His gaze went from the accidental portrait of him that I had drawn to me, and I felt my body flush with heat as his green eyes pierced mine. My heart started to race, and I wanted, no, *needed* to be closer to him.

After a moment of silence, I regained my composure. I didn't even know how I felt about him yet. It was just the remaining effects of being frozen and the amnesia that were making me feel this way.

"I mean, you are the most interesting thing in the room," I said, wincing inwardly at how awkward that sounded.

He snorted and turned away, tapping on the screen to clear the image. "So, I may have accidentally—"

"Accidentally what?"

"Accidentally connected your weird tech-brain thing to my computer systems."

I shrugged. "I don't see that as a big problem."

He grimaced, and my stomach started feeling queasy.

"It would be a big problem if, say, you happened to be connected to a network that was city wide and someone else was trying to access it."

"You're afraid someone's trying to access the city through my *brain*?"

"Well, along those lines…"

"So this blob of color you think is another human?"

"Um, actually, no…"

"An *alien?*"

"Uh, yeah." Apollo ran a hand through his milk chocolate hair, and I watched as it fell into place. At least that old habit hadn't changed.

I wasn't going to say he was wrong about the alien thing—if they existed—but he hadn't had sleep for at least two days.

"You need sleep." My wings appeared, tucked into my back, but shifting, anticipating a flight.

Apollo glanced at my wings. "I'll take my mini jet."

"Suit yourself."

"Do you have a place to stay?"

"I've been staying with my nurse, but it's a little crowded. Why?"

"I have a place. It's small… modest… Out of the city a ways." He ran his hand through his hair again.

I grinned and started walking over to the broken window.

"Sounds brilliant. What are we waiting for?" I fell backward out of the window, just to be dramatic. Flipping over and spreading my wings, I rose in the air, flapping hard to gain altitude.

Apollo ran from the office, turning off the light, and a few minutes later, I saw a little, white, mini jet rise from the roof.

I flew myself over to the little craft, and as soon as I was close, Apollo smiled wickedly and took off. Enjoying the challenge, I rose in the air, easily able to keep sight of the fast-moving craft. I flew after it, clearing large amounts of space with the powerful beats of my wings. I was slowly getting closer, but the craft suddenly took a nosedive. Reacting quickly, I tucked my wings and went after him.

I saw the mini airstrip he was heading for and smiled.

Angling myself toward his front porch, I snapped my wings open and let the air slow me down to where I could land softly on my feet. My wings disappeared as I craned my neck to look at the house.

"Modest, my ass," I commented to myself.

It was pretty tall, with lots and lots of windows, and designed on the outside like a… a… wait a second…

"You hate castles," I sputtered out, turning to face him.

"You don't."

He then walked past me to the front door, leaving me speechless. Pressing his hand to a pad by the door, I heard a *click*.

"My lady," he said, mock bowing and holding open the door.

I half-heartedly slugged him in the arm, then walked into the home. "It looks like a fairytale in here," I breathed, taking in the fae-themed room. "Is the whole house like this?"

Murals of trees were painted on the walls, making me feel like I was in a forest. The floor looked like green carpet on first glance, but felt like springy moss under my shoes. A bright, sunny sky was painted across the ceiling. Unique pieces of wooden furniture was scattered about the area, welcoming me to sit and enjoy my time there. Other ends and odds hung on the walls, and were scattered across the tables and countertops. I felt like I was at home.

"Every room except my office and the hangar."

I walked over to a low-hanging light and touched it. "No heat?"

"No heat. More energy efficient that way. You wanna see the rest?"

A smile crept across my face. "Lead the way."

I followed as he headed toward a tight spiral staircase. He walked me through the house, showing me every single room: all were decorated the same way except his office, which stood out in stark contrast by being more blah (and more organized, but whatever).

When he showed me the guest bedroom, I was in love. The floor had a mossy texture and color, and the walls were painted with the image of a forest, full and rich with color and life. The bed was dressed with cream-colored sheets and green curtains, with wooden side-tables. I walked forward to touch the walls, imagining I was in the forest.

When I turned back around to talk to Apollo, I found the door shut, and he was gone.

My heart dropped, and the wonder slowly drained away. I dropped my hand back to my side and sat heavily on the bed. I started to think about why he had just left me in here but pushed the thought away. He probably just wanted to give me privacy.

Laying back, I closed my eyes and focused.

AIHNA? I asked, curious to see if I could connect to her.

Eryn, Celestina is worried about you. She's wondering where you are, came the reply, the voice the exact same.

Tell her I'll be staying at Apollo's house tonight. I need to be around him.

When I finished, I sat in silence for a few seconds, waiting for a reply, but never getting one.

I sat back up and took off my leather jacket. Rolling my shoulders, I got up, then walked out of the room.

Down the hall and the stairs, I kept an eye out for Apollo. Not finding him, I searched the whole first floor. Nothing.

Unnerved, I climbed the stairs back to the second story, and checked all the rooms.

Nada.

I climbed the last set of stairs and checked out the third floor.

No one.

Worried, I ran back down the stairs and out the front door, sprinting to the hangar. Hauling the large door open, I looked inside. The lights weren't even on. When I backed out, the door banged shut in my face when I let it go. Where was he?

Then it felt like someone was beating my skull. I screamed at the sudden pain and fell back against what I assumed was the hangar door. My vision went black, but I was still awake, my brain in extreme pain. I panted, grabbing the door handle digging into my hip and gripping it tight. Then, the black lightened and focused. The pain in my head reduced to a dull ache.

"Can you hear me, human?" a creature in front of me asked, punching buttons.

"What the hell?"

"I'll take that as a *yes*," the creature said, clacking its weird beak... snout... whatever it was. It stood in front of me, very tall and stick thin. Its skin was partially translucent, and I could see what I assumed were its organs. Tucked against its back were a pair of bat-like wings. Its face was vaguely canine and avian. And it was *blue.*

And my head still felt like it had a bunch of angry ants inside of it.

"What the hell?" I repeated.

"I assume that's an expression of disbelief in your culture?" it asked, typing on a screen thing beside it.

"No, I'm asking a question. What is going on? That's what that means!" I yelled at it.

It was silent for a few seconds, typing, then its yellow eyes turned back to me. "Oh, sorry. I was trying to connect to you earlier. You have a piece of hardware in your mindspace, and it didn't have the right software, but it had the right connection. So, I downloaded the software on it so we could communicate."

I sat there, and I felt my mouth gaping and closed it with a snap. "You *downloaded* software onto the chip in my brain? Was that the excruciating pain in my head?"

Pushing the door handle down, I opened the door and carefully walked in. Once I was clear, I let it go, then searched for a chair with my hands.

"*Shlito,* yes. Sorry, it wasn't supposed to hurt. What's your name?" the creature asked.

A breath whooshed out of my body as my midsection ran into something hard.

"Eryn."

"That's a very short name, very easy to say." The creature continued typing, ignoring me for a moment.

My hands finally found something that felt like a swivel chair, and I sat down on it. This was too much all at once. How was I seeing this…person in my brain? Who was he? Also, who the hell knew that aliens existed? "Okay, let me ask a question: do *you* have a name, or will I just have to keep thinking of you as *it* in my brain?" I asked, crossing my arms over my chest. That seemed simple. Definitely something you would do if an alien appeared in your head. It turned to face me again.

"Sorry, my mate says I'm scatter minded. I'm Muroha." He nodded, a sort of bow, I realized, and tilted his head.

"Nice to meet you, I suppose. Although I won't thank you for this headache."

"Of course, of course, that is my fault. Should have checked for biological compatibility first. However, I don't know how long the connection will last, so I must move on, if you are okay?"

I sighed. "Go on."

"I have attempted, multiple times, to contact people in your life-station…"

"City?"

"If that is what it is called, yes. Ci-tyyyyy," Muroha said, playing with the word.

"And?"

"And our sensors tell us that your life support in the life-station is failing. However, your planet is also at high risk of failing and turning in on itself."

I tried to focus through the pain in my head. "What does that mean?"

"Your large star would reach a critically hot temperature and explode, bringing your planet down with it."

"The sun? The sun would turn into, what, a black hole? One of those space things that sucks in everything around it?"

"Correct. According to our estimates, you have approximately thirty rotations of your planet before this occurs."

"A month?" I sputtered, the pain in my head dulling for a moment.

He set his little screen down and started typing again. "I'm an… engineer, I think is what your species calls it… for the Intergalactical Conservation of Species and Planets. We step in to preserve species when events such as this occur. I suggest your people build something to get them to another planet, fast."

And all of a sudden, I could see again. Muroha was gone.

Apollo was kneeling in front of me, worried. "Eryn, thank god. You were in a trance, and I've been yelling at you for at least thirty minutes."

I looked at him and gave him a distracted pat on the head. "I'm fine."

I stood and moved past him to the hangar door, then paused when I realized he wasn't following. I looked back at him and saw him staring at me like I was insane.

"What's wrong?" he asked, walking along beside me.

"I talked to a blue alien," I said normally, as if I had said, *I want some cake.*

"The fuck?" Apollo said, shaking his head. "Has the freezing given you brain damage? We should get you to the hospital." He grabbed my arm.

Within seconds, I had him pinned on the ground. "Apollo, look into my eyes and tell me I'm insane and should be given medication." I stared at him until he lowered his gaze.

"You're sane," he admitted. "Can I get up now?"

I got off of him and offered my hand. He took it, and I hauled him up, then beat the dust off of his shirt.

The door was still unlocked, so I opened it and walked through, then led the way to his office. He sat at the small holoscreen, while I grabbed another chair in the room.

"Do you have access to satellite readings of other planets? Is there anything up there that does that?"

Apollo nodded. "A couple. Both are co-operated by myself and the government."

"Pull up the readings from today. Or yesterday."

"Why—"

"Just pull them up, please."

He stared at me, then turned to his holoscreen and logged in. After going through a few things, he pulled up a chart full of pictures and numbers.

I scooted closer and looked for any section that said *sun.* My eyes wandered over the paper, and I had to have Apollo scroll down once before I found what I thought was the correct section.

"There, do any of those readings for the sun look abnormal to you?"

He squinted at the screen and tilted his head this way and that. Finally, he shrugged. "Looks normal to me."

"Is it possible for someone to have tampered with the readings?"

"I mean, there's always that potential, why?"

"Because the blue alien in my head said the sun was going to explode."

"A supernova?" Apollo sucked in a huge breath, then looked back at the holoscreen. "Wouldn't it show up?"

"Would it show if the explosion was a month away?"

"Yes."

I gestured to the screen. "So these numbers could have been tampered with. Can you request a reading that goes straight to you?"

Without another word, Apollo took over and began tapping on the holoscreen. A loading bar popped up, and when it reached 100%, I saw another report like the one we had just looked at.

Apollo scrolled down to the same section, and I heard him draw in a breath.

The numbers definitely looked different to me, and by Apollo's reaction, I assumed that Muroha had been right.

"Temperatures are higher than normal. I can't calculate the rate of the increase, because it seems like all my other files have been tampered with."

"Would the government do this?"

"Absolutely," Apollo replied without hesitation. "Things are a lot worse than they seem on the surface here. It's the same old pattern of 'Give them something shiny to distract them.' These politicians don't give a shit about people. Just their own fame. Particularly this new bloke named Henry Marsher. He's this businessman that somehow was elected by some turn of luck. Marsher sweet-talked me into letting his men have access to my satellites, since I used to work for the government, and I agreed. Damn it, I never should've let him have access."

I leaned forward and cautiously laid my hand over his. "Hey, it's all right. You're not to blame."

Apollo looked up at me with puppy dog eyes, and I had the urge to hug him. But I stayed in one spot, unsure if he would welcome the gesture.

"You know, even when we were overseas, you always took care of others before yourself. Thank you," he said, running his hand through his hair, giving me a sad look. I had a feeling he meant more than me comforting him now, but he didn't continue, so I didn't push it.

"We need to do something about this. Can the others come here?"

"Others?"

I scratched the back of my head. "My reorientation nurse and… Well, the people making that other house so crowded."

"We can take care of that tomorrow, I think. Look at the time."

The clock read 23:00.

"Fuck it's late."

"And you need sleep, or else you'll be grumpy."

I stuck my tongue out at him and stood. He laughed and said a quick good night, and I walked past him get to my room, where I stripped off my shirt and yanked off my boots. Not feeling like undressing further, I climbed into the bed and stared at the ceiling.

Closing my eyes, I felt the tight pressure of my pants and the band of my sports bra. Shifting, I tried attaining a more comfortable position, to no avail. The past day ran through my head on repeat, my stupid brain over-analyzing anything to do with Apollo.

Finally, I gave up on sleep, went to the window, and fiddled with the latches until it opened. Breathing in the cold night air, I shivered as my wings materialized on my back.

I dove out the window, pumping my wings to get altitude. I looked at the three-quarter waning moon in the sky, at the bright, cold white standing out against a gray canvas. I couldn't see any stars, and that hurt my heart. The Big Dipper was even gone, its stars faded from our sight. Sighing, I flew, exerting myself as far as I dared. The night was especially chilly, and I could feel the goosebumps rising across my skin.

I circled the house, then soared upward, tightening my circles until I was basically spinning in midair. I stopped abruptly, wings spread, then dropped, angling myself into a dive. I slowed enough at the last second that I could hit the ground and roll, coming to my feet.

"That was fancy!" I heard from above me, and I craned my neck to see Apollo's head sticking out of his window.

"Gotta learn how to do it with wings!" I yelled back.

Apollo leaned on the window frame, seemingly content to watch me. "Aren't you cold in that scrap of fabric?" he yelled down, part of his voice taken by the wind.

I flipped him the finger in reply. He laughed and grinned as I took to the air. I climbed a bit, then, on a whim of an idea, turned and dove toward

Apollo's window. He moved aside as I slipped through and rolled to standing, making my wings disappear.

I felt a blanket being draped over my shoulders.

"Thanks," I said, slowly turning to face him and drawing the blanket around me.

He was shirtless now, and I could see how good his body looked. He had added weight since I last remembered, but it wasn't bad. Apollo looked more muscular, in a strong man kind of way instead of a bodybuilder kind of way. Which happened to be exactly my type when it came to masculine bodies.

My brain short-circuited, and I'm pretty sure I blushed, but I at least had the composure to keep the same, bored expression on my face. My assessment that he had gotten better looking definitely still applied with his shirt off.

"Are you sure getting an eight-pack was a great use of your time?" I asked, raising an eyebrow.

He had the nerve to laugh at me as I sat there staring at him with a mixture of amusement and confusion.

"Why, if I didn't know better, I would think you were jealous of my body," Apollo said, poking me in the arm.

"Ha, ha, ha," I clipped out sarcastically. "If you'll excuse me, I'm going to bed."

I left the room without another word, dragging the blanket with me.

Well, this was even better. If any drop-dead gorgeous, witty woman showed up in my life right now, I would be doomed.

Chapter 10

The next morning, I woke curled up on one side with my head in my hands. Groaning, I wiped the drool off my hands and yawned as I hauled my legs over the edge of the bed.

When I tried to stand, my legs collapsed underneath me, and I cursed. My skin prickled with needle-like stabs as my legs woke up.

I heard the door creak open and laid my head against the side of the bed.

"Hey, I heard loud noises. Are you okay?" Apollo asked, coming around the side of the bed. He was still shirtless, but my brain didn't have enough energy to care.

I yawned again. "My legs are asleep."

I gestured toward the useless things to emphasize my point, which were still prickling in an effort to wake up.

He sighed, and my half-lidded eyes didn't fully catch his expression, but it looked like it bordered on tender. He approached me and easily scooped me into his arms. In normal circumstances, I would tell him to let me down, but I was so sleepy that I wanted to fall asleep against his chest.

To my barely functioning brain's disappointment, he laid me on my bed. "Sleep."

My eyes closed of their own accord, and unfortunately, I didn't exactly fall asleep.

It didn't hurt this time when Muroha appeared in front of me.

"Can I not *sleep*?" I moaned, wishing I could strangle Muroha at the moment.

"Sorry, I can't exactly tell when a good time is for you. I contact when the satellite is in the right position. Do you know anything about engineering?" he asked, typing something beside him.

"Basic knowledge, yes," I replied, struggling to stay aware.

"Excellent. We need to go over the basics of spaceship building."

I sat there, my mind absorbing all the new information and storing it, even though I was as tired as hell. When Muroha was done, he mentioned something about storing blueprints in my chip.

"Okay," I said, wanting him to finish his lecture so I could sleep.

When he finally finished, the connection shut off with an abrupt *click*, and as I came out of it, the light hit my eyelids.

"Damn it!"

I screamed into the pillowcase, the fabric muting the sound. Forcing myself to get out of the bed anyway, I yanked open the window that Apollo must have closed. I jumped out, my wings spreading to slow my descent. As my bare feet touched the dirt, I looked toward the sun.

I stretched, turning my face to the soon-to-be-exploded sun.

"Hey, you're awake."

I turned to see Apollo approaching, carrying something in his hands. He smiled at me, and I swear, it was far more beautiful than the sunrise or the moon last night.

"What do ya got?" I asked, nodding at his hands.

"Breakfast. But it looks like you're busy waking up still."

Feeling a sudden rush of mischief, I grabbed the bag out of his hand and took off into the sky.

"Hey, that's not fair!" he yelled as he started chasing me.

I laughed, dancing through the air, watching Apollo on the ground. He made several grabs for my foot to bring me down, but each time, I pulled up before he could touch me.

When I had decided he had enough, I glided down.

Apollo quickly stopped in front of me, his chest rising and falling as he took in breath.

Our eyes met for just a moment, and it felt as if the world held still.

We both started to lean in, closing what space remained between us.

Then the sound of gunfire. Ryan running. Pain, blood, and death.

I pulled away quickly, nearly falling over. Taking in deep breaths, I sat on the ground and put my head between my knees.

"Eryn, are you okay?"

"I'm fine," I replied, voice muffled by my legs. "Flashback."

Apollo didn't say anything, but I felt the light touch of his hand on my back. I paid no further attention to him and focused on my breathing, trying to calm myself down.

"We should probably call your friends here. Have the nurse look at you."

I nodded, unable to give a better answer.

Damn flashback. Damn trauma.

AIHNA? I asked, concentrating, pushing all other thoughts away.

The artificial intelligence responded almost immediately. *Eryn. What do you need?*

Can you get Celestina and the others to this address?

On their way, AIHNA replied, then went silent.

"Let's get you inside, it's starting to get hot," Apollo commented, patting my back.

I got up with his help and went inside.

Apollo set the breakfast on the counter after helping me to a barstool, and I immediately reached for it and pulled out what was inside.

I grinned and took a bite of a chocolate chip muffin. Within seconds, it was gone, and I had another one in hand. Apollo joined in, much slower than me, and we ate in comfortable silence.

When I had cleaned the muffin off my hands, I refocused on what I needed to do. I felt less tired than I was this morning.

"Do you have anything to draw with?" I asked Apollo, right as he took a bite of his muffin.

He side-eyed me, then swallowed his muffin. "Yeah, what for?"

"The blue alien gave me spaceship schematics with their deadline."

Apollo snorted. "You don't have to draw them. We can just download them from your brain chip to a compatible device."

"Is that safe?"

"Well, we'll have a source that isn't connected to the rest."

"The base," I said, snapping my fingers. "Of course."

He nodded and stood from his chair. "Yep. I'm going to go change real quick. You're welcome to do whatever you want."

I gave him a thumbs up, and was soon by myself in the first floor of the house. Hopping off my chair, I wandered, peeking my head around doors and checking things out until I heard a knock at the front door.

I heard the knock at the same time Apollo came downstairs, hair wet and wearing different clothes. When I opened the door, Celestina stood outside, along with Theo, Marc, Marl, and Kimi.

Celestina stepped in and hugged me. I hugged her back, suddenly feeling grateful to have her, even if we hadn't known each other that long. When I finally let go, I stepped back so they could see Apollo.

"This is Apollo. Apollo, this is Celestina, Theo, Marc, Marl, and Kimi," I said, pointing to each in turn. Marc and Marl both shook Apollo's hand, Kimi kissed him on the cheek, Celestina patted him on the shoulder. Theo gave me an awkward side hug, and then I had to watch him give Apollo the most awkward fist bump of my life.

I grimaced, but since there wasn't much I could do, I shooed everyone inside and shut the door.

"Okay, you guys, here's the situation." I gave a short version of the blue alien in my head and what he had told me.

"Are you okay?" was the first question out of Celestina's mouth.

I nodded. "Could be better, but I'm surviving."

Then everyone started asking questions.

"What do you mean Earth is going to die?"

"How are we supposed to build a spaceship in a *month*?"

"How does this guy even know this? He could be lying!"

"Woah, stop!" I yelled.

Everyone quieted instantly.

"Apollo and I checked what the alien said, and we were able to confirm it. Someone has been editing the reports to hide the readings. It's a lot to take in, so I don't expect you all to be immediately okay with helping out, but if we're going to survive, we have to band together and bring in as many others as we can."

"Why are you in charge?" Theo asked. "Shouldn't this be like the government's job, or the CI? This is a foolish thing to do."

"Because I need to be. I don't have any power at the CI anymore. And we think one of the government folks was the one who messed with the readings. Additionally, I have more freedom without all the paperwork in the way."

"So what do we do next?" Celestina asked, gesturing. "This place isn't big enough to build a spaceship."

"I go restart an old base. You guys get in contact with as many people as you can who can help. I don't care if they're an engineer or a baker. We need all the help we can get if we don't want to suffocate or be caught in a black hole."

"Do you think people will believe us?" Celestina scratched their head. "It does seem a bit of a far stretch."

I shrugged. "Take them to the edge of the city to see the plants with their own eyes. But we can't do nothing."

"What about the CI?" Theo chimed in, crossing his arms. "Ever think that they might be listening in?"

"Are you spying for them?" I asked directly.

"No!"

"Then, unless Apollo's house is bugged…"

Apollo shook his head. "Not bugged. No one but me has been here in years."

"Then I think we're okay. Being the director had its perks; you knew that everyone, without proper organization, is essentially glorified police. The amount of times I had to keep my mouth shut when someone said something dumb is unable to be counted at this point."

"Well, I'll make sure to get my friend Rubi. They're the one who built AIHNA. They'll be a lot of help. Amazing engineer, and always so stylish," Celestina nodded. They sounded envious of Rubi's fashion choices.

After that, one by one, each person pledged their help. It was almost like I was in a movie. Kind of weird.

When people started chatting about who they were going to contact, Apollo pulled me off to the side.

"How are you planning to get into that base?" he whispered, glancing at the others. "You and I both know the reason why that base was abandoned."

I cleared my nose. It had been abandoned the year after I visited it, with reports that concluded a malfunction in the air conditioning system was to blame. Five people dead, but I had wanted to shut down that base anyways. This had given me the excuse to do so.

"I know," I whispered back. "I have an idea."

"A good idea?"

"An idea."

"What are you two talking about? And why was the base abandoned? And which base?" Theo asked, causing everyone to stop talking and look at us.

I took a deep breath. "I'm not going to name it right now, but you wouldn't know about it. It's wiped from all records. And let's just say it's very dangerous to be in."

"But you're going there. And we're going to go there," Kimi said, pointing at herself. "How is it going to be safe for us?"

"I'm going to figure that out," I responded, beginning to move myself slowly toward the front door.

"How?" Theo asked.

"I've got an idea," I replied as I pushed the door open and took off before they could say another word.

I climbed high and flew over the city, watching the sparkling silver buildings and the multitude of plants pass below me. As I got closer and closer to the edge of the city, I could see the plants beginning to turn brown, and some that just looked dead.

Then I hit a junkyard on the edge of the city, full of rusty metal bits and sad, dirty plastics.

Finally, I hit the desert, the hot wind scorching what skin wasn't covered. I could feel my lungs struggling to get enough air for a few moments, and I nearly panicked.

My breathing evened out after a couple more moments, and that tightness in my chest disappeared.

I glided over the sand, squinting through the dust that had been kicked up by the wind. Did I have any idea where I was going? Nope. Did it feel like I was going the right direction? Surprisingly… yes.

There was no life in this place at all. Just sand, and wind, and sun. I had no idea how much time had passed.

Finally, I managed to spot a gleam of metal and landed on top of it. Brushing sand away from about where the seal was, that's when I knew it was the right one. The CI seal stared out at me, glaring lines etched into the metal.

I started searching for the manual catch to the hangar door, knowing that there was one, but never having to use it before… let's just say I didn't know where it was. Kicking away sand, my boot revealed a depression *filled* with sand.

"Damn," I said, kneeling.

I began to scoop out the hot sand, cursing every time my bare skin touched it, and eventually revealing a keypad. Punching in what I thought was the code, I hoped it still worked.

After a pregnant pause, the hatch under me rumbled, and I launched off of it to hover over it. The hatch slowly crept open, making a weird grinding noise that didn't sound good and probably meant there was a lot of sand inside the mechanisms.

As soon as the hatch stopped, I stared at the large circle of darkness below me. I slowly let myself down, pulling a flashlight I had nabbed from Apollo's place during my wandering out of my pocket.

I breathed in deeply but didn't feel any warning tightness. It creeped me out how dark and silent it was, but I didn't dare to try turning on the lights and air conditioning. Not yet.

I searched for a gas mask, trying to stay in the main hangar. Luckily, I found one that had been thrown in the corner, and I strapped it on, making sure the apparatus still worked.

After securing my gas mask, I hit the light switch, grimacing as the bright ones pierced my eyes. I didn't hear the air conditioner kick on, which was a relief, considering my hunch that someone may have left a trap in the air vents.

I finally landed on the ground, sending a big poof of dust up into the air, making me cough. I walked toward the central hall, hoping I remembered the way to the central control room.

I used my flashlight, not wanting to push my luck with the AC, checking each door for the CI sigil that would indicate the central control room.

My footsteps echoed down the hallway, the sound bouncing off the stone. I felt like the darkness had eyes, and I felt the hair raising on the back of my neck.

Finally, after some turns, I came to the door marked with the CI sigil. Praying that the biometric recognition system was still functional, I blew the dust off and put my thumb on the pad. I heard the mechanisms whirr as it came to life, and a weak, blue glow emanated from the pad as it scanned my fingerprint. It beeped, almost sounding tired, and then I heard the lock *click*.

Since the mechanism to open the door clearly wasn't working, I wedged my fingers in between and pushed it open. It resisted, letting out a high-pitched squeak that hurt my ears.

I just hoped it wouldn't jam on the track.

But of course, it did, so I only managed to get it halfway open. But that was far enough. I went through, shining my flashlight on the main controls.

They were still fairly old-school, all manual, and one old, dusty laptop. The multiple TVs were still set up on the wall to form an overall picture. I hit the *On* button, and the machine came to life.

It tried to putter out on me, but I kicked it a couple times, and then it ran like new. The interface pulled up on the screens, a blue screen with nine app options.

"Welcome, Director Eryn. How may I help you today?" the voice asked, sounding rough and gritty.

"I need a scan of all the air vents, without turning the heating and cooling system on. I need to know if there are any foreign objects," I ordered, beating the old, leather swivel chair to get off the dust.

"Of course, Director," it replied, going silent. I continued beating dust off the chair, scratching something off the arm that looked suspiciously like puke. Well, hundred-year-old puke. After I deemed it clean enough to sit on, I sat down, coughing as another cloud of dust rose into the air.

"Director Eryn. There is a spherical foreign object inside the air vent closest to Hangar One-A. Made of a metal compound. Uncertain how dangerous," the machine reported, showing its scan. The green blob looked about the right size to be a bomb, but it was still intact.

"Thank you," I said, standing up and brushing the dust off of my ass. I went back into the hallway and considered whether I should try to close the door. Deciding that could be fixed later, I headed back to the main hanger.

When I reached the main hangar, I hung a right and went to Hangar 1A, our cargo plane hangar. The hatch for that one was huge, and the only time it had been opened was on the first day the base was operational. I went to the air vent in the corner, unscrewed the hatch, and set it to the side.

Taking a deep breath and praying I wouldn't pay for my half-cocked idea, I slithered into the vent on my belly. About ten feet in, enough for me to feel both claustrophobic and idiotic, I spotted the device.

"Damn it all to hell," I whispered, shaking my head. It was a modified gas bomb.

It was connected to one long tube that I assumed was connected to canisters filled with carbon monoxide throughout the base. Scooting forward, I managed to wiggle my arm into my pocket to retrieve my Swiss Army knife, military version, and pulled out the scissor attachment and the screwdriver attachment.

Inching forward, I searched for the detonator, hesitating to touch the thing just yet. After squeezing myself along the right side of the bomb, I found the detonator… already torn out. "Fuck," I muttered, putting away the Swiss army knife. Sighing, I squirmed toward the main tube.

I grabbed the tube and bent it, like you would for a hose. Luckily for me, it was flexible enough to bend back all the way. Then, before I could think on it, I yanked the tube off of the bomb.

It made a little hissing sound but didn't do anything else. I let out a breath that I didn't know I was holding.

Then I stared at my hand. What the hell was I going to tie this off with?

"What the hell," I muttered, twisting the tube into a knot, pulling it as tight as I could.

I turned back to the bomb and pulled my Swiss army knife out again, and used it to carefully remove the top panel. Looking at the insides, I chose the wires I needed, then cut them quickly.

The bomb didn't react.

Relieved, I unscrewed it from where it was attached to the vent, then squirmed out of the vent with the bomb.

As soon as I was clear of the vent, I straightened, then went to work dismantling the bomb. It was homemade, I could tell, by military grade skills. But it was the sigil on the inside panel that caught my eye. It was a chimera, a monster with three heads: a lion, a goat, and a snake. Some versions of myth warned that the creature could breathe fire or fly. This one did neither, but it tightened my stomach all the same.

I recognized it.

It had been on the uniforms of the people that had killed Ryan.

Now that those memories were brought to the surface, I realized it had also been on John's that same night, after my fingers had ripped the fabric of his uniform to reveal an odd, or what I thought was odd at the time, sigil under the sewn-up jacket.

"What the hell?" I asked myself, holding the panel in my hand.

Before I could do anything more, my vision went black. "Muroha," I said, leaning back against the wall. He appeared in front of me, sitting in a chair this time.

"Eryn, how is it going? Is the building going well?" he asked, leaning forward.

"Not yet. I'm currently in the process of trying to make one of our secret bases safe enough to live and build in." The sigil flashed through my memory for a brief moment, but I saw it show up on one of his screens as I thought about it. "You have one of the screens hooked up to what I think?" I asked, focusing on that screen.

"Indeed. It's to help me visualize images that you have words for, but I do not. It does not convey thoughts such as 'I'm hungry,' but if you were thinking of an apple, I would see an apple," Muroha explained, using his hands to animate what he was saying.

"Hmm." I digested the information. "Would you happen to recognize this?" I pictured the sigil more clearly and held it in my mind.

Muroha turned to face the screen, and then I saw him jerk violently, causing him to fall out of his chair. "That… that's… that's… that's the Mark of Fire! Where did you find it? How is it on your planet?"

I allowed the sigil to fade from the forefront of my mind, then showed him where else I had seen it. He watched the images in rapt attention, but by the end, he was trembling. "You have seen terrible pain, Eryn. I am sorry. How you humans go through things such as that, I will never know. I am still confused as to how the Mark of Fire is on your planet. It is—"

Then the connection dropped.

"Damn it!" I yelled, letting my head fall back against the wall. The satellite must've moved too far out of range. I took a deep breath, letting myself rest for a moment.

Why couldn't something be simple for once? I wake up from a hundred years in a cryostasis and get to enjoy less than a week before I find Earth is dying, and there's some Mark of Fire that's clearly not good news.

Why am I the one who has to fix things?

Even in the field, when things went wrong with a mission, they looked to me. I was always expected to come up with a solution.

I was supposed to know everything.

I don't want to get up.

I don't want to crawl back into the vents to remove the carbon monoxide canisters. I don't want to oversee construction of spaceships to get us away from here in four weeks. I just want to sit here. I want someone else to do the job. I want to rest.

I took a deep breath and thought about Apollo rushing to hug me, his tear-stained voice as he said my name.

Closing my eyes and leaning my head against the wall, I took a few more deep breaths before I gritted my teeth and pushed myself to my feet. Every cell of my body was telling me to stay down. To sit it out. But I pushed myself up anyway.

Because that's why I needed to clear the canisters. The reason I need to lead. Because of the people I love. My mother. Apollo and the others. They believe I can.

So, I will.

I stood and gathered the disassembled parts of the bomb and dumped them in a spare parts box, keeping the panel with the sigil. After tucking it into a pocket, I laid back down and scooted into the air vent. These were the times that I was glad I was small.

I came to the knotted tube and scooted past it, farther in the vent. I followed the tube until I came to the first canister. It was a weird design. The canister was filled with something liquid and had a row of small, closed hatches on the side facing the air vent panel.

I found a lever on the side facing me, attached to the protrusion that held the tube. Pushing it, a little panel dropped into place, sealing off the tube attachment. I smiled, then continued making my way through the air vents.

Hours later, I was dusty and sore, but all of the carbon monoxide canisters had been closed off, and the only thing left to do was remove the system. Making my way through the air vents, I eventually came back to the main hangar. It was still open to the sky.

I yanked the tube off that canister, pinching it until it was flush with the vent panel in front of me. Then I let it go. The gas hissed out, but escaped harmlessly into the air. I smiled in satisfaction, and then sighed when I realized I still had to retrieve all the canisters.

I rolled my shoulders and grabbed the canister in front of me. Scooting backward, I made it back to Hangar 1A and finally flopped onto the floor, dusty and tired.

AIHNA, notify Apollo that I need him to come to the base at once, I sent out, stretching out my arms and legs.

Of course, Eryn. A pause. *He's on his way.*

Thank you, I sent back, then sat up and set the first canister against the wall.

"One down," I said to myself, running my hands through my hair. It was full of dust and who knew what else, but it was worth it if I could remove the entire system in the vents.

I heard a low buzz and looked up into the glare of the sun to see Apollo's mini jet descending into the hangar. Once he had landed, I watched him climb out and run toward me.

"Are you all right? AIHNA… whatever she is… said you needed me urgently." Apollo knelt beside me. "Why are you covered in dust and… is that lint?" He picked off a ball of lint from my jacket.

"Yeah, I've been crawling around in the vents. I need you to help me retrieve the rest of the canisters," I explained, showing him the canister I had.

He glanced at the one I was showing him. "How many are there?"

"Twenty, minus this one." I set it against the wall again. Turning to the vent, I began to crawl back in.

"Wait, we have to crawl through the air vents?" he asked, sounding exasperated.

"Yep," I crawled in, working my way around the tube.

"Well, at least I have a great view," Apollo commented behind me.

"You've had a better view than that before, as I have had of you," I replied, continuing along the main vent.

"You're referring to the sewer fiasco, aren't you? The one where our clothes kept getting caught on the pipe walls and got ripped to shreds? From what I remember, you weren't that badly affected. You, at least, still had most of your underwear. Although, I'm sure seeing Ryan mostly naked was something you'd seen before." Apollo's chuckle echoed through the vent.

"Oh, shut it. You all complained so much about having sewer slime all over you, but do you know how long it took me to get that out of my hair?" I replied, hanging a right when the air vent turned.

"I know exactly how much fun you had. I was in the room next to you, remember? You were cursing for an hour straight, until Ryan went in to, uh, see if he could help. That's when I put in the earplugs."

I blushed, glad he couldn't see my face.

I was about to give a snarky reply when we finally reached the branch in the air vents. "All right. I'm going right, you go left. You should have only nine more, I already got the one from the main hangar vent," I ordered, already moving along my tunnel.

"Got it," Apollo replied, the banter paused for now.

I crawled forward, and at the farthest canister, I pulled off the tube and began to roll the flexible tubing. I did this for each canister, until I had an armful of five. I crawled one-handed back to Hangar 1A, where I stacked them against the wall. Then I went back in to retrieve the other five.

As soon as I had them, I crawled back out and stacked them with the rest. There were eleven against the wall, stacked neatly. I sat next to them for a while, maybe ten minutes, before I started to get worried.

Crawling back in, I took the left branch and continued along it. I passed the main hangar vent, and two more hangar vents, all with detached canisters.

It was a bit longer until I came across the next three canisters. Like the first two, they were detached. I crawled quicker, banging my knees against the metal shaft.

I passed another two detached canisters, adding up to a total of seven so far.

When I reached the eighth, I saw Apollo's legs sticking out of the shaft. I quickly squeezed in beside him, checking for a pulse. Thankfully, there was one, although it was weak.

I glanced at the canister he had been detaching. It was still attached, his limp hands fallen to cither side of the canister. His right hand was slightly swollen, with a needle sticking out of the wrist. This canister must have been trapped. But why this one?

I shook off the thought and focused on his arm. Apollo first. Questions later.

"Shit." I cursed, moving farther up to reach his arm. Holding it against my body, I pulled the needle out and took a look at the syringe it had come out of. There was a little liquid left, and it was one I recognized.

"Son of a bitch." I squirmed back down his body.

Who knew how long he had been laying here?

After pulling him out of the shaft, I ripped open his shirt to listen to his lungs. To my relief, he was still breathing strongly. I shrugged off my jacket, pulled off my shirt, and made a makeshift tourniquet next to his elbow, hoping the venom hadn't gone that far.

Taking a deep breath, I focused. I had to get him out of the air vents. I glanced at the air vent we were in front of, which overlooked an old, dusty morgue. I knew the medical bay vent was two down from where we were at, but that vent was significantly smaller than the one in front of me.

I moved back into the shaft and removed the canister, needle, and tubing, setting them farther down the vents. Pulling out my pocketknife, I unscrewed the vent, and cursed when one of the screws jammed.

I moved myself so I was sitting on my ass and kicked the vent until it clanged to the floor below. "All right, Apollo, hang on. You're not dying on me," I muttered, turning and dragging him toward the vent.

Jumping out, I steadied myself and grabbed him under the armpits, to pull him out of the vent. He was heavy, but nothing I couldn't handle.

Apollo's body flopped against mine, making me stumble to the side. I held on to him and my balance, standing rock steady again. I carried him out of the weapons locker and to the medical bay, where I kicked open the door with my foot.

After laying him down on a bed, I ran to the medical cabinet containing the medications and other antidotes. "Antivenom, antivenom, where the hell are you?" I said, the words erupting from my mouth like a spurt of lava.

Finally spotting the one I needed, I grabbed the bag and an IV, and rolled it as fast as I could over to Apollo. After hooking up the bag to the equipment, I grabbed the needle, and then took a deep breath before putting it in his arm, hoping like hell I did it right.

I started the IV, praying that it still worked.

And it did, the beautiful thing sputtering to life. I closed my eyes and searched for the mini jet's computer system, eventually finding it. Praying that my brain would connect to the city-wide internet like Apollo said it would, I mentally hit the "on" switch. I was rewarded with the buzz of the engine and the GPS view on the plane.

I configured the autopilot so it would fly back to Apollo's place and give Celestina a message. I was rewarded with an agreeable hum as the plane took off.

Opening my eyes, I watched the IV and Apollo. After a decent amount of time, I sensed the return of the mini jet. Deciding I could leave Apollo for two minutes, I sprinted to the hangar. As I was coming out of the hall, Celestina was climbing out of the jet.

"You said he was injured?" they asked, hopping to the ground.

"Yes, this way," I replied, jogging back down the hall.

They easily followed, and we made it to the medical bay in no time.

"He was injected with a very small amount of cobra venom. I administered the correct antivenom as quickly as I could, but I don't know if I did the IV correctly."

We reached the medical bay, where Apollo was still lying on the bed, shirt open, my shirt tied around his arm. Tina approached him and checked the IV as I stood on the other side, nervous to high heaven.

"Damn. You got it, first try. Are you sure you haven't done this before?" Celestina asked, tapping various things on the IV module.

"Well, we practiced it in training, but I've never had to actually do it before." I clenched my fists as I watched him laying on the bed. Apollo was breathing shallowly, but I was glad he was breathing at all.

Taking a deep breath, I waited until Celestina turned back around. "Is there anything I can do to help?" I prayed that there wasn't, because the adrenaline was fading, and I started feeling a little nauseous.

"No, there's nothing you can do for him. I'll watch and make sure the antivenom is working. Go." They shooed me out of the room, and I was left outside, doing my best to keep the contents of my stomach in place.

Once I felt as though I could walk without throwing up, I headed back to the open hangar. I needed a way to distract myself, or all I would do was worry about Apollo.

The mini jet sat where it last landed, in the middle of the hangar. There were large piles of sand from when I opened the bay doors, most of them covering spare parts. I climbed over one of the bigger piles to the panel that controlled the doors.

Searching the buttons, which were all meticulously labeled, (thanks past person who did that), I found one that simply said, *Landing Walls.*

I pressed it and immediately heard a labored grinding noise.

"Fuck," I cursed, looking upward to see if I could spot the jammed mechanism. It was right above me—a pair of wheels with a broken belt.

Taking off, I flew up to the jammed belt, which was broken with one end stuck between a wheel and the wall. I grabbed the belt and yanked it, dislodging it. It smacked me in the belly, and I hissed at the sharp sting.

After coming back down, I buttoned my jacket so that wouldn't happen again, then went to find a spare belt.

Luckily, there was a spare that was the exact same as the broken one in my hand. I flew back to the wheels and put it on, making sure it was tight.

I went back to the button and pressed it again, watching the mechanism with a wary eye. To my relief, it worked, and the most wondrous thing happened. A circular wall rose from the edges of the bay, keeping more sand from falling in.

Leaning against the wall, I surveyed the room. Everything was dirty, covered with sand, and generally disorganized. And I had forgotten that the rest of the canisters had to be removed. The cargo plane hangar also had to be cleared. And the living quarters. And every other damn room in the place.

"No time like the present," I said to myself, then went to work.

Chapter 11

I was utterly exhausted and covered with dirt. My stomach was growling, my hair was a matted mess, and I probably looked like hell. But it was done. Two plane hangars, a cafeteria and attached kitchen, four bunk spaces containing four beds each and two bathrooms, the control center, and the engineering room. All clean, free of sand, dust, and spiderwebs, and somewhat organized. Even if that was just piling everything into one corner.

Of course, now I was wearing the grime from all of those rooms, and desperately needed a meal, a shower, and *sleep*, although not necessarily in that order. But first, I had to check on Apollo. The last time I had dropped in, he was still unconscious, and Celestina had shooed me out.

Walking back to the medical bay, I left a trail of dusty boot prints behind me, which I would have to clean up later.

When I finally pushed open the door, I saw him sitting up, leaning against a pillow.

He turned his head toward me, and his eyebrows shot upward. "What happened to you?" he asked, breaking into a weak laugh.

I smiled, approaching the bedside. "Something called cleaning. How do you feel?" I asked, noticing that my shirt was lying on the table next to the bed.

"Like a couple of bricks were dropped on my chest. Repeatedly. Celestina told me what happened." He grimaced as they adjusted the IV. His shirt had been taken off completely—it had probably gotten in Celestina's way—and his chest was half covered with the heart monitor patches.

They backed away from him, turning to me. "He's doing good. The antivenom worked beautifully, but he has to take it easy for at least a week. No heavy lifting, no cardio; he needs to heal. Is there any food here?"

I grimaced. "The only food I found were MREs and a couple cans of various vegetables. And trust me, I checked for more." I walked over and grabbed my shirt, pinching it between two fingers so I didn't get too much dirt on it. "I'll go grab three MREs though. Something is better than nothing."

I exited the medical bay and headed toward the kitchen, dropping my shirt in my quarters on the way over. When I entered the kitchen, I shed my jacket and hung it on an apron hook. Sticking my hands in the sink, I hit the knob for water and hissed as the ice-cold liquid hit my skin. Honestly, I was just grateful that it *had* water, even if I didn't know how it was still on. They must've never disconnected everything when they shut down the base.

Once I had less dust on my hands, and a nice little line on my arm dividing "clean" from "dirty," I went back to the storage room and grabbed three MREs, grimacing at the titles. Sometimes you just had to make do.

I grabbed "Beef Ravioli," "Chicken Chunks," and "Chili with Beans" and prepared all three after finding trays to put them on.

Carrying all three trays, I made my way back to the medical bay. As I entered, Celestina and Apollo were talking, but stopped abruptly.

Apollo made a face. "Not *Chicken Chunks*, I *hated* that one."

I shrugged, then offered him the chili. He took it reluctantly, and I turned and gave the beef ravioli to Celestina. "This one tastes slightly better. Take it."

They took it from me, grimacing at the sad MRE.

I sat down with my *Chicken Chunks*, hoping my gag reflex didn't kick in. "*Bon appetit,*" I declared, then dug into the MRE. It tasted like puke, but I ate it anyway.

Apollo also managed to swallow his but coughed a couple times. Celestina, unaccustomed to the taste, spit their first bite back out.

"This is nasty! How the hell do you guys eat it?" they asked, wiping off their tongue.

"We had to." I shoved another forkful in my mouth.

"Never said it would be good. These things are designed to last in a nuclear fallout shelter, I swear," Apollo added, taking another bite of his MRE.

I nodded in agreement, then took pity on them. "Pinch your nose when you eat. That's how I did it until I got used to the taste." I pointed at her food with my fork. "Now, eat."

They made another face but pinched their nose and took a bite.

I ate another forkful, then asked, "What were you guys talking about when I came in?"

Celestina swallowed her mouthful and replied, "The spaceship."

I narrowed my eyes. "You're lying." I pointed my fork accusingly.

"Am not."

"You scratched your nose."

"It was *itching.*"

"It was a nervous tick. I think you were talking about something else." I shoved another forkful into my mouth to shut myself up.

Apollo rolled his eyes. "There's nothing you can get past her. Yes, we were talking about something else." Then he shoved another forkful in his mouth, swallowed, and gave me an evil grin.

I waited. Neither said anything else, so I decided to leave it alone.

For now.

Instead, I reached in my pocket for the bomb panel with the Mark of Fire. "Seen this before?" I asked Apollo, tossing him the piece.

He caught it one-handed and examined it, his eyebrows furrowing in concentration. Then his eyes widened in recognition. "It was on the uniforms of the men who killed Ryan."

I nodded. "And it was on John's uniform, hidden underneath his flag patch. I tore it off when we fought that night." I motioned for the panel, and he tossed it back.

"I take it that it's not a good thing?" he asked, setting down his fork.

"I'm really not sure." I shoved the last forkful into my mouth and stood. "But right now, I'm going to take a shower and sleep. I'll talk to you guys in a few hours." I left the room and dropped the tray off in the kitchen.

After trekking through the base back to my quarters, I immediately stripped and hopped into the cold shower. It took an hour to get all the dust off, but once it was, I grabbed some random workout clothes and passed out on my bed.

And this time, I actually got to sleep.

Chapter 12

When I fell asleep, it wasn't exactly peaceful. Instead of nightmares or strange dreams, I heard static and then I could see.

I was looking down at Apollo and Celestina, like I was looking down through a camera.

"She's stressed, Apollo, but not showing it. I'm worried."

Apollo nodded. I never did feel comfortable showing my feelings, but I didn't think it had been that obvious. Of course, Apollo did have like a sixth sense for when I was stressed.

"I know," he told Celestina, scooping another forkful of the chili into his mouth. "She'll keep going like that until she breaks down, which takes a lot, but it's happened before."

Celestina tucked a strand of hair behind their ear. "That time after Ryan died and John betrayed you guys?"

He shook his head. "No, this was after. When they made them director of the CI. There was this situation and… everyone else was failing… They took it upon themself to fix the situation, but afterward was not a pretty sight. It was like someone had hollowed them out and took all their emotions. It was worse than what happened to Ryan, but I understand why they beat themself up about it."

Celestina fixed his IV, making him squirm. Then they bit their lip, staring hard at him. "I want to ask, but I'm not sure I want to know," they said, releasing their lip.

Apollo bent his head to look at his hands, then looked back up at them. "If you want to know, I'll tell you. She refuses to talk about it. Well, she did. I don't know if she will now. It's not easy to hear."

Celestina nodded. "Tell me."

Apollo took a deep breath. "It all started when a mom got a call that her daughter had been kidnapped, and unless the ransom was paid, the girl would die. The girl was eight years old. The mom was frantic, and her husband was a lower-ranking agent in the CI. He begged for the CI's help, and Eryn set people on it.

"Then we found out several other people had gotten similar calls. A total of twenty kids were being held captive, ranging from three months to twelve years. Eryn doubled the agents on the case, not yet stepping in because there was something else she had been working on. She didn't want to be in the field again, because of obvious reasons.

"Then we got wind one of the kids had been killed. To this day, we don't know if that first death was an accident or on purpose. But it got Eryn's attention, and deciding that it called for desperate measures, she forced herself back into the field.

"It took a toll on her. She went out at five a.m. every morning, returned to the office at ten-thirty p.m., and worked until one a.m., at which point she slept in her office. I had to force her to eat most of the time. This went on for two weeks until we got our lead.

"She suited up and went out with a team of our best agents. They arrived at the place the kids were being held, only to find two kids alive, holding each other. Dead bodies surrounded them; the floor was covered with blood. It smelled like decomposing flesh. The kidnapper was there but shot himself before he could be arrested.

"The two kids were returned to their parents and had to attend some pretty intensive counseling. But Eryn… She was like a walking corpse after that. It took me hours to get her to tell me what had happened. It was like she had lost all hope. At one point, I sent her home, because she couldn't do anything, not even fight.

"It broke my heart to see her like that. And there was nothing I could do. Then, about a month after, she came back to the office, acting like normal. I never knew what returned her to me, and when I tried to ask, she wouldn't tell me." He ran a hand through his hair and laid his head on the pillow behind him.

Celestina's eyes were wide, and their mouth was slightly open. "Holy shit," they said, and I could hear the roughness in their voice. Celestina was about to cry.

"Are you gonna need tissues? Cause the way Eryn ripped my shirt would make it pretty good tissue material." He joked. I laughed too because I had ripped up his shirt pretty good.

Celestina laughed. "She did do a pretty decent job of ripping your shirt. Bet you wish it was for another reason though."

And they winked at him. Oh no.

I woke up abruptly, feeling a headache coming on. Had I sleep…connected? To a camera?

It wasn't worth thinking about at the moment. I got out of bed to once again wander the halls, stumbling upon a laundry room.

It was old, and dusty, and the machines were probably broken, but it would occupy my mind for now. I sat down and began pulling the washing machine apart.

Apollo was right. I didn't like talking about what happened at the warehouse. There had been a reason I stayed out of the field after we came home. I knew my mind couldn't take any more. The darn thing was at its limits with trauma that no person should have to deal with. Trauma I certainly hadn't wanted to deal with at the time.

As my hands moved on their own, I let silent tears roll down my face.

Those two kids. Brother and sister, holding each other tight, covered in other children's blood. The rest of the children…

I had beelined for the kids that day. To protect them. *You shouldn't have to see this. You're too young.*

And all I could remember in that moment was my sister's body flying like a ragdoll and hitting the ground. Glassy eyes staring up at me, with nothing left behind them.

The terror in the siblings' eyes as they held each other.

Other CI agents had run to train their guns on the killer. I still remembered the shot and the *smack* of his body hitting the floor.

I had attended every single one of the funerals held for the children who had died. Many parents were grateful to see me there, and I held them awkwardly as they hugged me, lost in their grief. Others hissed at me to go away, so I would leave and stand a mile away to pay my respects.

The washing machine was finished when my train of thought finished. My cheeks were tear-stained, my headache had grown more intense, and I really needed to sleep.

I stood back up, brushed off the dust, and headed back to the dormitories. If I could, I would try to find a hot bucket of water to stick my feet in. That always helped my headaches.

Most of all, I would leave the rest of my thoughts for later. There wasn't time now, and no energy, to begin to process everything.

So, it would have to wait.

Chapter 13

I woke up the next morning feeling so clean, and it was amazing.

After rolling out of the bed, I yanked on my combat clothes, my clean ones, and ran to throw the others into the washing machine I fixed last night. I would have to fix the drier too, but that could wait. I left the jacket off, simply because it would be too hot.

I headed to the kitchen again and pulled out three more MREs, some Vienna sausages, and some dried jerky. Grabbing three more trays, I divvied up the food and headed to the med bay.

When I finally turned into the med bay, I found Apollo sitting up in bed, talking quietly with Celestina.

They both became silent when I came in, smiling at me like they shared some sort of secret.

"What?" I asked, wearing a ridiculous grin.

"Why are you so happy? You spent all yesterday doing manual labor by yourself." Celestina raised an eyebrow.

"I guess I tired myself out. Tends to happen when you actually do physical labor." I winked at them.

They mock gasped, clutching their chest as if they'd been wounded.

"How are you feeling?" I asked Apollo, my heart melting at his soft smile.

"Better, but still like I've been run over by a four-wheeler," he replied, yawning.

"Well, here you go." I set a tray down on his lap and handed the other to Celestina.

"Eat up." I commanded, giving both of them the Mom Stare.

They both started eating, Celestina grimacing less than they did last night. I finished mine in record speed, bidding both Celestina and Apollo a "see you later" as I left to investigate the storage rooms.

I had to break the padlock on the first one, because I couldn't find a key, and none of the ones I had in my pocket worked. Once I hauled the large doors open, I immediately regretted my decision to go through the storage rooms.

"This is some *Indiana Jones*-level shit," I muttered to myself, staring at the room full of boxes that were stacked in rows from floor to ceiling.

Sighing, I pulled the flashlight out of my pocket and started toward the back. By the time I reached the back, I was again covered in dust, cobwebs, and something I was pretty sure was not dirt.

Thankfully, I was able to find the electric panel and turn on the lights, which helped somewhat.

Before I even started deciding which box to open next, I heard another pair of footsteps echoing on the concrete floors.

"Eryn? Where are you?" Celestina yelled out, their voice bouncing off of the walls.

"Here!" I hollered back, and they turned the corner a few seconds later.

"Need help?" They were dressed in a T-shirt and a pair of overalls they had found somewhere.

"That would be much appreciated, but shouldn't you be watching Apollo?" I stepped to the nearest box and heaved off the lid.

"He's out of the danger stage now, so he'll be fine, just bored. I figure you shouldn't be working to death by yourself, so I came to help." Celestina grabbed the discarded lid and dragged it off to the side.

"All right then, let's get to work," I said, bending over the lip of the box to start pulling out the items inside.

We worked for a while, in silence, although there was an occasional smatter of conversation when I found something especially interesting.

Celestina was in the middle of breaking down a cardboard container, and I was digging through another one when I came across a small metal box hiding in the corner.

"Celestina, come here!" I yelled, tucking the box under my arm and jumping off the edge of the box.

The runes on the box were familiar, and I felt myself reaching for the keys in my pocket.

"What is it?" Celestina asked, coming around the corner.

They watched in silence as I chose a small, silver key on my key ring and opened the lock. The lid popped open, screeching because of unuse. Inside laid a silver Vue Dragon sigil, shiny and nestled in red velvet.

"What's that doing in here?" Celestina commented, reaching out a hand to touch the sigil.

"Maybe I used it for something, like maybe a key or as a part for a machine." I picked up the small, hand-sized object. I flipped it over, seeing again the runic symbols that were carved on the box.

"How would you use it as part of a machine?" Celestina muttered

I kept silent, studying the runes.

"Would Raven, by chance, know ancient languages?" I brought the sigil closer to my face, as if that would help me decipher it.

"Yeah, she knows tons of languages, but she's probably working right now," Celestina replied, holding their hand out for the box.

I gave it to her, sticking the sigil into my pocket.

We spent the rest of the day unloading boxes, with Celestina occasionally leaving to check on Apollo. After the sigil, we didn't find much of interest to us, but lots of mechanical and electrical parts that might interest a mechanic or engineer.

When we were both tuckered out, we left everything where it was and headed to the mess hall, where we fixed MREs. Again.

After eating, Celestina took a MRE to Apollo, and I went to the control room.

When I reached the half-open door, I pulled tools out of my pocket and just took the door down, leaving the doorway bare.

I sat again in the old, disgusting chair, and fiddled with the wires beside me until the old TV came on. It was grainy, and it took a few tries to tune it to the right channel, but I managed.

It started playing the news, where a robot anchorwoman was giving announcements.

"Doctors are recommending everyone purchase masks to continue breathing oxygen. We also have an offer from Untold Incorporated on their special colony launch…" and she went on.

My stomach clenched. How dare they make people pay to stay alive?

The screen shifted to a tall, average-looking man standing in front of a microphone.

"There's no need to worry! Doctors at the Vue Institute, the top medical professionals and bioscientists, are on the job! Also, the city is just fine! There is nothing to indicate we won't recover from this," said the man, grinning with weirdly white teeth.

A shiver went down my back. So this was Henry Marsher, President of Lorina City. Not the one I'd choose.

I hit a comm button on the panel in front of me, hoping it still worked. "Celestina, report to the control room ASAP," I said over the intercom system, grimacing at the feedback that came with.

They were in the control room within minutes.

"Yeah, what's wrong?" They stood beside my chair.

"How big is the city?" I pointed at the TV screen.

Celestina squinted at the TV. "The population of the world has decreased, so about five thousand?"

I whipped my head toward her.

"Five thousand? What the hell happened?" I asked, eyes wide and still trying to process the fact that there were only five thousand people left in the *world.*

"Eh, several things. World War III, mass shootings, unavailability of resources, disease, a weird trend of families only being able to have one child, and some more I can't remember" Celestina shrugged. "It's not that bad. At least our city is better than it used to be."

I felt ready to throw up. "The population of the world used to be billions! How are you so nonchalant about it?" I said, still in shock over the news.

"I've grown up like this. I've never known anything else," Celestina told me, turning to face me.

I just sat there, keeping my mouth shut and thinking about all the people that had died.

Then my vision went black, and Muroha appeared in front of me.

"Eryn, how goes it?" he asked, leaning forward in his seat.

"Um, okay. What were you going to tell me about the Mark of Fire last time?" I replied, hearing Celestina ask if I was okay in the background.

"It's an intergalactic federation that kills planets and uses the energy and resources from said planets to build their own. They're a nasty group, and we've been trying to get rid of them for a long, long time," he told me, holding up a blurry picture of a planet.

"It's blurry," I said, feeling Celestina shaking me.

"Well, my mate wasn't able to get the clearest of pictures, as she was trying to escape their defenses," Muroha commented, tilting his head.

"I'm sorry, I didn't know…" I trailed off, swiping my hand at Celestina's hand.

"It's quite all right. By the way, I found out the ICSP can send two ships that house about a thousand humans each. You're lucky you're so small. They should be there within a week. How many humans are left after that?"

"Around three thousand." I grimaced.

"Here are plans for ships that are similar to the ones we're sending, but smaller," he said, typing, and then I felt a stinging sensation in my head.

I hissed, but the pain faded quickly. Were these not the ones he had given me earlier?

Then my vision came back, and Celestina was standing in front of me, arms crossed.

"What happened?" they asked, obviously annoyed.

"Oh, that was Muroha," I said, standing, "You know, the blue alien."

"That's still so weird" Celestina muttered, arms falling to their sides.

"He contacted me through my brain, and he's been giving us blueprints for ships." I put my hands on my hips.

"How is he putting them in your *brain?*" Their eyebrows furrowed.

I stepped backward to start heading out of the room, but tripped over a cord in the process. "Well, I have this thing," I said from my spot on the floor.

"What thing?"

"This thing I can do with electronic things. I can… connect with them. Control them. I've been able to do it for as long as I can remember."

"There's no way. No one can do that."

I looked at the old computer and opened a program. Celestina glanced between the computer and me several times.

"That explains things."

"Explains what?"

"AIHNA. Do you remember your first night back at my house?" Celestina offered a hand.

I took it and pulled myself to my feet. "Yes, what about it?"

"Rubi hasn't been able to get the system that nuanced to read hunger and thirst. Yet AIHNA was able to tell that you were both when you came home with me. You must have been interfacing with her without knowing, and that's how she knew," Celestina explained, drumming their fingers on their face. "But no one can do that that I know of. How would you interface with tech? I suppose a brain chip could work in theory, but I didn't see one when I did a scan…"

"A brain chip? Like an actual piece of metal in my brain?"

Celestina nodded. "They ran some experiments a few years back. It was supposed to be the latest and greatest innovation. But they never could quite get it to work. And I'm told many of the animals they used died under weird circumstances."

"Now that I have that terrifying information, why don't we go find some MREs, or maybe get more people here to help with all the boxes?" I gently pulled Celestina out of the control room.

"Sure," they agreed quietly, staring off into space.

I led the now silent Celestina to the cafeteria, where I gave them a couple MREs and pushed them over to the stoves. They silently worked on preparing them while I fit on a headset I had found in the control room.

"Testing, one, two, three," I said, tapping the mic.

I heard feedback in my ear.

Grimacing, I pulled it away from my ear, then rolled my eyes.

I only had the one headset. Ding dong.

Considering myself tired and not thinking straight (of course, I was never thinking *straight*), I left the cafeteria to find the rest of the earpieces. Walking through the hallway, I went back to the control room. Deciding the drawers would be the best option, I started there.

After combing through every inch of the drawers, I moved on to the desk.

Unless the missing earpieces were disguised as gum wrappers, I found nothing.

Leaning against the wall, I surveyed the room, passing over every inch and hoping to find something. A weird configuration on the wall caught my eye, but I ignored it for now.

Giving up on the headset, I left the control room and meandered down the hallway. Soon, I was in the section of the base that I hadn't cleaned, coughing on the clouds of dust that flew up every time I stepped. It was dark, so I pulled out my flashlight to illuminate the hallway better.

The tall doors looked eerie in the dim space, and my footsteps echoed around the hallway, making me pull myself in to appear smaller. When I reached the end of the hall, I stood in front of a massive door, big enough for quite a few elephants to pass through. There was a control panel to the right of the doors, old and rusted.

After rubbing off some of the dust, I discovered it was an old biometrics system. I tapped it a few times, and the only thing I succeeded in doing was making more dust pile on the floor.

I took my multitool out of my pocket, opened the screwdriver attachment, and took off the panel to expose the wires beneath. It took some fiddling and a couple of shocks, but I finally managed to hotwire the system.

The doors screeched like some sort of massive monster in pain but managed to open. When I stepped around the edge I stopped in my tracks. My stomach dropped, and I felt ready to throw up.

There were space suits scattered all over the large room, various different types and sizes and styles. But that wasn't the problem.

The walls of the room were covered with rectangular drawers, ranging from several feet wide and tall, to only a few inches. They had silver outsides, and I heard a faint humming from the refrigeration unit behind them. It was the morgue I had seen earlier through the vent where I found Apollo.

Walking shakily to the first drawer, I pulled it open.

I had to find a trash can immediately after that.

After dry-heaving for a minute, I managed to compose myself and forced myself to look at the contents of the drawer again.

The creature was close to seven feet tall with long, spindly limbs and pale, translucent skin. It had three sets of arms, one pair of legs, and large eye sockets like a squid's. The tag attached to its foot read:

Date Found: January 5th, 2026

Discoverer: Rancher in Texas

Species: Cavern-dwelling type

I pulled out the file in the pocket at the end of the drawer, steadied myself, and opened the file.

NOTES: This extraterrestrial was found in Texas by a rancher who was searching his property after noticing his cattle herd was suspiciously depleted. He found the creature feasting on one of his cattle, and in a panic, shot it. He noted that "it didn't seem real intelligent, so it was like shootin' a coyote." When he realized "it wasn't from around here," he contacted authorities, who in turn contacted us. We came in, removed the carcass, and did an autopsy here.

William A. Buckner

UPDATE: The corpse was moved into this new base in the year 2029, due to secrecy issues at the former location. Another autopsy was done, and it was found that this creature lived in a place that was oxygen-deficient and had adapted a respiratory system to counter that. We are trying a similar idea on spacesuit C27, for low-oxygen/aqueous environments.

John Dwight Jones

I threw up again into the same trash can.

I closed the file, put it back in the drawer, and closed the drawer.

Then I sat down and cried into my hands, trying to keep myself as silent as possible. Every time I thought I would be okay, all I had to do was look at the drawers again. How could I never have known about this? I had been the director of the CI; nothing had been a secret from me. Something like this should have been in the records.

Pulling myself up, I started going through the work desks, reading papers, blueprints, and the few journals I could find. Most held scientific data from the space suits or the aliens, which really tested my gag reflex for the third time in the past hour. I did manage to find a journal that was semi-personal and one entry in particular that shed a little bit of light.

10-20-2030

We received more specimens today and nearly got yelled at by site director Jones. Apparently, the aliens had nearly been seen by Eryn Vue, who seems to be a semi-legendary figure around here. When I asked who that was, one of my colleagues explained to me she was the director of Core Intel and was renowned for being a bit of a hardass, and dangerous to boot. Apparently, she knew nothing about this part of the organization, and we had to keep this place a secret. According to Jones, she would "kill you all and make sure your remains were given to pigs!" However, I don't really believe that, especially if what my colleague told me is true. Even though I just started working here, I'm already starting to feel uncomfortable. I really don't like my rotations on the cages; some of those creatures really freak me out.

It wasn't signed, but the manner of writing triggered a memory. A note, left in my office, saying *A soldier should know everything happening, especially when locked behind bars.* At the time, I had simply ignored the message, unsure what it meant, if anything.

Cages?

I looked up from the journal and surveyed the room again. There were just drawers and tables, no cages.

Getting up, I walked along the walls, listening.

There was a humming noise behind the first wall, an indication the refrigeration unit was working.

When I reached the second, I didn't hear anything.

Tugging on a drawer handle, I found it fake.

I yanked on all the drawers I could reach, but none of them activated any sort of trigger.

Going for a different tactic, I tried pushing all the handles.

No luck.

I ran through every possibility, including opening most of the real drawers, which I felt awful about.

Finally, I screeched in frustration. "Why won't this damn thing open?"

And then I heard a *click*.

I froze as one of the fake drawers popped open, revealing a voice recognition panel.

"Welcome Director Jones. Please say the password. If you need a hint, say 'hint,'" said a pleasant female voice that sounded eerily like my own.

"Hint," I said, on the off chance that he'd simply password protected it and didn't use a voicewave recognition.

"You have selected: Hint. Your hint is: the organization you work for," the panel said.

I gaped at the panel. Organization he worked for? This base used to belong to the CI, so I tried that.

"Incorrect."

I tried a couple other things, including Mark of Fire, but none of them worked.

I made an exasperated noise and tried to remember what, exactly, was on that patch. If I were an evil organization with a symbol like that, what would I call us?

"Chimera's Fire?" I asked.

I heard something *click*, and the panel slowly retreated into the wall. Hopefully, that was the right password and not the panel giving up.

A door silently opened in front of me, letting out a blast of freezing cold air. I shut my eyes and scrunched my face until the gust stopped, then peered inside the door.

Inside were enclosures, all roughly seven feet tall and maybe ten feet wide and deep. There were only fifteen, which was a small amount compared to the drawers in the room behind me. The glass outside was frosted over, making it impossible to see what, if anything, lay inside.

Hooked up to the outside of each enclosure were giant IV bags with tubes that led inside each enclosure. They were all about a quarter full, and when I stepped close to one, I heard the mechanical noise that told me it was still working. This room might explain why the electricity and water in the base was working.

I took the bottom of my shirt and rubbed a circle in the frost, then peered inside.

Squinting, it took me a moment to process what I was seeing.

The creature inside the enclosure looked like a cross between a large, furry man and a wolf, but it was hard to tell details from the way it was laying. Standing, I would guess it would be somewhere close to seven feet, and it was bulked with muscle. Its entire body was covered in a thick, gray and white pelt, and its face looked like a cross between human and wolf. It wasn't exactly facing me, but I could see the wolf-like ears and a short snout.

Backing up, I went to the next enclosure and did the same thing: wiped a circle and looked inside. I found another creature like the first, with a black pelt, slightly smaller than the first.

Moving along, I also found a little creature that looked like some sort of sugar glider, except it had three tails and bat-like ears and was roughly the size of a cat.

The next six enclosures I looked in were empty.

Another enclosure held a lizard-like humanoid with webbed hands and feet and a tail that wrapped around its waist twice.

Then there were two enclosures with little, dragon-like creatures, except they were the size of horses and had no wings.

The last three shocked me the most and made my stomach churn.

When I wiped a circle in the first of the three and pressed my face to the icy glass, I immediately reeled back in shock.

Blinking my eyes a couple of times, I looked again, and this time, I knew what I was seeing was real.

Standing, it would be around six foot tall. It had legs with knees that bent the other direction, like the legs of a Tyrannosaurus. It's skin was light blue and translucent, which meant I could see muscles and organs. And the face looked exactly like Muroha's.

The next two also held similar beings, except both the others were green and somewhat taller.

I felt sick to my stomach, and I could feel bile crawling up my throat. I was so stunned I couldn't really process a coherent thought. They came in pieces: *But how-why-no-can't-this shouldn't...*

I took deep breaths, then made myself move to try and find the temperature control unit. With any luck, the IVs had kept them all alive, and I could wake them up. My hands were numb from the cold, as was most of the rest of me. I couldn't really feel my nose either.

It took a bit of searching, but I found the control unit on the far side of the room in an obscure corner. The temperature was currently set at a ridiculously cold temperature, and I turned it up to forty to start. Those wolf-like creatures... I didn't want them to overheat.

While I was waiting for the room to heat up, I went back into the first room, where the heat made my body buzz, and then turned into pain as my body adjusted. I grabbed the journal I had found earlier and sat down to read it, hoping the person had more information about the creatures in the enclosures.

No such luck.

I searched all the tables until I found a small journal. Scanning it, I saw dates of arrival, medical reports, and various facts about the different creatures. They had numbers, no names. I flipped pages until I found one about the creatures that looked like Muroha.

November 23rd, 2050

New arrivals

A spaceship crashed in Roswell, New Mexico, on November 20th, 2050, containing three aliens. One is blue, and the other two are green, and they're a cross between some sort of dog, a dinosaur, and a human. The green ones deferred to the blue when they were awake. They spoke English, but it was poor

English. They are all in good physical condition, and their spaceship was taken to a holding facility in DC.

It wasn't signed, but the handwriting was the same as on the tags. My gut churned reading it, and I was ready to go back in time and punch this guy in the face.

How could he treat these beings and these other creatures like unintelligent beings, when they were clearly more advanced than we were? And to harp on their English was just wrong. They probably learned by tapping into satellites and using what they found there.

Then I heard a howl from inside the other room, which made me drop the book in surprise.

I got up and ran inside the other room, which was bearable now. Hurrying, I reached the enclosure with the first wolf-like creature, where some of the frost had melted, making it easier to see inside the enclosure.

It looked like it was trying to rise but couldn't. All I heard were its howls and an occasional clank of metal. I searched for some sort of door but only found a set of rungs leading to the top of the enclosure.

The creature's eyes were open, and they were a pale blue and humanlike. It growled when it saw me, the vibrations making the enclosure shake. I had an idea that probably wasn't the safest at the moment, but it felt like I had no other option.

I climbed the rungs quickly and found the trapdoor on top. There was a harness rig with a winch next to the trapdoor, along with a flexible metal ladder. I peered down into the enclosure, where the creature was staring up at me and sniffing.

"Do you understand my language?" I asked in a low, soothing voice.

It sniffed again and wagged a bushy tail.

"I do, even though the language you speak is my secondary one," said the creature. Their voice was deep, one of the deepest I had ever heard.

"May I come down there and undo your IV and metals?" I asked, looking for signs of possible hostility. After all, he had no reason to trust anyone like me after what he had been through.

"You ask if I will harm you? No. You do not wear the uniform of the others, the ones in the white robes. You seem like me, a warrior. So please, come down. I would be grateful if you would undo these," he replied, pointing his nose toward his metals.

I climbed through, holding on to the edge, and lowered myself until my arms were extended, where I dropped and landed in a crouch.

"You are a warrior. What is your name?" the wolf asked as I approached his massive form.

"Eryn," I replied, placing my left hand by the IV needle and using my right to slowly withdraw it. "What about you?"

The wolf grinned, which was a bit freaky, but I figured he meant no harm. "I'm known as Stormfighter, or at least that's the nearest translation in your language," he said, growling a little as the needle left his arm.

I knelt by his left hand, my deft fingers undoing the metal catch, which would have been too small for Stormfighter's massive fingers to work with.

"No need to worry, I will not harm you," he told me, catching my glances back at his face.

After all four metals were opened, Stormfighter stood slowly. The fur on his head brushed the top of the enclosure. He seemed even bigger upright, and I made sure to keep my gaze on his face, which might give me a crick later, but would save me from embarrassment now.

"It feels good to stand again. May I have permission to lift you out of this glass enclosure?" he asked, hands palm up toward me.

"You may," I responded, inclining my head.

He gently grabbed my waist and lifted me until I could reach the edge of the trapdoor, which would hopefully be big enough for Stormfighter to climb out of. I pulled myself out and climbed down the rungs on the outside of the cage.

Stormfighter followed, pulling himself out and dropping to the ground from the top of the cage. Some more of the frost had cleared, and Stormfighter accompanied me to the cage where the other one was held.

"My son!" Stormfighter yelped, then ran forward in a few bounding steps. In seconds, he was on top of the cage, flipping open the trapdoor and dropping inside.

"Dad!" I heard from the cage, slightly muffled due to the glass.

Stormfighter moved to hug his son but stopped. "Eryn, would you mind coming in here? My fingers are too big to release my son," he said, sounding a bit embarrassed.

I quickly climbed the rungs, dropped in, and knelt next to the kid. "What's your name?" I asked, gently taking out the IV.

He looked at his dad, who nodded encouragingly. "Lightningborn," he said, watching as I released him from his metals. When he was free, he stood and bowed to me.

"Thank you, Eryn, for helping me and my father," he said respectfully, glancing at his dad.

I smiled. "You're most welcome."

Stormfighter leaned down and whispered in his son's ear, although I could still hear what he said. "Good job," he whispered, a touch of pride in his voice.

It made my heart warm to see the father-son duo. Stormfighter again asked permission to lift me out, and I again accepted. I waited on the floor of the room until they were both standing next to me.

The other glass cages were almost completely clear, and it looked like the dragon creatures were beginning to wake.

"May we? They're our companions, Mulsker. They're creatures from our world and are similar to hunting dogs on yours," Stormfighter explained.

"Go ahead," I said, heading toward the cage with the sugar glider.

This time, I lowered the ladder and climbed down, then scooped the creature into my arms. It opened its big eyes and blinked slowly. I felt its tails touch my neck and shoulders, light, probing touches to discover what I was.

Then it hooked its tails in my shirt and climbed to lay across my shoulders. Taking that as a sign that it trusted me, I climbed up the ladder and back into the main room. The…Mulskers?…were out of their enclosures and swatting playfully at Stormfighter and Lightningborn. They wagged their short, pointed tails in time with the wolves bushy ones.

As I approached, they smelled me and stepped in front of the two wolves, growling. Stormfighter and Lightningborn both pulled them back by the scruffs of their necks and whispered words of assurance. They eventually calmed down and even let me scratch behind their scales.

"If you can," I said, "try and find your spacesuits. I assume they're adapted to keep you a comfortable temperature here?"

"They are," Lightningborn replied. "However, we can stand temperatures up to sixty of...Fah-ren-hiiiiit."

I raised my eyebrows and nodded. "That's helpful. I'm going to turn up the temperature then, try and wake up the lizard guy and the others."

Stormfighter glanced at the hibernating forms. "You know the transparent-skinned ones?"

As I was walking to the temperature control, I threw over my shoulder, "Yeah, I have one that's been helping me. There's a lot I need to catch you guys up on, and some of it, you're not gonna like."

Chapter 14

After awhile, the lizard guy woke up. He panicked a bit, until I got in there, undid his metals and IV, and explained who I was. He introduced himself as Ythea and told me his race didn't really have set genders, so it was fine whichever pronouns I used. When I told him that male pronouns were typically the default, he asked what the female pronouns sounded like.

Well, she decided she liked those better, so I would introduce her with those pronouns.

I moved her into the first room, and Stormfighter and Lightningborn followed. After scrounging for a bit, I found a suit that might belong to Ythea.

"Is this yours?" I asked, holding up the tan suit made of some sort of meshy fabric.

"Yes, and I will change into it. Thank you." Ythea replied, taking the suit from me.

The Mulskers were sniffing the drawers while I searched for suits that might be the wolves, but none that I found were big enough.

"Well, you guys will have to go natural for now. Are you okay with that?" I questioned, my eyes tracking back to Stormfighter.

"We're fine with that," Stormfighter replied.

My pocket buzzed. Glancing down, I reached in and pulled out the phone. I held the small thing up to my ear.

"Eryn, where the hell are you? We've been searching for you for hours!" Celetina yelled into the phone, which I took away from my ear.

"I found a secret room at the back of the base. You'll know more later. I'm still waiting for some of them to wake up."

"What?"

Then I hung up, and the three humanoids were staring at me.

I heard a scream from the other room, and my body reacted instantly, sprinting toward the sound. It was the blue one, who was staring at the IV needle and screaming in fear.

"Hold on!" I yelled, pulling myself rapidly up the side. I dropped the ladder and scrambled down. It was breathing rapidly, too fast. It was trembling, and I could hear quick swallowing, probably trying to keep nausea down.

"Hey, hey, look at me," I commanded, putting power in my voice.

It trained its eyes on me, which were wide with fear.

"Breathe. I need you to remind yourself to breathe," I said soothingly, placing a gentle hand on its arm.

It stared into my eyes, and I could hear it slowing its breath down, and the trembling stopped.

I quickly turned and took the IV out, then tossed it to the side. "What's your name?" I asked, undoing the metals.

"Maesha, and you?" it said, with a soft, lilting voice.

"Eryn. Can you stand?" I asked, standing myself.

She pushed herself to her feet and wobbled a bit.

I caught her easily. "Can you climb?" I guided her over to the ladder.

"Yes, I can, I think. Last thing I remember was a man with a cruel grin stabbing me with the IV, and then it was cold, really cold." Maesha began to climb the ladder.

I followed her up and out, then moved to the next two cages and took out IVs and released metals. They were all able to climb out on their own, much to my relief. The two green ones were named Scia and Shirmra, and they both seemed to be very loyal to Maesha.

I sensed a tight bond of friendship between the three, not unlike the bond of friendship between Apollo and me. And once they were all next to each other, I noticed something strange. They all bore the same tattoo on their left arm. It was a scorpion, poised to sting.

Leaving the idea alone for now, I gathered all of them in the other room and began telling them the news.

Giving them the short version, I explained they had been in hibernation for at least a hundred years, give or take, and that Earth was going to die in less than a month.

They took it relatively well, and once I told them what my group was trying to do, they agreed to help.

"Well, we don't have much choice, do we?" sassed Scia. "You have no idea where our ship is, so we couldn't leave without you, even if we wanted to."

"Scia! Eryn just saved us from those cages, and you belittle all she's been through! Look in her eyes; they're the eyes of a leader," Maesha snapped, pointing at me.

Scia mumbled something under her breath, but I chose to ignore it.

"Will you come with me to meet the others?" I asked, gauging their feelings.

"We will," said Stormfighter, slinging an arm around his son.

"I will accompany you," said Ythea.

"We will come with," Maesha said, obviously speaking for herself and her friends.

"Let's go," I said, leading the way out of the room.

We silently made our way down the hall, and I felt like some sort of weird superhero. Except there wasn't any dramatic music, and I certainly wasn't heroic, not to mention I had a sugar glider thing laying across my shoulders.

The silence was awkward, and the only sound was our footsteps.

When we reached the cafeteria, I ducked my head in to see if Celestina was there but moved on when I saw the kitchen empty. I headed next to the med bay, where I found Apollo and Celestina talking.

I felt the dull stab of jealousy, and then shame. Celestina was just relieving the boredom for him, because I hadn't been.

"Hey, guys, I have a small surprise," I said, stepping inside the med bay, and watching their priceless expressions as the rest of the people followed me in.

"Shit," Celestina said, and Apollo's jaw dropped.

After they both recovered from their shock, I introduced the crew behind me to them.

"They were in a secret room in the back of the base?" Apollo asked, eyeing Stormfighter. "I didn't know there was a secret room."

"I didn't either, or the cages never would've happened. Do you remember a John Dwight Jones?" I asked, moving farther into the room so the rest could file in.

"Vaguely. He was a dick and wanted to talk directly to you a lot, but his matters were petty. He was the site director for this base. I was pretty sure he had some sort of stalker crush on you," Apollo commented dryly.

I made a noise through my nose, then turned to Celestina. "Are the others on their way?"

"Yeah, I called, and they're working on getting here. Are we gonna get started today?" Celestina flipped a stylus between their fingers.

"Sooner is better," I replied. "How many of those capsules do we have left?"

"Five," came her curt response.

"Okay. Maybe you can get that ingredient list from Mom, just in case we can make more." I turned to the crew behind me. "Are any of you good at anything engineering or mechanical?" I looked at each in turn.

"I am." Ythea held up her thin hand.

"We are as well." Maesha gestured to herself and her friends.

"We need to get started on bigger ships, which I have schematics for, because we only have four weeks," I told them, tapping my head. "I'll download them and print out some paper copies. The tech here is relatively old."

Leading them out of the med bay, I took them to Hangar 1A, and then asked them to wait while I went and dealt with the schematics.

A headache and several curse words later, I had finally managed to figure out how to download files from my brain and got the printer working.

Running back to Hangar 1A, I noted with pride that it was completely cleared in the middle and ready for work.

I stopped in the middle of the room and unrolled the schematics for the ship, and the rest gathered around me.

"All right, this is what we need to build. And we need to build two by four weeks from now." I passed the paper off to Maesha.

"I recognize this design. Where did you get it?" she asked, looking up at me and trembling.

"A being named Muroha. He's been contacting me through my brain thing…" I trailed off when Maesha dropped the papers.

"Muroha? Are you sure?" she whispered, while her friends looked at her wide-eyed, obviously shocked.

"Yeah. That's what he told me."

Maesha threw her arms around me. My hands dangled uselessly for a few seconds, then I wrapped them around her. I patted her back as she trembled against me and silently cried. Still confused, we stayed like that until she let go.

"Are you okay?"

"Muroha…is my father." Maesha gulped, and a tear leaked out of her eye. "It's good to know he's okay."

I thought about patting her on the shoulder but decided against it. "Do you need a moment to sit down?"

"No, I'm fine. Let's get to work," she said, straightening her spine and picking the papers off the floor.

I mentally shrugged and followed her. Sometimes it was better to throw yourself into things to cope.

She took us over to a worktable and laid the papers down. After studying them for a moment, she nodded. "Right, this is what we need." She listed several items, and then looked at me. "Do you think you could retrieve our ships, or their parts? Anything will help."

I nodded. "Once Apollo is back on his feet, I'll take him with me to find your ships. I think I have an idea where they might be."

Maesha rolled up the sleeves of her spacesuit, then started directing everyone else, completely ignoring me.

I left her to it and let the sugar glider climb onto the table beside her before returning to the med bay.

"Hey how long until Apollo can be on his feet?" I directed the question at Celestina, bouncing on the balls of my feet as my blood started coursing, excitement building over a mission.

"A day." Celestina glared sternly at me. "He can't get up any earlier."

"Deal. Will you help me move the storage room stuff to Hangar 1A?"

They glanced at me, then at Apollo, then at me again. "Sure."

Celestina followed me out of the med bay, and we walked in silence until we reached the storage room. Once we got inside, she stepped in front of me.

"Eryn, do you know Apollo has a crush on you?"

I froze and watched them warily. "I have an inkling, yes. Why are we discussing this now?"

Celestina stared at me curiously. "Well, I thought if you knew, you would've, I don't know, said something? Or acted on it if you liked him back?"

"I guess, but I didn't know for sure until you said something," I pointed out, hauling the door to the storage room open. "Besides, it's not like I've had the time or the luxury of pursuing that. Or even the time to think about it."

"That's fair," Celestina said, nodding. "Would you act on it now?"

"No."

"Why not?"

I sighed. "There's too much going on right now. Romance is the least of my priorities."

"That's... reasonable," they said, but hearing the tone of their voice, I side-eyed them.

"You have something to say?"

"Nope. Well... honestly, I think it might take some of the weight off your shoulders. You're stressed. Give yourself this."

I nodded but didn't say anything. Thankfully, Celestina didn't push further. We were silent after that, working on taking all the stuff to Hangar 1A. It took several trips, since there were only two of us, and the majority of it was large and heavy.

After we finished, Celestina went off, I assumed, to talk to Apollo. A little bit of jealousy started slithering up my throat, but I quickly blocked it off. *They're right,* my mind whispered, but I gritted my teeth, pushed the thought away, and started fast-walking toward my old office.

The door was still where I had left it, unfixed, so I ran and grabbed some tools and rehung the door. The work didn't help me any, just gave me something to do while my feelings were jumbled and I tried to keep them organized.

Then I stepped inside the office and started to take down and disconnect all the computing systems, since they might have possible parts we could use, when my eye caught the weird thing in the wall again.

I stood from where I had been kneeling and walked closer. It was an indentation in the wall, and now that I stood in front of it, I could clearly see *something* was supposed to fit in there. Something kind of circular, with a weird, angular protrusion toward the top...

Of its own accord, my hand reached into my pocket and pulled out the dragon sigil. On instinct, I maneuvered the sigil until I was holding it from the piece in the back, then placed it inside the depression in the wall. Hearing a quiet click, I stepped back, and the sigil remained in place. Then, a piece of the wall in front of me started moving upward, and I was hit with the smell of wet dirt.

"What the hell?" I muttered, touching the slimy wall. I took a few steps forward, and the dank smell hit me again, but I also smelled metal. I took a few more steps, then heard a *click* under my foot.

Before I could do anything, the door slammed shut behind me, echoing down the hall.

"Please let there not be any rolling rocks, I am *not* Indiana Jones," I said to the air, and then shut my mouth. If I said anything more, it would probably jinx me.

Walking forward, I pulled out my flashlight from another pocket. When I turned it on, a military grade beam of light illuminated my way, which was nothing but hallway. Chills went up my spine as my footsteps echoed. As I walked, the smell of metal became stronger, until I reached another door. This was more modern-looking and had a biometrics panel on the right side.

Out of curiosity, I placed my hand on the biometrics screen, and it scanned my hand. I fully expected it to beep and turn red, but of course it did the exact opposite. The door gave a hum and opened, and I stepped inside to find…

I didn't know what it was.

Around the edges of the room lay parts, half-finished projects. Some were just wires, but many looked vaguely human. There were also bones, and things in jars, and I soon recognized they were organs. Human organs.

Fighting the urge to retch, I turned my focus to the center of the room, where there was a giant set-up of machinery, tables, and wires. The tables held computers and papers, stacks that covered the entire space. The machinery was all made to form some giant thing with a delicate crystal tip that was pointed at a crib.

I stepped around a table to look at the crib more closely. It was ordinary, made of some type of wood, with a mattress, pillows, and blankets inside. There was also a little doll, with yellow yarn hair, pink glasses, and a blue denim sundress. Her shoes were red, and when I picked her up, I saw that one of her soles had been worn thin, where the beads inside were pushing against the remaining threads.

My thumb absentmindedly rubbed the sole, and a wave of peace washed over me. I looked down at the doll, and a tear leaked out of my eye.

Baby Doll. That was her name.

The tears started falling quicker as I hugged the doll to my chest and started looking for something that would confirm the memory that was bombarding me, one I shouldn't be able to remember.

I noticed a camera, sitting behind a computer, forgotten. I grabbed it and stuck it into a pocket, and did the same for Baby Doll, then got out of there before my brain could overwhelm me.

The door was open when I made it back, and when I stepped through into my office, it shut behind me and the sigil fell to the ground.

I fell heavily into the rolling chair, placing my head in my hands. It couldn't be true. This couldn't be right. My hand fluttered toward the pocket with the camera but stopped. I drew my hand back and forced myself to stand.

Robotically, I walked out of the office and to Hangar 1A, where they were working on pieces of the first ship. I went over to Maesha and asked what she needed me to do, and she handed me some tools.

"Ever build a cryo-unit before?" she asked, ruffling through blueprints.

"Nope." My voice sounded monotone to my own ears.

She found a blueprint and pulled it out of the stack, then handed it to me. "Here's the main part of the cryo-unit, the system that'll regulate everything else. If you need help, it seems Ythea is pretty good with wires."

I took the blueprint with a huff and went over to a workstation. After searching for the parts I needed, I went to work, letting my mind wander as my hands easily went through the motions.

My mind went places I didn't want it to go.

"Mommy, why can't I play with the others?" I asked, tilting my head to one side.

"You've been sick, honey, and we don't want the other kids to catch it," Mom told me, walking over and picking me up.

"You're lying," I said, picking up on the fact that she had glanced toward Daddy, and her heart rate and breathing rate had increased.

"No, honey, I'm just not telling the whole truth. Forget about it." When she ordered me, I could no longer remember what we had just talked about.

I adored my little sister. She was five to my nine, and the most adorable thing ever. She loved horses, and dragons, and princesses. She always told me she wanted to rescue the princesses, that the knights never treated the princesses nicely. My sister also dragged me into gymnastics with her. She loved flying through the air and doing flips and tricks. She was a natural, and I always teased her that she would do well in the circus.

I was good, but not a natural. I mainly went to protect my sister, which was what my parents had ingrained in me since she was born. We went to gymnastics for a year, and then the current gymnastics teacher resigned, and they hired a new one. I was immediately suspicious of him. The way he looked at my sister gave me a weird feeling, and I kept a closer eye on her and him.

Then, one day, my sister was called to his office. Something about her performance. I wanted to come with, but he told me the discussion was between her and him, and that my sister would be out in fifteen minutes.

So I stayed outside the door, to make sure nothing bad happened, and I'm glad I stayed.

After a couple minutes and some low-pitched murmuring, I heard a muffled scream that could only be my sister. I turned to the door and ripped out the knob, leaving a jagged hole. I pushed the door open and saw the man had torn my sister's leotard and was forcing himself on her and covering her mouth with his hand.

With a scream of fury, I leapt on him and bit his arm, then threw him off my sister so hard that he hit the wall. After rebounding and hitting the desk, he was knocked out, so I grabbed my sister, wrapped my jacket around her, picked her up, and hauled ass out of there.

When I got home, I took her immediately to Mom and told her what had happened. Mom nodded, took my sister from me, and started soothing her.

Five weeks later, my sister was better but more subdued than she had ever been. She had quit gymnastics, but still did flips and stuff in our backyard.

I decided, one day, that I was going to teach my sister how to ride a skateboard. So I took her to the sidewalk and the street and taught her the basics. She was having loads of fun and was matching me in skill.

Then, behind me, a car came down the road, going way faster than it should've been. Me, with my great hearing, didn't notice because I was having too much fun.

My sister did, and in the split second she had to react, she chose to push me out of the way.

The car hit her going thirty-five miles an hour, and her body fell like a ragdoll one way, her skateboard the other.

I saw the driver. It was the gymnastics teacher that had hurt my sister, the one I had thrown against a wall.

I saw him slam his fist on the dashboard when the car stopped, and then he got out and came toward me.

My sister was lying in a pool of blood, arms and legs twisted in different directions. I had to get her to Mom, but before I could get over to her, the teacher had grabbed my arm.

"It was supposed to be you. But you'll work," he said, then he started dragging me toward his car.

Instead of anger, I felt calm and focused.

I hit the spot where I had bit him, and he yelped and let go. I climbed his body until I was sitting on his shoulders, and with my little hands, grabbed his head and broke his neck.

And that's how Dad found us. I was holding my little sister, who was dead and cold by that point, and I was covered in her blood. The man was still in the middle of the street, dead.

After everything was cleaned up, Dad sat me down in a chair. "You don't have to remember all this, so I'll only give you pieces," he said, pulling out the machine and placing it over my head.

I came back to myself and found the unit halfway finished and me covered in grease and other stuff.

My stomach rumbled, so I stood and headed to the kitchen, passing the others working on various projects. I felt as though I wasn't entirely in this world, like I was outside of myself.

When I reached the kitchen, I washed my hands and dug into the cans and MREs and got to cooking.

Chapter 15

I managed to whip up a decent lunch. It wasn't the greatest, but it would do for what we had. I took the trays to everyone, leaving Celestina and Apollo last, because they would definitely notice something was off.

When I finally got up the courage to take them trays, I found them deep in conversation.

I didn't care what they were talking about this time.

"Hey," I said, which brought them out of their conversation, and both turned toward me.

Celestina took the tray and said, "Hey." They left the room, glancing at Apollo as they left.

I didn't care.

I handed him the tray. "I'm sorry for not coming and talking to you more."

"That's fine. I understand you're trying to get all of this done. You're the person for the job, which means you're responsible, and you take responsibility seriously." He took the tray from me and began to eat.

"Yeah," I replied, sitting heavily in the chair beside the bed.

His fork paused on the way to his mouth. "Something's wrong," he said, then set the entire tray off to the side. "Tell me."

In response, I pulled the camera out of my pocket and handed it to him.

He scrunched his eyebrows, confused, while he opened the side flap and turned the camera on. Scrolling to a video, I watched the video sideways as it began to play.

It was focused on the crib, and the contraption, and a man in the background, one I recognized as my uncle after a couple of seconds.

Then my mom also came into view.

My uncle stepped in front of the camera.

"This will be the final trial for this experiment. We will be using a robotic baby created out of nanites…" He picked up the camera and aimed it into the crib, where we could see a skeletal robot baby and a real baby, side by side. The real baby was holding Baby Doll and looking innocently into the camera.

"And a human subject, known as Eryn Vue."

I heard Apollo gasp quietly, but we kept the video rolling.

"With all the calculations fine-tuned, we should create a strong, smart, tech-human hybrid. She will be the instrument for our final step in achieving our goals. When this works, we can create many, many more like her."

He set the camera back on the table, went over to the computer nearest to the crib, and started fiddling with the controls.

Mom walked up to the crib, and I saw her smile and reach in, then pull her arm back out and walk over to my uncle.

"Ready?" she asked, leaning on his chair.

"In three… two… one…" My uncle flicked a switch.

A low hum began. It gradually increased in pitch until it was a silent scream. I could hear baby me crying as the tip of the contraption began to glow.

Two beams of light shot out of it, and I watched as they steadily merged into one beam, then shut off, smoking.

My mom went over to the crib, and my uncle grabbed the camera and ran to stand beside her.

The camera was, again, pointed inside the crib. But this time, there was just one baby, one that looked purely human, one that gurgled and reached for her mother.

"It worked," my uncle breathed, as my mom reached in and picked me up.

"It did, but I didn't expect her to look so… human," my mom replied, cradling me.

"She'll grow, then, and we'll see how well this worked," my uncle said, and that's where the video ended.

Apollo and I sat there in silence for what seemed like hours. Then, he snapped the side thing shut. "Are you okay?" he asked softly, turning his gaze to me.

"I… don't know. When I was younger, I knew there was something off about me, but I never knew what, until now." My throat constricted. I felt a weird sensation in my nose, and then tears started silently falling from my eyes. I let them fall, feeling the hitch in my breathing as I quietly sobbed. I closed my eyes, not wanting to see pity on Apollo's face.

Then I heard the creak of the bed and a quiet "Shit," and then Apollo was pushing me over and sitting down beside me.

"I'm here," he said, and then I broke.

Wrapping my arms around his waist, I buried my face in his shoulder and cried, a real cry, with all of the ugly faces and noises.

When I finished, I sat back up, knowing my face was red, my eyes were puffy, and my nose was runny.

"I'm sorry for getting your shirt dirty," I apologized, grimacing at the giant wet spot.

"Not a problem. All I have to do is this," he said, taking off his shirt, "and find the washer and dryer. Would you happen to know where those are at?"

I let myself glance once at his body, then met his eyes and stood. "Of course, I found the washers and dryers. I didn't want to be wearing dirt," I snatched a tissue pack from the medicine cabinet.

He laughed, and then stood and followed me out and to the laundry room.

To break the silence, I started talking about what I had found in the base, to talk about anything else besides the camera that had ripped me apart inside. Apollo commented when he remembered a part of the base, and even laughed when I made a really bad MRE joke.

After finding the laundry room again and throwing his shirt into the wash, we found him a new one, and I took him to Hangar 1A with me.

Maesha glanced up from her work for a moment when we came in, but then ignored us and went back to work. Ythea was busy crawling over something, and everyone else was sitting on various parts of the floor eating their meal.

I went over to my project and showed Apollo the blueprints, and then we started working on it together.

It took a little bit, but we were soon moving in perfect unison, one leaning over the other, leaning away when sparks flew, moving to the side when one had to crawl underneath. We finished the first one quickly, and by the end of the day, finished the second.

At that point, we were both dusty, greasy, and tired, and when we headed to our beds, I handed the blueprints back to Maesha.

"The main units are done. Tomorrow, we'll get gear together and go find everyone's ships," I told her, watching Apollo carefully as he walked slowly to the main hallway.

"Excellent," she said, rolling the blueprints and following my line of vision. "You care for him." She tapped me on the shoulder with the rolled blueprints.

"I do."

"Do you have a relationship with him?" Maesha asked, sounding genuinely curious.

"He's my friend, but other than that, no."

"You do not want a different relationship with him."

"I… don't know," I said, taking a moment to think about how weird it was to have this conversation with an alien.

"Hm." Maesha turned back to her work.

I took that as a cue to leave and headed back toward my quarters.

Along the way, I ran into Celestina, who was looking significantly less dirty than earlier.

"Hey."

"Hey, I heard you got Apollo out of bed and you two worked on a cryo-unit together. You made him really happy, Eryn." Celestina stopped in the middle of the hallway.

I stopped in front of her. "I'm glad I made him happy. He needs that. I need that. And I'll take care of the whole crush thing later. Promise."

"Okay, I'll accept that for now," they said, sticking their tongue out at me. "Also, you need to get cleaned up. You smell like WD-40."

I stuck my tongue out at them as they walked away laughing, and then took the sleeve of my shirt and smelled it. They were right; I did smell like WD-40.

I made it to my quarters, entered, and took stock of the empty room. I noticed my bed, at the far end of the room by the bathroom, was exactly how I had left it this morning. The bed next to it was rumpled and had dirty, greasy clothes lying on the chest at the foot of the bed.

As I walked closer, my ears caught the sound of running water.

I let out a large sigh.

Maybe *that's* why Celestina insisted that I go take a shower. Although I really did smell like WD-40.

Reaching my bed, I pulled out a robe and towels, then stripped and put on the robe. Padding silently, I passed the sinks and turned left to reach the showers. There were three of them on that side, two regular and one handicapped. The first regular one was the one running, so I passed it and the one next to it and stepped into the handicapped shower.

I hung my towels on the hook inside the door, and did the same with my robe, then stepped into the shower and started running the water.

It was freezing at first, but it gradually warmed to a decent temperature. As I washed my hair, thoughts of Apollo came into my head. They started out normal, just working through different thoughts as they came, until my mind decided to go off the rails.

At one point in my life, I had loved Ryan. Or I thought I did. It could've been just physical: after all, who knows what would've happened to us after coming back to the States? We could've found that we weren't compatible after all, and that it was always the adrenaline and hormones talking.

But that part of it didn't matter now. He was long gone, and as much as I missed him, the what ifs weren't going to reanimate his corpse.

Apollo was the here and now.

Even back before the cryostasis, I knew Apollo liked me. Hell, when I first met him, I knew he had a crush on me. At that time, I hadn't really paid attention. He was just another guy on my team. But after the Ryan and John incident, he had been there for me. Apollo made sure I ate and drank, gave me tons of hugs, and somehow pulled me out of my depression.

My view of him began to change, and I saw him less as another team member and more as… this weird gray character that was more than a friend but less than an intimate partner. During the worst period of my career as CI Director, when those kids had been killed… I broke. I'd had enough. I was going to kill myself. Put a bullet in my head, end it all.

I had been moving things around in my house, preparing to take my life, when I found a note written to me. It had fallen out of a book that Apollo had bought me on our return to the States. I read the note, which consisted mainly of Apollo telling me how I'd changed his life and how much he loved me.

It changed my mind. I decided I was going to work through the suicidal thoughts and the depression and the anxiety. Not only was I worth being on Earth, but I wanted to love Apollo back.

So I went back and acted like everything was normal. I took a week to adjust to being back, and then I was going to ask him on a date. On a real date, wine and dine him, the whole nine yards.

Then I never got to.

Going through all this pain again, the cycle starting over. Now, I had the strength to resist, to put everyone else first like I always did. But was the cost of my strength the breaking of my heart?

Was I worthy enough to love him, even?

"Hey, you aren't drowning in there, are you?" I heard Apollo ask, feet slapping on the floor as he walked toward my shower.

"No, I'm fine. Besides, I'm pretty sure it should be me worried about you. You can't swim, remember?" I forced out a laugh.

"Ha ha ha, very funny." He stopped outside my shower.

I reached between the shower curtain and the wall and grabbed my towel, making sure he couldn't see me. After wrapping the towel around myself, I stepped out. "What's up?" I asked, trying to contain my reaction to him standing in front of me with just a towel.

Don't think about it, don't think about it, don't think about it.

"I'm checking on you. You got some pretty shitty news today, and that would screw up anyone," he said, head tilted to the side.

I shrugged.

"Come on, you know talking about things helps." He made one of his goofy faces.

I couldn't help it—I burst out laughing. Apollo stared at me like I was crazy for a couple seconds, then eventually started laughing himself, until we were both leaning against the wall, out of breath.

"I... I... think I'm okay," I said, trying to draw breath into my body.

"Good... to... know," Apollo replied, breathing a bit harder than I had been.

When I could breathe again, I adjusted my towel and grabbed my robe off the hook. Glancing at him once more, I walked to my bed, where I quickly dropped the towel and tied on the robe. He followed a few seconds later, silent.

I swallowed, and then opened my mouth before I could talk myself out of it. "How do you like me?"

"What?" Apollo replied, looking at me in shock.

"How do you like me?" I repeated.

He blinked a couple of times and sat down on one of the beds. "Well, for me, I like you... Damn it, I sound like a teenager again." He snorted. "I like you because you're... you. I don't know how else to describe it. You've always done your best to make sure everyone else was safe before you were. You've been through so much you shouldn't have had to go through. You've come out the other side that much stronger. I tried to help you as much as I could, but you pretty much had it handled."

"You helped me more than you think. After those kids were killed, I was going to kill myself..." I said, and saw his eyes widen "But I found the note you left me in that book and decided not to."

His eyebrows scrunched for a couple of seconds. "I had forgotten about the note. I never thought you'd read the book, it being a romance and all." He ran his hand through his hair.

"But I still don't understand. You know how broken I am." I sat on my bed. "Don't people like people who aren't... messed up like I am? I don't know if I'm even human."

He scooted over so he was right across from me. "You've been through a lot of shit. Of course ,you're going to feel the aftereffects. That doesn't mean I love you any less," he said, leaning forward. "In fact, I think you're more amazing because you face it head on instead of running from it."

I looked into his eyes, feeling almost hypnotized. "You're romanticizing it," I said, shaking my head.

"I'm not. I mean every word."

My heart started beating faster, and I felt the tears brimming for the second time that day. Staring into his eyes, I could sense his honesty in his words. He believed every word he said. I couldn't hold myself back any longer.

I kissed him.

My hands went to his hair, burying my fingers in the strands and pulling him closer. He responded in kind, his hands going to my waist and pulling me onto his lap. It felt so good to kiss him, having his hands wander over and under my robe. I loved the little moans he made when I ground myself against him just right.

"I want you," I said. "I have ever since I saw you in your office."

Apollo moaned and moved his lips from my mouth down to my neck, kissing and nibbling, making me gasp and grind against him harder. My hands went to his shoulders, where my short nails dug into his skin. The rush of emotion through my body made the feelings more intense.

His hands fumbled with the ties on my robe, and I dropped mine to help. Soon, the robe was on the floor.

"I've wanted you, too, since, well… I first met you," he murmured against my shoulder. He kissed that spot, and took his time moving his hands and mouth over my shoulders and collarbone. I gasped, and I felt…wanted. Needed.

I got up. "That towel needs to come off."

Apollo smiled and stood. He untucked the towel and let it drop.

With a grin, I placed one hand on his chest and the other in his hair and pushed him back against the wall, kissing him again. I wanted to show him how much I needed him, wanted him, too. He chuckled and buried his hand in my hair, pulling gently. I bit his lip, enough to cause a bit of pain, but not enough to make him bleed.

"Oh, you wanna play that game?" He play growled, which made him even hotter and turned me on even more. Then, he *picked me up.*

I was about to protest because I wasn't kissing him anymore, but he laid me on my bed and whispered in my ear, "Let me pleasure you."

He kissed me again, slow and sweet. Then he started moving down, finding the sensitive spots on my neck again. He stayed there awhile, bringing his head up eventually to murmur words of praise. "You're amazing. Your body is strong, and beautiful, and I want to make you feel good. May I?"

"Yes."

I could no longer think. But I felt safe. And loved.

Then he finally started moving downward, teasing me with his tongue and fingers. I squirmed under his touch. "Please."

Apollo obliged, kissing my belly and my hips, then nibbling the insides of my thighs. Then he stopped.

"Why are you stopping?" I asked, my voice coming out more high-pitched than normal.

He met my eyes. His eyes almost seemed to shimmer. I thought he was more beautiful than ever before, and I needed him. Not just for the pleasure, but to feel that I wasn't *alone.*

"Eryn." My name was a sweet music coming from his lips. "You will always be loved with me."

Then he bent his head between my thighs, and I was in heaven. My thoughts were a jumbled mess. I felt pleasure, but more than that, I felt *loved.*

I shook, and felt myself fall over the edge, squeezing his head between my thighs.

I lay there panting, feeling like I was floating on a cloud. When I was able to focus, I found him beside me, his head on my chest.

"Your turn," I said, mustering the strength to push myself up and to roll him on his back. He needed to feel the way I was feeling, safe and loved, and blind with pleasure. I leaned down to kiss him, mimicking how he had kissed me earlier. I ground against him, sliding easily across the hardness.

Kisses and nibbles were left on his neck as I loved along his body. He gasped, and let out these breathy little moans that made me smile. He was feeling more than good, if I were to guess.

My hands had a mind of their own, wandering over his body, feeling the strength and softness. When he started asking me to make my way further down, I obliged, but went very slow, which made him sass me and made me laugh. But I soon had him gasping and moaning as I sucked and licked and stroked until he came. A few moments later, I rolled out of the bed to grab a washcloth to clean both of us up.

I tossed the cloth aside and climbed into the bed. Snuggling close, I threw one leg over his and tucked my head on his chest. He wrapped an arm around my waist. At peace, I easily slipped off to sleep.

Chapter 16

I woke up with my head still on Apollo's chest and the sheet covering both of us. He was snoring softly, and I smiled at his sleeping face and didn't move. He needed his sleep. I nearly glanced at the clock on the wall, but there was a good chance it wouldn't display the right time.

Luckily, Apollo started shifting and opened his bleary eyes to focus on me. He gave me a lopsided grin. "Morning."

"Morning. Now that you're awake, we can get dressed and go find some ships," I replied, sitting up.

"Can I at least have a good morning kiss?" Apollo asked, giving me a shy grin.

Smiling, I arranged myself so I was straddling his lap and took his face in both of my hands and gave him a good, long kiss.

When we pulled apart, he looked more alert.

"Now I'm awake," he said, smiling brightly.

Laughing, I got off him and found my clothes. I chose a bulletproof vest instead of my normal leather jacket. Once I was dressed, and my combat boots were tied, I turned to Apollo. He was dressed similarly to me, minus the vest.

"I outgrew mine," he explained, blushing.

"*How?*" I replied, raising an eyebrow.

"Uh... I hit a second puberty?"

I shook my head and sighed. Motioning for him to follow, we walked out of the dorm and headed toward the med bay. Thankfully, Celestina was there, humming happily to themself.

"Hey," I called out, cautiously entering the room.

They looked at us, and then gave us a big grin. Winking at me, they grabbed something from their pocket and walked up to me. They pressed the object—*objects*—into my hand.

"For next time," they whispered in my ear.

I glanced down at my hand to see condoms. I made a face at her and quickly shoved them in a pocket.

"Is everyone else here?" I inquired, zipping that pocket shut for good measure.

"Yeah, they came in late last night. Kimi, Raven, Theo, Marc, Marl, and Rubi are all in rooms and have been given a quick tour of the important locations," Celestina responded, nodding.

"Great. Have I shown you the conference room?" I headed toward the door.

"No, but if you could show me where it is on this map, I can find it." They picked up a tablet from a side table and showed me the screen.

"That one, there. Have you been mapping the base?" I queried, taking the tablet.

"Yeah, I got bored."

I chuckled and handed her back the tablet. "Have Maesha, Theo, and yourself in that conference room at ten. I'm going to go with Apollo to get food and gear. We'll meet you there." I grabbed Apollo's arm and pulled him down the hallway.

Celestina leaned out of the doorway and gave me a thumbs up.

I let go of Apollo's arm, and he dropped it to his side.

"What did Celestina give you?" he quizzed me, glancing over at my zipped pocket.

"Condoms."

Apollo raised his eyebrows.

"So does that mean I'll get laid again sometime soon?" he asked with a wink.

"Depends," I replied, smirking.

"On what?"

"On whether we get the ships back to base in a timely fashion."

He mock gasped, putting his hand over his heart. "All work, no play?"

I raised an eyebrow.

"Okay, I can wait," Apollo acquiesced, leaning over to give me a kiss on the cheek.

I smiled back and winked, then pushed open the door to the gear room. It wasn't all that big but had racks of vests on one side and shelves filled with gun boxes on another. The last wall had a couple benches and non-standard weapons.

It only took a few moments to find a vest that fit Apollo well, and then I was searching for guns and ammo. He joined in, searching the top shelves while I searched the bottom.

"Hey, Eryn, these yours?" He pulled a box down from one of the shelves.

I glanced up at the box and noticed the Vue sigil. "Yeah, those are mine. Why are they here?" I reached up and took the box from him, then set it on a bench nearby. When I opened it, I found my shoulder holsters and my special-issue handguns. I shimmied out of my vest, then slipped the holsters over each shoulder and clipped them to my waistband. I took my guns out and checked them for rust or other problems. Thankfully, they were both in excellent condition.

After grabbing ammo, I loaded my guns and made sure they were both on safety before I put them in my shoulder holsters. They clicked when they locked in place. I grabbed more magazines and ammo and put them together in another pocket. This was why I had cargo pants. *Pockets.*

I put my vest back on, relieved it had been specially made for me. Apollo soon found a pair he liked and put on his own holsters, then replaced his vest, which he had to wiggle to get over the holsters. I took one last look at my box and my eye caught a glimmer of metal.

"What is this?" I reached in and pulled out a pair of small, silver armbands. Curious, I slipped them on my forearm, panicking for a moment as it clicked and expanded to cover my entire arm, but went around my hand like a fingerless glove, leaving my fingers free to move. I slipped the other one on while Apollo checked the box.

"Hey, a note. I don't recognize the handwriting." He handed me a folded piece of paper. On it was my name, in very familiar handwriting.

I opened the note and read.

Eryn,

A gift. Use it well.

My throat closed as I refolded the note. I would recognize that handwriting anywhere. "My dad. He made these for me."

Apollo's eyes widened, but he didn't say anything. But he did place a hand on my shoulder and left it there.

I put the note back in the box and closed the lid, then placed it on the shelf where it came from. "Let's go get breakfast," I said, my throat closing and my nose tingling.

Somehow, I managed to hold back tears as I led Apollo out of the room and to the cafeteria. We each grabbed an MRE, fixed it, and ate it, grimacing the entire time.

"We really need to get better food."

"I'm not disagreeing," I replied, setting my fork down.

Soon enough, ten rolled around, and we headed to the conference room.

When we reached the open door, I looked in and saw the long, oval conference table surrounded by comfortable rolling chairs. A TV had been set up on the far wall, but it was currently black. Celestina and Maesha were in there, but there was no Theo.

"Where's Theo?" I asked.

They both shrugged.

"I told him to show at ten," Celestina replied, looking at the clock on the wall.

"Well, we don't have time to waste, so let's get started." I took the chair at the head of the table. Apollo took the chair next to me, and Celestina and Maesha leaned forward.

"All right, Maesha, where are we at?" I asked, turning my gaze to her.

"At the rate we're progressing, we won't have these built in time. We need more hands," she said, clasping her hands in front of her.

"I'll work on that," I said, making a mental note.

"I've been working with Raven and Kimi on things that aren't… all that stuff… and we've got a good list going. Foremost among them is a clothes maker so everyone can have working clothes." Celestina gestured at her own clothes to prove the point.

"Noted. I'll get on that. Apollo and I are heading out to find the ships and hopefully get them back here," I told them, glancing at Apollo and nodding.

He smiled and nodded.

"All right, if there's nothing else, we have work to do," I said, standing.

The others stood. Celestina gave both me and Apollo a hug, and Maesha shook our hands.

"Be careful," Celestina said to me and left the room, Maesha not far behind.

I turned to Apollo and raised my eyebrows. "Ready?"

He took my hand in his. "Let's do this."

We let go and exited the room, heading toward the smaller hangar that Apollo had parked his jet in.

"Where do you think the ships are?" he asked, breaking the silence as we walked.

"Someplace I *really* don't want to go back to." I pulled my phone out, typed in an address, and showed it to him.

"Shit, you think… Shit."

"Yeah. I think it's in the highest security base we had, which…"

"Is under the city."

After that exchange, we walked in silence until we reached the hangar. My wings appeared, tucked against my back, and I turned to Apollo.

"We rendezvous at your offices," I said, spreading my wings to stretch them, grateful for whatever helped them avoid the vest and shoulder holsters.

He nodded, getting in the jet and buckling himself in.

I eyed the hood of a nearby Jeep, tucked my wings, and ran at it. I leapt and used the hood to push myself upward, where my wings snapped open and propelled me into the air. I glided around the room, then, when the hangar doors were open far enough, started climbing.

Apollo's jet rose after me, and I climbed even higher, until the jet was clear of the hangar. Swooping down, I hit the close button, then leapt up again, climbing enough to start gliding. The jet shot past me, but I stayed at the same pace.

Soon, I was flying over the junkyards again, and then over the city. There were people on the streets, dressed in bright and drab colors, like a collage of cultures. The buildings caught the rays of sun and glimmered, making the colors swirl together if I stared long enough. It was art, from my point of view. If only they knew what was coming.

I easily found Apollo's office buildings again and landed on the roof this time. He was waiting for me, a grim look on his face.

"What?" I asked, keeping my voice low.

"I can get us where we need to go, but we stand out like a sore thumb in this gear. We're gonna have to go through the sewers," Apollo replied, scrunching his nose.

"And how are we going to get to the *sewers* without anyone noticing?" I shot back.

"We have to get to the second floor. There's a waste chute we can use, and we'll land in garbage, but we'll be okay," he said, not responding to my snark.

"Stairs?" I asked.

"Yeah, not very many people use them." Apollo motioned me to follow him to the staircase entrance on the far side of the roof. After unlocking the door, and then shutting it firmly behind us when we were inside the stairwell, we started down the stairs, every footstep echoing.

"Are you sure no one uses these stairwells?" I asked, grimacing at every sound.

"One hundred percent. They're only for emergencies, and we haven't had one of those in ages," Apollo responded from behind me, his boots echoing more than mine.

We kept silent as we traveled down the many flights of stairs. As we reached the door that had a big number two beside it, I rolled my shoulders back. Apollo was breathing hard beside me, and as soon as his breathing evened out, I cracked the door open to see if there was anyone in the hallway.

The hallway was empty, as far as I could see, so I opened it farther, allowing Apollo to go first.

We walked into the hallway, and I immediately started scanning one side, and then the other. There wasn't really any danger, but it never hurt to be safe.

I followed Apollo to a small door in the wall, which he opened. "Ladies first?" he asked, grinning.

I narrowed my eyes at him, but climbed in, crossed my arms, and slid down.

It wasn't too long of a slide, and I landed in a mountain of garbage. After rolling down the side, I came to my feet in a pile of sticky green stuff that didn't smell so great. Apollo soon followed, getting several banana peels stuck to his arm. After peeling them off, he led the way through the garbage rooms until we reached a sewer hole.

"It's bolted."

"Not for me." He pulled out a small device about the size of a pen.

"What? Are you gonna write *Help me* on the walls?"

"No, I'm gonna do this." He pointed the pen at the sewer grate. I heard a *click* as the device switched on, and a focused beam of light shot out of the tip. After focusing it on each bolt, he shut it off.

"Try to lift the grate." He nodded at the circle.

I grabbed the bars and pulled. It easily came up, and I set it aside, then leaned over to look down the hole.

"What was that thing?" I asked, standing straight again.

"A focused, pocket-sized welder, complete with several different settings for heat and size," he said proudly, flipping it end over end.

"Hm." I raised my eyebrows. "You'll have to get me one."

"In your dreams."

I snorted, then climbed into the sewer hole, trying not to think about what exactly was on the ladder I held onto. After about seven rungs, I was in six inches of murky, nasty liquid, which squelched under my boots. Trying my damnedest not to grimace, because the smell wasn't that great either, I moved out of the way so Apollo could stand behind me.

The tunnel was a decent size. About six feet tall, with flowing, yucky water at the bottom, and chunks of who-knows-what covering the walls. It went off in both directions, both ends cast in shadow.

I pulled out my flashlight and switched it on, aiming it down both ends. "Which way?"

"Umm… from where we are, we need to go… this way."

"Lead the way."

We took off, shining my flashlight in front of us, Apollo behind me. The water sloshed around our feet, echoing down the tunnel. With every step, I felt chunks break under my treads. I was going to have pieces of feces in my shoes. Fun.

I checked my coordinates to our current location and followed the sewer until we came to a four-way.

I turned right, trudging through the sludge. To keep my mind off the disgusting nature of the tunnel, I replayed memories of last night. And then I thought about how good it would feel to take a shower after this… and have Apollo join me.

I smiled to myself. Maybe I would do just that.

We walked in silence for a long time, taking a turn when there were options, or just going straight when there weren't.

Soon enough, we reached the general area of the coordinates, and I started searching for a ladder. Once I found it, I climbed up and pushed on the grate. This one came off easily, and I moved it to the side with one hand. Climbing out, I found myself in what looked like a workshop. Luckily, it was empty, so I motioned Apollo to follow me out of the hole.

After he climbed out, I replaced the grate and put my phone away. Grabbing a nearby hose, I quickly washed off my shoes, and then took care of Apollo's.

"You know the way from here?" he asked, pocketing his flashlight.

"Yeah." The hairs on my arms lifted in anticipation.

We walked through the basement of the building, keeping an eye and ear out for anyone else. It was eerily silent compared to the sewers, which at least had dripping water and the occasional rat. The only sound I could hear was my breathing and our footsteps.

I changed my gait every few seconds, in order to hear other footsteps that

I might miss otherwise. We were doing great until we rounded the final corner and found the hangar.

It was still as I remembered it. A large, organized space that contained everything deemed too weird or too important for the general populace to know about. I easily spotted three ships that could be the ones we were looking for: they looked mostly intact, although only one looked flyable.

And it was abandoned. Or at least looked that way.

We walked cautiously up to the ships. No alarms were triggered, and no people were showing up. But it was too clean to be sure that no one was still in the base.

"Is this it?" he whispered.

I felt the uncertainty in the air too. Better to be safe than sorry. "I think so. But let's stay as quiet as we can, just in case."

I walked up to the ship. The one in the center looked relatively untouched, while the other two looked like they had the outer panels of the hull ripped off. Like someone had been trying to get into the ship from the outside, without being successful.

"Eryn!"

I leaned around the ship to look at him. "What?"

"I think this is a curio storage room."

In the CI, we had fondly nicknamed some storage rooms as "curio" rooms. They contained odds and ends that we either didn't care to work on anymore, or stuff that we couldn't figure out. If I were to guess, this room filled both criteria.

"Makes sense. Keep an eye out for hiders – I'll see if I can get the ship working."

The ship was completely smooth, like one big piece of metal, except for the window spots in the front. No panels, not even a crack to indicate a door or hatch. Not even a ladder for a ceiling hatch.

This one would be a doozy.

I scrambled up onto the top of the ship and walked around, searching for anything that could indicate a door. When that was unsuccessful, I plopped down on the ship to think. I couldn't spend too long trying to get it open.

The longer we were here, the more likely it was that hiders would come in here for a private place to have some fun.

Then I thought about AIHNA. And the jet. Maybe…

I placed a hand on the hull and closed my eyes. My palm pressed against the cold metal and my mind felt as though it was tracing a path to where I wanted to go. Everything was intact in the ship. With a nudge in my mind, the ship hummed to life.

My eyes shot open and I launched myself off the side of the ship and ran to the back. A door was slowly opening, coming down to let us into the ship.

"Apollo!" I whispered as loud as I could. "Come on!"

I ran up the ramp into a room with spacesuits hanging from the walls. At least, I assumed they were spacesuits. There were some benches, and a sealed door at the other end.

As I stepped toward the door, it hissed and opened for me, and I walked through, into a long hallway with multiple doors down either side. It ended in the pilot's compartment.

I passed all the doors and stepped into the cockpit, where there were three stations. As I investigated, everything made sense to me. Like how the station on the far left was for the weapon and defense systems. I suppose it made sense, since these systems were the same as the blueprints in my head.

Sitting down in the front pilot's seat, I surveyed the controls in front of me. Did I have the knowledge to man this craft? Yeah, somewhere in my head. Could I pilot this craft? *Don't know, but we're gonna find out.*

Apollo came up behind me, his footsteps even and unhurried. "Woah."

"You think you can help me try to fly this?"

"I can try." He scratched his neck and sat down at a station. "Better to try and fly out than stay here."

Glancing out the front window, I silently cursed. They had gotten this craft in through the top, but said doors were currently closed. And the panel to open them was on the other side of the damn room. Once those bay doors started opening, someone would come running.

"Ready to fly it?" I turned to face him. "Once we open those doors, we're going to have a party."

"Yeah, it's not like we have much of a choice. Hope you remember your crash course in flying planes."

I grimaced. That had been over a hundred years ago. My body could handle all the tumbling about that happened in a jet. But the chances of the old plane controls being similar to a literal alien ship?

Guess I would just have to wing it. "I'm going to run out and press the button, and run back in. We'll need to get this off the ground as fast as we can."

"Got it."

I jogged off the ship and toward the panel, and scanned the labels next to the buttons.

Well. That was new.

I pressed the button with the label *bay* and sprinted back toward the ship as soon as the doors began to screech open. That would be sure to get someone's attention.

Dirt fell in my hair as I crossed the distance to the ramp, which I ran up and immediately slammed a button near it in hopes that the ramp would close.

My luck held and the ramp began to rise.

I hurried to get myself in another seat next to Apollo, and stared at the controls. Some of it looked similar to what I knew. Most of it didn't.

My gaze went to the front window, and I saw a door at the far end begin to open.

"We need to take off. Now." I grabbed the joystick-looking parts and felt energy surge through me. My hand moved of it's own accord, as if I had done this a million times.

"Taking off. Please ensure you are in your seat," came a sweet voice from the ship's walls.

"Does this have an AI?" Apollo stared out the front window. "You know what, we'll table that for now. Just get us out of here!"

People were starting to rush through the doors, and I could hear bullets *ping* off the side of the ship.

The ship lifted off the ground, slowly rising towards the doors. When I risked a glance upward, I saw that the doors were barely open enough to get the ship out.

"Fuck. Go!"

Not knowing if that came from Apollo or me, my hands slammed the controls and we went rocketing out.

"The yellow button with a cloud on it! Hit it!" I yelled, excitement rushing through me. "We're flying!"

"Eryn."

"Yeah?"

"There are mini jets following us."

I went still as a statue for a moment, searching through the plans in my head. Then, I hit a switch for a rear camera, and a picture appeared on a little screen in front of me.

Three mini jets were following us, keeping up pretty well despite the fact that the craft we were in was far more advanced.

"Did you not press the button?" I yelled, jerking the controls to the right as the jet fired at us.

"What button?"

"Yellow button, with a cloud!" I banked, seeing all three jets lined up briefly before they turned to follow.

Apollo would've responded, but I pressed down on the thrusters and we *moved.* Within seconds, we were up in the cloud cover, even though it wasn't all that thick.

"Where is that damn button?" Apollo yelled.

"Find it! I'm driving!" I yelled back. "Also, how strong is your stomach?"

"Pretty strong, why?"

"Are you buckled?"

"Yes, Eryn, what are you planning?"

"Just hold on!" I hollered, taking a deep breath. "I hope this works."

"What'd you say?"

Ignoring him, I sent the craft into a very fast barrel roll, feeling the G-forces pull on me in a tunnel type fashion. As we spun, I tilted the nose of the plane downward.

"Found it!"

I breathed a sigh of relief when I heard him, and pulled out of the dive. The mini jets were still there, but flying randomly above us.

I heard the sound of Apollo throwing up behind me. Oops. "You okay?"

No response except for more hacking noises.

Once I realized where we were, I navigated back toward the city, to the junkyards, keeping an eye on my rear camera for the minijets.

"Eryn, why did you do that?" Apollo said, continuing to make weird hacking noises behind me.

"The hope was to make them dizzy by watching us, and then, when they couldn't focus, cloak and escape," I explained, grimacing.

"Well, did you forget I was human, too?" Apollo snapped, and I heard him throw up again.

It felt like a punch to the gut. "I asked you if you were buckled and if you had a strong stomach," I said coldly.

"Did it occur to you that you could have warned me about what you were about to do?" he said, the angry tone still in his voice.

"I don't have to explain everything to you. I guess my non-human brain works differently from yours." I snapped my mouth closed.

We sat in silence for the rest of the ride, which wasn't too awfully long, thankfully. When we arrived at the base, the bay doors were already open, and I carefully lowered the craft down, parking it easily.

After I turned it off, Apollo basically ran out of the cockpit and off the craft. By the time I got out, he was gone. However, Maesha was waiting for me, along with Scia and Shrimra.

"She still works fine," I said, smiling at Maesha.

"Excellent. Did you have any problems getting her out of wherever she was?" Maesha asked, running a hand along the side of the craft.

"The only real problem was getting inside in the first place," I commented, patting the back of the craft.

"Oh, I'm so sorry, I forgot to tell you how to open the hatch! Since our preferred method of communication is usually telepathy, that's what our ships respond to," Maesha explained, her cheeks turning a deeper blue.

"Wait, you mean there was a chance I wouldn't have been able to get in?" I asked, raising my eyebrows.

"Yes…" Maesha grinned nervously.

"Well, past is past, we got it." I brushed it off.

"I am sorry. I truly meant to tell you," Maesha apologized, her cheeks still a dark blue.

"No problem. Don't worry about it." I nodded. Raising a hand in goodbye, I started heading away from them, so they could check over their ship. Before I could get very far, Celestina ran up to me and hugged me very tightly.

"Hey, you guys are back in one piece! Apollo told me you did some crazy piloting moves or something?" They grabbed my hand and towed me toward the hallway.

"Yeah, did a barrel roll maneuver, stopped, and dove to lose some mini jets," I said, allowing myself to be dragged along.

"He seemed pretty angry, and… Hey, are you okay? It looks like something's bothering you." Celestina stopped abruptly and studied my face.

"It's nothing, really." I started moving again, hoping they would drop it and follow. No such luck.

"Tell me," they ordered, standing their ground.

I sighed. "Well, before I tell you what's bothering me, there's something else you need to know."

"Literally nothing could shock me, so go for it," Celestina dropped my hand and crossed their arms.

"I'm not… entirely human."

"What?" Celestina asked, eyes wide, standing stock still.

"I'm essentially a cyborg."

"That… that's not possible, Eryn," they replied, still frozen.

"How do you explain the tech thingy I can do then?"

"No, no, they've tried to make a cyborg before and they *failed*. People *died*. If it is true, how the hell are you alive?" Celestina moved their hands to their hips.

"The experiments, were they done on adults?"

"Yes, because adults are the only ones who can consent to such a thing!" they burst out, pretty much yelling in my face.

"Well, this was done when I was a baby," I said quietly, staring at them.

"What… who… why… Well, that could potentially work since babies heal extremely quickly… Who would do that to a *baby*?" Celestina shook their head.

"My uncle," I said, taking a deep breath. "And my mom."

"Dr. Vue? What… no… no… What?"

"Yes, my mom. It's all on camera."

"Okay… It'll take time to wrap my head around that, but you're my friend, and I believe you. What does this have to do with you and Apollo being in a foul mood?" They crossed their arms again.

"He asked if I'd forgotten he was human," I reached a hand back to scratch between my shoulder blades.

"What? And he knows?" Celestina gaped.

"Yes, and he was angry, but… it hurt."

"You need to tell him! That's not okay!" they insisted, grabbing my hand again.

I tried to protest, but every time, they made a noise so loud I couldn't say anything over it.

They finally dragged me to the dormitory Apollo and I shared, threw me in, and slammed the door.

I looked at the door, considering if I should try opening it, but it wasn't worth the effort. So I sat on a bed and waited for him to come out of the bathroom, assuming he was in the shower since it was running.

I put my head in my hands until I heard the water shut off, and then heard the slap of feet as he walked out of the bathroom.

He came around the corner, wearing nothing but a towel. He saw me and ran a hand through his wet hair. "Hey," he said coldly, walking over to his clothes and just dropping the towel to put them on.

"Hey, I needed to talk to you about something."

"Well, I'm listening," Apollo said, sounding irritated.

"Remember after the whole crazy piloting moves and throwing up thing, you were mad at me?" I asked, resting my chin on my hand.

"Yes. I'm still annoyed about that, actually" he replied, turning to face me with his pants on, shirt off, and hands on his hips.

My brain got distracted for a moment, then I focused back on the task at hand. "Remember how you asked if I remembered that you were human, too?"

"Yes. What's the point?" Apollo asked, crossing his arms.

"The point is… I felt like you thought I'm not human, and that it was a bad thing. It hurt."

There was silence. He moved closer to me.

The bed sank as he sat down next to me and wrapped an arm around me.

"Eryn, I'm sorry. I wasn't thinking, and I was scared. I don't like being chased in a ship on the best of days. And I think you're beautifully unique. You don't have to be the same as anyone to be beautiful. I lashed out, and I'm sorry." He squeezed me tight against him.

I stayed silent but buried my face in his chest. He took the hint and stayed quiet, too, keeping his arm around me.

Finally, I spoke. "I'm sorry I got mad at you, too. I know you don't like heights. I'll do better."

"I love you, Eryn," he said, resting his chin on top of my head.

I looked him in the eyes. My heart warmed, and I felt a sense of peace and calm.

"I love you, too."

Without warning, he kissed me, and I responded by climbing into his lap. As much as I didn't want to, I eventually pulled away.

"I wish we could do more right now, but we don't have the time." I leaned my forehead against his. "How long have we known each other?"

"Not including the time you were in the cryolab?" he whispered, staring into my eyes. "Nearly eight years, I believe."

"I never want to lose you," I whispered, closing my eyes.

"I don't want to lose you, either," he said, and I could feel the vibrations of his voice through my body.

Gulping, I opened my mouth… then shut it. That could wait.

"We should go help Maesha," I said, climbing off his lap.

In silence, he stood and put on his shirt while I changed into my work clothes.

We left the room and headed toward the hangar, walking so close we almost touched. I could still feel the heat from his body, and I wanted to reach out and take his hand.

Well, what would be the harm in that?

I reached for his hand and intertwined my fingers in his. He squeezed my hand and looked over at me. Then he smiled and held up his other hand, and it took me a second to realize he was signing *I love you.*

I copied the gesture, grinning back at him, then continued onward toward the hangar. We walked in and saw pretty much everyone, minus Raven and Kimi.

They all gave us glances, then continued on with whatever they were working on. Celestina winked at me, then continued talking with Theo.

I dragged Apollo over to Maesha and asked what she needed us to do, and she handed me the blueprints and told us to go.

Chapter 17

We spent the next three days working on the first ship. You would think that, with nothing else to do, we'd make a lot of progress very quickly. Not the case, apparently. We kept having to stop to make covert trips to get more materials or redo a section when someone read the blueprint wrong. At one point, I suggested just bringing the entire junkyard to an unused hangar, but was met with some sarcastic laughter.

Apollo and I were working on the pilot's compartment on top of the ship, along with Theo and Celestina, when I finally did something brilliant.

"We're never going to get this done in time," Theo said, handing me some of the screws.

"Not unless we have help," Celestina chimed in.

I climbed up to the next bar and laid down a panel. "Well, how can we get more help?"

"Well, we'd have to broadcast it out: that would be the easiest way to find help," Apollo said below me, looking up from working on the floor.

"And how would we do that?"

"Could talk to the president," Theo suggested, drilling in another piece.

"Are you crazy? That would *not* go over well," Celestina said, shaking their head. "There's gotta be another way."

"Hey, it could work. We have Mr. Famous Guy over here," Theo said, nodding at Apollo.

We all silently stared at Apollo until he realized Theo was talking about him.

"He and I aren't exactly on speaking terms. I've never actually met the guy, just spoken to his rep." He shrugged. "Besides, I'm not sure I'd *want* to meet him, after all you've told me."

"Privilege is a bitch, huh?" Kimi called out from down below, handing up more panels. "He's done some terrible shit to this city."

Apollo nodded, leaning down to take the panels from Kimi. "I'm sorry he did that. Being closer to it blinds you more."

"But it could be possible to get an audience, especially if you have the actual Dragon, the daughter of the Vues, the one that literally has a statue in the CI Museum… That would pretty much guarantee facetime." Theo gesticulated with the drill.

"I'm not sure he'd want to help us, from what you've told me. Isn't he in on the whole thing that is making people pay to get off the planet?"

"There's a good chance he is, yes," Celestina agreed. "Is there a way to maybe hack into something?"

"I don't know." I turned back to the panel.

We all sat in silence, working on the ship for a moment before Apollo suddenly shouted.

I turned to look at him, Theo dropped his drill and cursed, and Celestina put down their tools.

"You can hack in. Remember?" Apollo said, looking at me.

I stared at him, then it clicked. "My electronics thing."

"What thing?"

"You know how AIHNA told you all to come here?"

"Yes."

"I asked her to do that in my head."

Celestina stared at me, not moving. Only blinking.

"Celestina?"

"How did you…?" Celestina trailed off, shaking their head. "That's impossible."

"Being… well, being half robot or a cyborg or whatever you want to call it, I can connect with electronics. That one…" I pointed at Apollo. "Connected my systems to the larger network. Technically, I have access."

"Can you be hacked back?" Theo asked. "Because that wouldn't be so good."

"I don't know." I shrugged, which stopped the conversation.

We silently finished the rest of the frame and outerworks of the pilot's hub, then climbed down to the ground. Everyone walked like zombies, with hunched backs, or in the case of Stormfighter and Lightningborn, dropping to walk on all fours. All the humans had dark bags under their eyes from working until the late hours of the night, then waking up early the next morning.

Luckily, none of us were dehydrated or malnourished. Although the only food we had was MREs, they were actually pretty nutritional, even if some of them tasted like puke.

Ythea came up to me as we were walking back to the table with the blueprints. "Lady Eryn, could we please find other food? I understand these meals-ready-to-eat are nutritious and last a long time, but it's been forever since I've had real meat, and I miss it something fierce."

I paused and gestured for the others to continue. "Of course, we can, and I don't know why I didn't think of that sooner. What did your diet consist of on your home planet?"

"Lean meats, like, um, birds," Ythea said, flicking her finger at me.

"Okay, we can get some chicken or turkey, that should be pretty close. Let me take preferences from everyone else, and then someone can make a trip to go get stuff," I replied, pulling out my phone and making a note.

"Thank you. And I must say, before, I didn't have a very good opinion of humans, but you have proven you're better than the others." Ythea gave me a half-bow.

"Thanks, Ythea. I appreciate your kindness and your aid, and I hope to someday repay you," I said, holding my hand out to shake.

Ythea enthusiastically shook it. She had picked up on human customs very quickly and loved using them.

Sighing, I took off to go talk to everyone else.

After that was done, I tramped back to my room and stripped out of the work clothes and put on my gear. Apollo came in a few minutes later in his work clothes.

"Where are you going?" he asked, walking to his own chest and pulling out clean clothes.

"To get some real food. You in?" I said, unashamedly watching him undress.

"We could go to my house. I have food there." Apollo caught my gaze and gave me a wink.

"Enough to feed all of us? I highly doubt even you have enough to feed Lightningborn and Stormfighter. Besides, you've been gone for a bit, and it's highly likely a lot of the food has gone bad by now," I snarked, poking his stomach.

"True, but there'll be something." He smirked and pulled on his shirt.

We sat there in silence as he put on the rest of his gear. I couldn't think of anything else to say.

"Ready?" he asked, clipping his belt into place.

I stood. "I was waiting on you."

He nudged me with a friendly elbow, then we walked out of the room to the hangar, and he took his mini jet, while I flew like normal. He easily outpaced me to his house, and I knew that he had already landed by the time I got there. As I flew close enough to see his house, I also saw small black dots that surrounded it.

I got closer and was able to make out they were cars. Sedans. Black sedans.

"Shit," I whispered, torn between the urge to go down and get Apollo back in the air, or stay up here, out of sight, and make a plan that wasn't halfcocked.

Little black dots swarmed the hangar, and I knew my decision had been made for me. There were too many for me to take down. I would have to set down somewhere else. The little black dots left the hangar and moved inside and around the house.

Carefully, I flew toward the hangar roof. The house was a decent enough distance away that I felt like I could pull this off. I carefully set down on the roof, lying flat and folding in my wings.

None of the CI agents were moving, which was good for me. I studied the house, eyeing the window I had dove through before.

I rejected the idea as soon as I thought it. There were too many agents, and I was way too obvious. There would be no way I could get us out quick enough. And I'd still have to find him in the house.

Then I felt a twitch behind my eye, and my vision went black, then Muroha appeared.

"Long time, no see," I said, grimacing.

"How's it going?" he asked, typing furiously on his holokeyboard.

I snorted. "Uh, it's going. When will those other craft be here?"

"*Skala.* The other craft."

"You *forgot?*" I hissed, feeling my anxiety begin to crawl up my throat.

"No, no, no... Yes, yes I forgot! I'm sorry, I'll send them right now. They'll take two weeks to get there," Muroha said, frantically texting on a wrist thingy.

"That's one week before the Earth's said to explode. Cutting it a bit close?" I snarked.

"Hey, I got... distracted. They'll leave port in two of your hours and make the trip there," he said, making a placating gesture.

Before I could reply, he blinked out, and I was looking at Apollo's house again. I squinted at the house, when Muroha's check-in gave me an idea.

Closing my eyes, I let myself seek out the house's wireless connection. When I thought "camera," I immediately was looking at the agents backs on the front porch.

"Next," I whispered to myself, and my view blinked to inside the house. It was Apollo's living room/kitchen area, where a bunch of people stood, surrounding a buff person and Apollo.

"We pay you to use your satellite system and technology, most of which you don't share with us. We're tired of you keeping your secrets. And then, to top it off, you go missing for a week. Nowhere to be found. Sorry, but we're taking you in and confiscating your stuff," said the buff person, voice muffled through their mask.

I pulled out. CI operatives, for sure. *Wonder if I still have any pull with them?* This wasn't ideal when we were planning to hack into their systems to broadcast things.

Gliding off the roof of the garage, I landed in front of the porch. The guards pointed their guns at me, ready to fire. I held my hands up, and one spoke into his comms. "Boss, we have a winged human in old CI gear out here on the front porch. What do you want us to do with her?"

The guy listened for a second while the other kept his gun pointed at me.

"Yes, sir, " he replied, and pointed his gun at me again. "Go inside. No funny business."

I smiled. "Of course not."

Walking inside, all eyes were immediately trained on me. I made straight for the man in charge.

One of them stepped in front of me and pressed a gun to my chest. "Not so fast, sweetheart."

I smiled at him. "Sorry. What's your name?"

"Ricky the Ripper," he said, and I could hear a bit of snickering from some other helmets.

"You can fight me later, Ricky, and we'll see who wins. I want to speak to your superior. Now." I dropped my smile and squared my shoulders.

He moved aside meekly, and I approached the commanding officer. "Rank, operative?"

They turned to me and replied, "Captain. What's it to you?"

"I want to introduce myself," I started, walking up to stand beside Apollo. "I'm Eryn Vue, Director of the CI. I assume the paperwork wasn't done to relieve me of the position. No one ever could remember to do that. So I rank higher than you, Captain."

I think the whole room collectively gasped. Apollo looked mildly proud. The commanding officer took a step back.

"No way," said the commanding officer, sounding a bit breathless. They took off their helmet, and I could finally tell that it was a woman in that suit. "I'm Caroline Strider, sir. Big fan. No offense, but how are you still alive? We thought you were dead years ago."

"Let's just say I was frozen in time. Can I have an audience with the president? Apollo and I both. I have a few words for him. Also, if you could get me in contact with the current director, I'd be grateful," I replied, sending her a quirky smile.

She put her feet together and saluted. "Yes sir, right away. It'll take them a bit to get here."

"Of course. Ricky," I called out, turning to the crowd of agents. "Wanna have that fight while we're waiting?"

The operative stepped forward. "With respect, sir, aren't I too big for you to fight?"

The others around him took a step back, as if they expected me to attack him right then and there. It pained me a bit to do this, but I wasn't one to back down on my word.

"Why don't we find out?" I pulled my guns out of their holsters and handed them to Apollo.

Some of the people around us snickered. I don't know if they were laughing at me or him, but it got my blood racing.

The others in the crowd hurried to move furniture out of the way, and within seconds, they had formed a makeshift fighting ring.

"Ready?" I asked, bouncing on the balls of my feet.

The operative brought his fists up. "Ready."

And we started circling. I kept a relaxed stance as I moved, not giving away the inner excitement I was feeling.

He threw the first punch, which I avoided with ease.

It almost wasn't even a contest. He would try to attack; I would move out of the way. Soon, he was tiring, and I wasn't even breathing hard.

I threw a flurry of punches, pulling them back so as not to hurt him. But they were still powerful enough to leave bruises.

He fell to his knees and held up his hands in surrender. "I yield."

I froze in place, and then held out a hand to him.

He accepted it, and I pulled him to his feet. We nodded at each other. There was no need to exchange words. I had proved my worth, and he couldn't back up his words. Simple as that.

At that moment, Captain Strider came back into the room. "Director, the president will see you now."

Chapter 18

After that statement, there was a whole flurry of activity, getting everyone into vehicles and driving somewhere else.

I rehearsed in my head how I would handle whatever came up, over and over for a million different scenarios, all the way until we stood in his office.

They had opened the big, fancy doors to let us in, and I had to keep myself from making a face. The opulence of the office made me a little sick. And it made me wonder exactly how much this man cared about the people he was supposed to serve.

And then I was facing him and nothing came out of my mouth.

"You claim to be Eryn Vue," he said, looking every bit as sleazy as I anticipated. "You're a little small to be a CI agent."

"I do well enough," I managed to say, meeting his eyes. "Never been much of a problem for me."

"Well, as great as that is, it's not you I'm concerned with. Apollo, we had a deal," President Marsher said, turning to Apollo, who was standing right beside me.

"We had a deal until you tampered with data coming in from my satellites. Not only is that a breach of our agreement, but it's unethical research, to say the least."

I became less impressed the more I stared at him. How did he get to sit in here? What did people see in this guy?

"Our contract. Right. Hm… Well, must've slipped my mind. Nevertheless, you tampered with government property."

"Un-tampering it, you mean."

"No, it was… adjusted. We can't have people panicking over this. Not yet. Not the right time. It all starts with the plants… slowly dying. There's nothing we can do, I'm afraid" President Marsher clicked his tongue and shook his head. "Then, the water will start disappearing, and our scientists will suddenly discover the sun is due to implode in a week. People trying to survive will do many things to stay alive. Of course, we have ships waiting to take them away—at a cost."

"And what, pray tell, will you do with the money once you have it?" I asked, huffing. "Money will be useless in space."

He grinned. "Who said anything about money? Oh, and I can't allow you to leave. Secure information and all that."

I tensed as I heard multiple guns cock around myself and Apollo.

I kept my breathing even, stifling the panic that crawled up my throat in that moment. Now was not the time for a flashback. I counted at least fifteen people. I would be fine, had I been by myself, but with Apollo around to get caught in the crossfire, it was just too much of a risk.

However, the operatives weren't set up very effectively. At least six had their guns aimed in a way that would hit the President if they fired at me. Still too risky though.

They began herding us toward the hallway, and I could hear the words "lock" and "no escape" as we were leaving.

I kept my breathing regulated as they got us out into the hallway and shut the doors. They still had guns trained on us. Apollo kept glancing at me, I assume to see if I'd thought up a way to get us out of this.

Glancing at the faces surrounding us as we trooped down the hallway to who knows where, I spotted the face of the captain that had greeted me earlier.

"Captain Strider," I called out, and she dropped back to walk beside me.

"Eryn, I'm so sorry about this. We have no control over this kind of thing, and—"

"I understand," I interrupted. "All I'm asking for is maybe a blind eye at some point, if it can be safely done. I don't want to hurt anyone, but what we're working—it could save everyone. Get them out. Without a cost."

Captain Strider raised an eyebrow. "Really?"

"I assume you know how they plan to reveal the sun's incoming supernova?"

She nodded.

"We know, too. And we want to make sure everyone survives," I said, listening to myself and thinking about how crazy I sounded. Why would she ever believe me?

Captain Strider glanced around at the other operatives, who were also glancing at each other with looks that I couldn't read.

"You didn't hear it from me, but there's a lot of fire escapes installed in this building," Captain Strider said with a wink.

The group moved down the hallway and kind of paused in front of what looked like an office door.

"Good luck, Director," Captain Strider said, and the rest of the group nodded at us.

I looked around in awe as every single one of them holstered their guns and formed a protective ring.

Before they could change their mind, I held out my hand for Strider to shake. They did, and I stepped away to grab Apollo's hand.

"Until we meet again."

I pushed down the handle and walked through the door with Apollo following behind.

We entered an empty office with one window, and after shutting the door, I promptly went to the window and opened it. Looking down, I saw the nearest fire escape was a window to the right of ours. The one directly below had one as well, but the one on our window had been removed or broken.

"Do you have a rappelling device?" I asked Apollo, stretching my shoulders and peering out at the ground three floors below.

"Not one long enough," he replied, pulling out the cable.

I took a look at it, then took it from his hands and pulled out some of the cable. Tying some of it in a harness around him, I locked the device and took it in hand.

"Rappel down to the next fire escape. I'll stay here and brace it, then fly down behind," I instructed, walking over to the window.

"Got it," Apollo replied, walking over to join me.

He quickly gave me a kiss, then climbed through the window and started to rappel down. I braced my feet against the wall and held the device taut against me, letting Apollo's weight slowly draw out the cable. I felt tugging on the cable, and then I went to the window and flew down.

After joining him on the fire escape, we quickly opened the ladder leading to the next platform, then made it all the way down the building into a side street. I tucked away the wings and undid Apollo's harness.

"Are we going to walk into the street in these?" Apollo said, gesturing at our clothes.

"Probably wouldn't be wise to, but we have nothing else," I said, looking down at my own clothes.

He grimaced and glanced at the street. "How long do you think we have until he sends people to find us?"

"Not long enough." I squared my shoulders and walked onto the street in the general direction of the junkyard. We couldn't go back for food now.

Apollo followed me silently as we made our way down the street. People moved around us and avoided looking us in the eye. It made my gut churn to see them afraid of us, but in this case, I was glad we could move quicker.

Our walking took us halfway to where we needed to go, when alarms started blaring from the buildings around us. Glancing at an electronic billboard that had been showing an ad for toothpaste, I saw pictures of Apollo and I with a flashing "WANTED" over it. My photo was outdated by a lot, as I avoided pictures at every possible opportunity, but Apollo's looked quite recent. Not to mention he was a familiar face because of his company and work.

"Keep moving." I stayed at a walking pace but sped up a little.

People still avoided us, but we were starting to get curious glances.

We turned a corner onto a side street to cut across to the train station.

And ran straight into CI agents.

There were four of them, and I had already knocked two out before they even started responding. Apollo barreled into another who was reaching for his comm unit, and I took on the last, who was reaching for his gun.

After knocking the gun out of his hand, I knocked him out and turned in time to see Apollo pistol-whip his guy with his own gun. He fell to the ground unconscious, and I quickly grabbed Apollo's arm and yanked him after me.

This time, we ran through the side streets, sliding around corners and sprinting down the alleys. In no time, we were at the train station, which was swarming with CI agents.

"No way we can even get near the train," Apollo said, standing so close to me I could feel his breath on my neck.

"There's one way," I replied, turning to look at him. "I fly and cause a diversion; you get on the train."

"No, I'm not letting you put yourself in danger like that!" he argued, running his hand through his hair.

I gave him a half-smile. "Got a better idea?"

He scrunched his face for a second, then slowly shook it. "No."

"Fine. Be ready to run." I shrugged as my wings appeared on my back.

Before I could take off, he grabbed my shoulder. "Be careful," he told me, looking into my eyes.

"I always am," I said, grinning, then took off.

I flew upward, then swooped over the platform, hollering my lungs out. The soldiers immediately turned their attention to me and aimed their guns. Bullets started whizzing past my ears. I kept rolling and climbing and diving, in an effort to make myself a hard target to hit, but still distracting enough that they weren't paying attention to a uniformed man walking through their ranks.

A bullet managed to hit me in the leg, and I hissed, but kept flying. Apollo had almost made it onto the train.

I paused for a second too long because another bullet hit me in the arm, burying itself there.

Hissing again, I climbed upward and left, hoping Apollo had made it on the train safely and that it was leaving.

Flying through the sky, I dodged a commercial airplane or two while traveling, but thankfully no CI aircraft. I tried my best to mirror the path of the train below, but it moved a lot faster than I could fly.

So I followed the tracks, then diverted my course where he would've gotten off.

Swooping lower, I glided above the rooftops, searching for a telltale sign of Apollo. Soon, there was nothing, and the houses got farther and farther apart, until I arrived at his house in the middle of nowhere.

I circled above the building, scanning for sign of CI cars, but it was empty.

Diving down, I carefully went inside, checking for cameras and bugs.

I found one bug under a kitchen counter, and one in a desk drawer, but after doing a sweep of the rest of the house, found no more.

Quickly, I smashed them, and then went out to the garage to see if Apollo was there.

After checking, a tense feeling crawled up my throat.

No.

I ran back inside the house and turned on the TV to see if there was anything there that might indicate what had happened to him.

After watching a commercial for a blender, and another for insurance, the news came on. There was a bit about the weather, and then the reporter introduced a message from the president.

"Hello!" he started, and an uneasy feeling rose in my throat. "Lately, there has been a lot of bad news, and many rumors about planetary issues, as well as the rumor that plants throughout the city are beginning to wilt. However, I would like to present some good news to you."

I held my breath.

"We have captured one of the main perpetrators of these rumors. Apollo, the legendary technology genius and inventor, has been caught trying to sow these pictures on the web." The president flashed pictures of plants in buildings wilting. "He has luckily been stopped before too much panic could be caused. It seems he has an assistant, a woman who claims to be a former CI director that has long been believed to be dead. She uses the name Eryn Vue, but she isn't who she says she is. We must be wary. Do not engage, but call the authorities if you spot her. Thank you."

And then the screen went to commercials.

My blood boiled with rage, and I felt my body shaking from all of the pent-up anger. Instinct was telling me to go. Go now, kill him, take back Apollo. But the rational side of me held me in check.

If I went in and dive-bombed the place, it would only serve to prove the president right. I would get nowhere. When the time came to get people off the planet, no one would believe me. And everyone would die.

How could I change their mind?

An audience with the president hadn't worked. In fact, it only made everything worse.

I never should have left Apollo's side. And now he was enduring who knew what because of me.

A straight-up fight was out. Sneaking in would be impossible. The only real way to get him back would be to get the public enraged. Even the president couldn't stand against the entire city.

I bit my lip, staring hard at the floor, trying to think. *How do you turn an entire city to your side?*

Without really thinking, I pulled out my comm unit and dialed Celestina's number. It rang three times, and then they picked up.

"Eryn, are you okay? Did everything go well?" Celestina spit out the questions like fire as soon as they were on the line.

"No, Apollo got captured and it was my fault. I can't retrieve him by myself," I admitted, feeling my heart sink.

"Shit. What do you need?"

"A way to turn an entire city to my side. The president went public and said Apollo was a traitor and I was a fake, essentially," I explained, reaching up a hand to rub my nose.

Silence on the other end of the line. "Well fuck," I eventually heard, followed by some very unclean muttering.

"Wait," Celestina said, gasping. "What about a journalist? An interview or something that I can guarantee would be on every single large airwave out there?"

"That could work. What, or who, do you have in mind?" I asked, grasping for the straw they just gave me.

"My older brother is a famous journalist. And he owes me a favor," they replied, chuckling. "I'll give him a call and see what I can do. Expect a text within a few minutes."

And with that, they hung up.

Chapter 19

Twenty minutes later, I was staring at the screen of my comm unit, waiting for it to light up. I had taken the first ten minutes to say a bunch of curse words and pull the bullets out of my arm and leg. They bled, but I slapped a bandage over them and knew they would be fine after a bit. I would get Celestina to check on them later.

Drumming my fingers on the countertop, I tried to resist pressing the button to check for notifications.

Be patient, I told myself, biting my lip, keeping my gaze on the phone.

Before I could catch myself, my finger was pressing the button, and surprise, surprise, no texts.

I sighed and hopped off the barstool I was sitting on, and paced around to get out my nervous energy.

Thirty minutes.

Every minute I waited meant Apollo could endure more pain. But unless I wanted to be captured, too, my hands were tied.

Finally, I grabbed the comm unit and went out to Apollo's workshop.

Hitting the lights, I squinted as harsh shop lights sputtered on. The area around the edges was covered with workbenches and tools and small projects that could fit on a tabletop. In the middle of the room was a large heap of electronic and mechanical junk. Probably salvaged from the scrap yards.

I climbed around the junk, seeing what I could pull. Honestly just keeping my hands busy.

Fiddling with the junk, I found a piece of metal that kind of looked cool, that I could cut maybe. I wasn't bulletproof, after all.

But I could be.

Dragging the sheet over to the tools, I chose one, geared it up, and began cutting.

An hour later, I had greaves. After fitting them with some ties, I put them on, bending my knees and elbows to make sure they didn't impede my movement.

Then, mercifully, the phone buzzed in my pocket.

Pulling it out, I glanced at a text that read: *It's a go. Ap pl in 10*

It's a go. Apollo's place in 10.

I exited the garage and went back to the house and into a bathroom.

Taking a look at myself in the mirror, I cringed. What I needed was a shower. But I didn't have time for one now.

I washed off my face the best I could and ran a hand through my hair, trying to make it look purposefully messy.

Then I walked into the living room to wait.

They were on time, as promised. Celestina and two men walked in through the front door. One man was dressed sharply in a suit, and the other carried a camera on his shoulder.

"Ah, you must be Ms. Eryn Vue," the man in the suit said, extending his hand to shake. "I'm Carl, Celestina's older brother. Celestina tells me you want an interview, and that you've got some juicy news."

I straightened, popping my back. "I do. Do you broadcast through the entire city?"

He grinned at me. "Oh, yeah. By the way, I've been wanting to stick it to that asshole president for years now. Thank you for giving me the opportunity."

"No problem," I said easily, giving him a matching smile as Celestina stood beside me. "But it wouldn't have happened if Celestina hadn't thought of it."

"True. I already promised them dinner at their favorite restaurant." He winked at me. "Ready to get started?"

"Let's do this," I said, before I could lose any nerve.

The camera man brought the camera up, and Celestina moved behind him. I stood a little off to the side, mentally rehearsing what I was going to say.

"Three… two… one… and… live," the camera man said.

"Helllllooooo, the prospering city! This is Carl, reporting from an undisclosed location on a topic I'm sure you've been wondering about. We've all heard the rumors. But are they true? Here to answer our questions I have the one, the only, Eryn Vue!" he said with a flourish, gesturing toward me.

I stood as tall as I could and smiled at the camera. "Thank you, Carl. I certainly hope I can answer everything you ask."

"I have no hesitation you will. So, tell us, Eryn: are you really the famous CI Director who we thought died all those years ago?" Carl pointed the mike in his hand toward me.

"I am," I said, flashing a smile at the camera.

"What were you doing all those years? You don't look any older than your statue, and it's been a hundred years."

"I was frozen for a hundred years," I said, raising my eyebrows. "It was a little chilly, to say the least."

Carl laughed at my joke, and I grinned in response.

"So, our audience wants to know: why now? Why come forward now?" he asked, and the camera panned toward me once more.

"Because I found out that while I had been frozen, the world was marching toward its death," I said, the words coming from nowhere. "You've all been lied to. Within recent weeks, the plants at the city limits have been wilting, slowly reducing the amount of oxygen this city has, and letting the temperature crawl slowly upward. However, there's a darker, more dangerous secret you need to know. For weeks now, the president and various rich people in your city have known about a supernova that will occur a couple of weeks from now. They plan to save you on their spaceships—if you pay their price. Anyone who can't will be left to die here when the planet is sucked into a black hole. We don't have long until the planet breathes its last breath."

"That's definitely not good. How do you know this?" he asked, and I got the message. The audience needed proof.

"Solar reports, which you should be able to see on screen, and my own eyes," I said simply, pushing the image of the solar report into the video broadcast by staring into the camera. "You can go to the edge of the city to see for yourself. And the president himself admitted to it moments ago when I spoke with him. Afterward, he attempted to imprison myself and my partner, Apollo, who I'm sure you all know. He succeeded in taking Apollo, but he will not succeed in hiding this all from you."

"Viewers, I encourage you to do as she says. Now, one more question, Eryn: Why are you warning us?" he questioned, leaning toward me.

"I don't want a single soul to die because they lack the money to live. My best friend has already been wrongfully accused of treachery. I've known Apollo since I was trained, and I can assure you he would never betray the people he loves so much. Those of you who have met him and know him can confirm this. He is wrongfully imprisoned, and you've all been wrongfully deceived. I'm trying to right those wrongs. If you want to aid me, go to the peacock among pigeons, and I'll meet you there," I finished, only then realizing that my wings had appeared and extended to their full wingspan.

"You heard it, folks. The peacock among pigeons. I'm Carl, reporting the truth, always for the people," he said, smiling, as the camera man then shut off the camera.

"Thank you," I said, holding out my hand to shake.

"No, thank you. You have a gift for words. You should be a reporter." He grinned, putting his hand in mine and shaking it.

"They were used for something else for a long time," I said, grinning grimly. "Will you join me?"

"Heck yeah. President is a douche. I'd rather follow you. I think most people would," he commented as Celestina came around the camera man.

"Good job," they said, giving me a hug.

I hugged them back tightly, then let go. "We've got to get to Apollo's tower." I shifted my wings.

"Peacock among pigeons. Clever. That's what all the street folk call it," Celestina said, winking at me.

"That's what I was hoping," I replied, grinning back. "Now, we're wasting time. Let's go."

After heading out the door, I took off into the sky, letting my wings take me high. I flew through the clouds, all thin and wispy. I watched the land as it passed below me, my heart clenching at the sight of all the yellow land.

My flying took me over the city, the silver buildings and their plants a harsh contrast to the blank ground outside the city limits.

I landed on top of Apollo's building and jimmied the lock to get in.

After walking down the stairs, I switched over to the elevator and took it to the first floor. When the doors opened into the lobby, I entered into a packed crowd of people. And more were still coming in.

I felt my eyes widen and my throat close. So many. And I would have to speak in front of them all.

Gritting my teeth, I walked over to the receptionist's desk, which had a young girl sitting there, eyes wide, staring at the crowd.

"Hey, what's your name?" I asked, making her jump as she turned to me.

Her eyes widened. "Lisa."

"You mind if I climb on top of the desk so everyone can see me?" I asked, giving her a quirky smile.

"No, go for it," she said quickly, gesturing at the desk.

I grinned in thanks and climbed atop the desk. Slowly, people turned to look, until there was a bunch of shuffling as everyone turned toward me.

Silence fell over the room, and then the only sound was the door falling shut.

"Hello," I said, suddenly feeling the nerves hit me. "Thank you for coming. I know I was vague on camera, but now I can tell you what I'm sure you want to know."

"Is it true? Is the city really dying?" asked a teenager, raising their hand.

I grimaced. "As much as I hate to say it, yes, it's true. And the danger of that and the supernova is very real, and imminent, and we need your help to save as many people as we can."

"What do we need to do?" said a guy toward the front of the crowd.

"There's a place outside the city where we're building spaceships. We're going to leave Earth and live somewhere else," I explained, feeling the silence that accompanied it.

"What's the other option?" asked someone from the back. "That seems like we're giving up a lot."

Other people started muttering similar things, but I felt my confidence settle into my body.

"The other option is staying here and dying in two weeks," I stated coldly, spreading my wings to emphasize my statement.

"No thanks," said a voice from behind me, and I turned to see Lisa standing up. "I'm with you."

I nodded at her, giving her a small smile.

"I am, too. I don't want my children to die," said a woman in the front.

"Me, too."

"I am, too," came the chorus from the crowd.

My hopes began to climb for the first time today. Pulling out my comm unit, I made a call.

Within minutes, a pair of buses were pulling up to the curb. I raised an eyebrow, wondering where they had managed to find buses, as there hadn't been any at the base.

I went outside and nodded at Raven and another person I didn't recognize, who were each driving a bus, then started directing people on the buses.

Within forty minutes, we were back at the base and settling people in. It surprised me how willing they were to start working, and how gung-ho they were about it all. The children stuck by their parents' sides and helped. It was so different from what I remembered of the time I was born in.

Celestina and Theo took care of organizing them all. I glanced up at the open sky, feeling the need to fly. Apollo was still imprisoned somewhere. I was going to get him back. If I could find him.

"Thinking?" Maesha asked. "I'm sure Apollo will be okay."

"I have to get him back. But I don't know how."

"Do you want help?" she inquired, tilting her head.

I raised an eyebrow. "What do you have in mind?"

"How about a team effort? My girls and I are well trained, as anyone must be to be an ambassador and government official." Maesha grinned.

"Let's see what you've got," I stated, smiling in return.

Chapter 20

"Okay. If the CI still uses the same holding place, Apollo will be here," I said, pointing to a building on the map.

Maesha had gathered her friends, and we met in the conference room to discuss the best way to get Apollo out of government custody.

"In the building?" Scia asked, chewing on her lip.

I shook my head. "Underground. The cells are in the basement. There are only two access points. One is the elevator, and the other is the emergency exit, which is a staircase on the west side, leading out into the yard, which is surrounded by electrical fencing."

"Electrical fencing?" Schimra repeated, tilting her head.

"Metal fencing charged with electricity. When you touch it… ouch." I grimaced just thinking about it.

"Got it," Schimra said, nodding. "The emergency exit is set with an alarm?"

"Yes," I said, tapping the map. "And the elevator has cameras. Plus, guards everywhere, and cameras outside."

"Cameras aren't a problem," Maesha said, reaching into her pocket and pulling out a small device that looked like a dog clicker.

"Jammer?" I asked, nodding at the device.

"Nope. Interferes with anything electric. So the fence, cameras, lights…" She trailed off, grinning. "Pretty useful."

"And the elevator," Scia mentioned, looking thoughtful. "How is the alarm triggered?"

"All I know is that if you open the door, an alarm will trigger. Apollo could maybe tell you more." I sighed.

"Could we scale the elevator shaft?" Schimra asked, raising her eyebrows.

"The elevator would have to be above the first floor, because the lowest level is the basement. We don't have any sub-basements or anything," I clarified, realizing my first statement was kind of stating the obvious.

"Hey guys, how's it going?" Celestina asked, sticking their head in the door.

"It's going," I replied, scratching my head. "Actually, do you think you could see if your friend Rubi or Raven know anything about how alarms work?"

"Sure thing, I'll be back!" Celestina said, giving me a thumbs up before shutting the door.

"How many guards are there?" Scia asked, rolling her shoulders.

"Outside, about ten to twelve. Inside depends on the floor. The first floor will have a guard every ten feet. The basement will have two or three guards per prisoner," I explained, pointing to spots on the building.

"So… lots of guards," Maesha stated.

"Yep, although if Apollo is the only prisoner down there, at most we'll have three guards," I said, crossing my arms.

"Unless they're expecting us to come for him," Schimra stated.

"Right," I said, biting my lip. "If they think that, they could've also moved him somewhere else. Fuck." I grabbed my hair and sighed.

Maesha placed a hand on my shoulder. "We'll find him."

I drew in a deep breath and straightened, smiling at her. "Thank you."

She nodded. Then the door opened, letting in Celestina and Rubi.

"You needed me?" Rubi asked, wiping a hand across her forehead. Her hijab was still perfectly in place, even though I knew she had been building ships all day.

"Yeah, can you tell us how door alarms work?" I asked.

"Sure, they're fairly easy." Rubi shrugged and grabbed a piece of paper on the table. After scribbling for a bit, she shoved the paper our way and left.

We all gathered around it.

"Wow, this is really easy to understand," Scia commented, picking up the paper.

"No joke. Alarms are that easy?" Schimra asked, looking over her shoulder.

I leaned over the table and stared at the map, trying to think my way into Marsher's head. Was he smart enough to pull that kind of trick, or not? Once we made a move, we would be showing our cards, and that could be a disaster.

The door opened again, but this time it was Theo. "Hey, Eryn, can I talk to you real quick?"

"Sure," I said, walking over and into the hallway. "What's up?"

"Are you okay? I heard about Apollo getting captured," he asked, his eyebrows drawing close together in concern.

"Yeah, I'm fine," I said, giving him a reassuring grin.

"Okay. If you need help getting him back, I'm always willing to help," he offered, smiling at me.

"I'll remember that. Thank you."

He nodded, then walked off down the hallway to the hangar. I glanced at the door to the conference room, then decided against going back in. I needed to clear my head.

I wandered down the hallway and into random empty rooms until I came to the hospital room Apollo had stayed in, and the video camera was still sitting on the table.

"Why did you make me this way?" I asked, picking up the camera and sitting on the bed.

When it gave me no answer, I set it back on the table and flopped onto my back. Then I cried. Bawled. I stifled any sounds to prevent anyone from coming in to see what was wrong, but let the tears flow freely.

It's too much. I'd lost one man I loved, and it seemed I might be unable to save another. A hundred years, frozen, and I woke up to a different world. My dad was dead. My mother seemed okay, but as it turned out, she'd experimented on me. Everyone else I knew besides my mother and Apollo were dead. *I have to get everyone off of Earth before it gets sucked into a supernova.*

Who decided I was the one to handle it all?

I was done leading. Everyone's eyes were on you, all the time. Any weakness, any breakdown, and they started losing faith. Hide your emotions, stay positive. Do your best even if you have no idea what the fuck you're doing because that's what everyone else expects.

I was done acting perfect.

But the problem was, I couldn't be done. They expected me to pull them through all of this, to always have a plan. Apollo was probably expecting me to rescue him. Which I wanted to do, but how would I tell the others that I was out of ideas? That I was dry?

I can't be dry, I have to think of something.

After staring at the ceiling for far too long, I got up and walked back to the conference room.

"Hey," Maesha said, nodding. "Head clear?"

I smiled sheepishly. "Yeah, blank slate. Any ideas?"

"Well, we have a plan for getting in and getting him out. If he's there," Scia commented, clicking.

"Can we hack into the system?" Schimra asked. "You know, to check if he's really there."

They all looked at me.

I shook my head. "Apollo's the hacker. Anything I know, I learned from him, and I don't know much. Just enough to do the basics with my brain thing. Anything complicated, like hacking into government databases, is beyond my level."

At that moment, Celestina and Theo came in.

"Hey, first ship is finished and ready for takeoff," Celestina said. "Any progress?"

"Kind of. We have a plan for this building, but no idea if he's actually in there," Scia said, crossing her arms.

"Can't hack?" Theo asked.

"Apollo's the hacker. Unless one of you knows how to hack?" I questioned him.

"No."

"Hey, what about your connection to the computer thingy?" Celestina asked, gesturing at my head.

"I thought about that, but I don't know if I'd be able to get into their systems," I ran my hand through my hair.

"Worth a try." Theo shrugged his shoulders. "You'd probably be the only one who could do something like this anyways."

Sighing, I sat on a chair next to the computer, and, cringing at the puff of dust that came up, I closed my eyes, placed my hand on the computer, and relaxed.

My mind was blank for a moment, and then I saw a series of 0s and 1s flashing through my head. Soon, it showed me what looked like a desktop. It had files and folders, and a background that was a giant sunflower. Without my will, I saw a file begin to load and opened a video.

It had no sound, but it did have subtitles. The video was of Apollo.

Eryn, I'm sorry about this. I made this video before they got me. I did almost make it back to the house, but I knew they were tailing me, thanks to what you taught me. I know you'll try to access this to find out where I am. There are...

The video cut off. There are what?

I exited out of the video. I began searching the folders, and it took me a few minutes to find one labeled "Conventional Holding Facilities." I clicked on it, and more code ran across my mind. Then a database appeared in front of me.

Quickly, I found their holding files, and thankfully found Apollo in the system... at the same facility I figured he was being held at. After glancing over cell number assignments, I left and closed it.

Opening my eyes, I had to blink a few times to reorient myself.

"Well?" Celestina asked.

"Good news and bad news," I said, grimacing.

"Good news first," Theo said.

"He's at the holding facility I thought they would put him in, in the basement," I replied, trailing off.

"Bad news?" Maesha asked.

"They've assigned fifteen guards to him. And he's the only prisoner there," I said, sighing.

"They know you're coming for him... but isn't fifteen overkill?" Theo asked.

"It would be, yes, but if they've had any look at my records, and if they expect someone to accompany me, it's a good amount. On the upside, it'll be crowded down there, and there will be more of them. More chance to be caught in crossfire," I added, folding my arms. "Theo, you feel up to going with me?"

"Sure. You need a good shot?" Theo asked, grinning.

"Yes, but we aren't going to kill them; they're just doing their job. We're going to tranquilize them," I said, giving him a look.

"Deal. Where do we get the tranq guns from?" he asked, studying the map.

"No clue. Maybe in one of the storage rooms?" I mused, cracking my knuckles.

"I think someone may have found something like that. Want me to check?" Theo asked.

"Yes. See if we have enough. If not, see if there are any veterinarians in the bunch."

"On it," he said, then ran out the door.

It only took a few minutes before Theo came back with a long box. "We have four."

"Great. You each take one, and I'll use my hands. Go get your gear," I commanded, heading out myself.

I went to my room, stripped and showered, then changed into black cargo pants and a black, long sleeve shirt, with a bulletproof vest over top of it. Black combat boots completed my gear. I stretched to get the nerves out, but it barely helped. I hadn't actually planned a mission like this in so long, but it still felt like second nature.

I returned to the command room and studied the map until my eyes hurt.

"We'll get him back," I heard Theo say behind me.

"Yeah, I'm still worried though," I replied, turning around. He was dressed similarly to me, but his gear looked newer.

"You really like him."

"Yes, I do," I said simply, and left it at that. We were silent after that, the only sound being the vents.

Eventually, Maesha, Scia, and Schimra came back, bearing an extra tranq gun and a box full of cartridges.

"After taking a look at these, we discovered these were ours," Scia said, handing me the gun she was holding. "One shot is enough to knock out most humans. I think our tips are sharper than yours and should easily pierce clothing. We had an extra on our ship, so we should now have enough for all."

"Thanks," I said, feeling the heft of the gun and getting used to the feeling.

"Each cartridge has three shots. It should be plenty for the men in that basement," Schimra explained. "You guys aren't bad shots, I assume."

"Nope, I'm quite a good shot," I replied, examining the cartridge.

"Me, too," Theo added, putting the gun in his holster.

I did the same and put the extra cartridges in an easily accessible pocket.

"We wait for darkness, then we go," I said, noticing Maesha also getting her gun ready. "You ready for this?"

"Yes," she responded, sheathing her own weapon. "I'm quite handy in a fight."

"Okay, sounds good. Can we take your craft?"

"Of course," Maesha said, smiling. "As long as I pilot."

"Deal."

We headed out, Scia and Schimra staying weirdly silent.

"It's been too long since I've been in the field," Maesha commented as we headed down the hallway.

"What do you do now?" I asked, curious.

Maesha looked at me. "Paperwork."

I snorted, and then got myself under control. "Glad to know it's universal."

"Ha, bureaucracy. Glad I don't have to deal with that," Theo added, grinning.

We both glared at him.

He chuckled and held his hands up in surrender, and we were silent for the rest of the walk. People passed us on the way to the hangar, lifting a hand or muttering a hello. The base felt like the old days, filled with working people. It didn't feel empty. It felt like home.

We boarded the ship with minimum fuss, and we were flying in no time.

I sat as Maesha's copilot, watching her and actually learning the controls. Theo was strapped in behind us, tense as a stretched spring. Turned out he didn't like planes, or by extension, spaceships. Most of the flight he looked fairly nauseous, and I think I heard him forcibly swallow a couple times.

"They'll be trying to find us, you know," Maesha said quietly, so only I could hear.

I sighed. "I know. I was aware of that, but I don't feel like we could do this without him."

"You've already lost enough team members," Maesha said, nodding. "I have as well, and then my father promoted me to a senior officer. Then the paperwork came," she said, smiling.

"I'm sorry. Losing your team is rough," I said, sadly smiling back at her.

"I appreciate it. And you. I owe you quite a debt for pulling us out of that freezer."

"Consider it taken care of," I replied. "You're helping me get Apollo back, when you didn't have to."

She nodded, then we fell silent for the rest of the journey.

Most of the city passed us by before we arrived at the holding facility. As we agreed upon, Maesha landed on the roof of an abandoned building, then shut the ship off, going dark.

We crept out of the ship and to the edge of the roof to look at the facility. All the guards patrolled the outer edge of the property, leaving the building free.

"Ready Theo?" I asked, glancing at him.

"No, but let's do this," he said, standing.

I stretched out my wings and stepped up behind him. I hooked my arms under his armpits and crossed them over his chest, my hands coming to rest on his shoulders.

"I'll be back for you, Maesha," I said, scooting Theo carefully forward until we were standing on the edge.

"Careful," she replied, then turned her attention to the guards, ready to shoot, should the need arise.

"Whenever you're ready, Theo, just fall forward," I instructed, making sure my grip on him was secure.

I felt him take a deep breath, and then we fell forward.

As soon as we were clear of the edge, my wings snapped open, and I started pumping them to make us move upward.

Soon, we were far above the building, and I began to glide us to the roof of the building, flapping every so often to keep us at the right height. He was heavy, but thankfully the distance was short.

The roof was quickly coming toward us. "Be ready, Theo."

He muttered something under his breath, but the wind blew it away.

As I flew over the roof, I dropped him and continued flying over. Wheeling around, I took a couple seconds to check that he was okay before flying back to Maesha. After picking her up and dropping her off, I repeated the same tactic with the rest of the members, then landed on the roof with them.

We all crept to the edge of the roof and looked down.

The guards were still circling the outer perimeter. Luckily, there were no dogs, but there were blindingly bright lights.

"We'll need to do this quick. When the lights go out, they'll notice. It needs to seem like a minor glitch. We need to scale down to the door and get it opened quickly. Theo, you'll be opening the door, so we'll start sending you down first. Once you reach the ground, Maesha will blink the lights, and we'll join you. Scia and Schimra will stay up here to cover us. Got it?" I asked, looking at everyone.

They all gave me a grim nod.

"Let's go," I said, pulling out my climbing equipment while Theo and Maesha did likewise.

Hooking it up to the ceiling, we began lowering Theo down, inch by inch. Every part of me screamed to go faster, but it was imperative we didn't draw attention. The rope was taut with his weight, and I kept glancing at the guards to make sure none of them were in any way alarmed.

Eventually, there was slack on the line, then two tugs. Theo had made it to the ground.

The next part was the riskiest. Maesha and I would both be dropping supremely fast in the darkness before she had to turn the lights and cameras back on. If we dropped too fast for too long, stopping would jolt us and send us flying into the wall. Too slow, and the guards would notice a pair of shapes descending down the wall.

Hooking up our own equipment, we leaned out over the wall.

"Ready?" Maesha asked.

"No," I said, then chuckled. "But let's do this anyway."

With a grin, Maesha held up the device. My breath started coming faster, and my heart began to race as I anticipated her pressing that button.

Then she pressed it, and the lights went off. We began descending, quickly and carefully, and as soon as our feet hit the ground, Maesha turned the lights back on.

The guards were swarming like ants in an ant hill, but when the lights came back on, they froze.

It took a couple minutes, but they went back to their patrols, while we stood frozen and pressed to a doorway.

Once we were clear, we relaxed a little.

"Alarm is disabled. Ready to go in when you are," Theo whispered.

"On my mark, open the door. Remember, tranqs only. No deaths. Don't let anyone trip an alarm. I'll take the left side, Maesha takes center, and Theo, you take right. Got it?" I checked, and when they nodded, I drew my weapon.

Crouching down, the other two followed. Maesha grabbed the door handle.

Lifting my hand, I counted down on my fingers. *3... 2... 1...*

Maesha pulled open the door, and I dove in, rolled, and stopped, in a crouch. I found my first target and shot. I took down three before I had to reload and they turned around.

The sound of gunshots rang out around us, stone pieces flying off the walls as the projectiles hit around us. I heard Theo and Maesha firing, but I kept all my attention on the enemies in front of me.

Three more shots. Then silence.

All the guards were out and down, but gunshots weren't silent. We needed to move.

I ran to the cell and looked in.

And cursed.

He was sitting on the bench, unconscious.

Theo tossed me the keys off a guard, and I hurriedly unlocked the cell. After opening the door, I ran in and hauled him onto my shoulders in a fireman carry.

"Go, go, go," I said, and we ran toward the door. After quickly passing Apollo off to Maesha, I ran through the open door that Theo had pushed and took flight.

Gaining height, I swept around and picked my target, then tucked my wings and dove.

The wind whistled by my face, and at the last second, I brought my legs in front of me.

I hit the man squarely in the back, knocking him down. His head hit the ground, and he was out like a light.

Before I could be seen, I climbed up again and picked another target on the opposite side of the building. Doing the same maneuver, I took him out as well.

I silently and efficiently did this for the eight guards patrolling the perimeter. Not a single one saw me coming.

When they were down, Maesha put out the lights, and I took Apollo from her. I struggled into the air with his limp body while Maesha and Theo sprinted to the fence and over. Scia and Schimra had scaled down the building to join us.

I followed, reaching the ship as Maesha started it.

As I landed, Theo caught Apollo from my arms and dragged him inside. I stumbled after, hitting the button to close the bay door.

I collapsed onto one of the nearby seats and strapped myself in, breathing heavily and willing myself to calm down.

Maesha took off, and my stomach lurched for a moment before remembering itself and coming back. Theo sat beside me and strapped in.

"You did a good job," he said, placing a hand on my shoulder. "Everyone is out without even a scratch."

I smiled weakly at him, then turned my gaze to Apollo.

Was he okay?

He hadn't woken up once in the entire rescue. What had they done to him?

Chapter 21

We arrived back at base in the early morning, just as the sun was beginning to peek over the horizon. Apollo had been unconscious for the entire flight and remained so throughout landing. Needless to say, I was worried.

When we opened the bay doors, Celestina was immediately inside. "Who's hurt?" they asked, hands on their hips. "I can sense it."

"Apollo hasn't woken up since we found him." I pointed a shaky finger at him.

Celestina was at his side faster than I could blink. "Good news, he's still alive. Bad news, I don't know why he's not awake. Yet. Let's get him to the infirmary, quickly," they ordered, and Theo went and picked him up.

The two exited the ship, and I let my composure drop and my head fall into my hands.

I felt a hand on my shoulder. "He'll be okay, Eryn, really. Your friend is quite a talented medic," Maesha said quietly.

I lifted my head and smiled weakly at her. "Thank you."

She smiled back, taking her hand off my shoulder. "Go get some rest. We will watch over him, and I will personally wake you if he stirs."

With a groan, I unbuckled myself and stood, joints creaking like an old woman. I made my way back to my bed, half-heartedly greeting the people I passed. When I got there, I fell onto my bed and stared at the ceiling.

Then the tears began to roll.

I sobbed silently, letting the tears and mess run down my face, but keeping the sounds inside. All the stress that had been on my shoulders since Apollo's capture melted away.

After I realized there were no more tears, I got up and dragged myself to the shower, where I rinsed the salt from my face and the sweat from my body. The hot water felt good, but I couldn't stand being in there too long.

I quickly got out, toweled off, and dressed, then went to where they were building the remaining two ships. There was no way I could sleep while I was still worried about Apollo.

I worked mindlessly for the entire day. People seemed to sense my bad mood and stayed away. Celestina and Maesha each approached me once with food, which I ate, even though it had no taste. When I finally felt tired enough to sleep, the garage was pretty much empty. The second ship was almost finished, and the third wasn't too far behind. We would finish in time.

Sitting down on an overturned bucket, I rested my head on my hands and stared at the ships, losing myself in the gleam of their metallic hulls.

What only felt like seconds later, Celestina shook me and told me to get up. "Apollo's awake."

I leapt up and followed them quickly to the infirmary. Upon entering, I saw Apollo hooked up to an IV, leaning back against an upraised bed.

"Hey," I said, smiling softly and sitting on the edge of his bed.

"Hey," he croaked, returning my smile. "Thanks for coming to get me."

"Of course, you goofball," I replied, chuckling. "How do you feel?"

Apollo grimaced. "Like I got run over by a car."

I raised an eyebrow and looked at Celestina. "So, what was wrong?"

Celestina scrunched their face this way and that, and finally sighed. "My best guess is some mixture of something. I couldn't identify it, but it had some things in common with chloroform."

I nodded, then turned back to Apollo. Brushing the hair away from his face, I kissed his forehead.

He leaned into me and snaked one hand to grab mine.

I leaned back but kept hold of his hand.

"I think I have to go do something," Celestina said, winking at me, and then turning to leave the room.

I turned to meet Apollo's gaze, and we both leaned forward and kissed.

"I was so worried about you," I whispered to him, looking down at our hands.

"I'm okay now. That's what matters. Hey, look at me." Apollo set a hand under my chin to tilt my head up.

I looked him in the eyes, and tears started falling from mine.

"I'm okay. Come here," he said, opening his arms.

I leaned into his hug, drawing a deep breath, and with it, the faint scent of his cologne. I could hear his heart beating, faster now that my head was on his chest.

"I was so scared," I whispered, feeling the tears leak out and onto his shirt. "I thought I was going to lose you."

He silently stroked my hair. "I knew you would come for me. You don't give up that easily. Especially when you want to shove it to an asshole."

I chuckled as the tears continued to leak out of my eyes. "Yeah, Marsher is a bit of an asshole, isn't he?"

"Just a bit," Apollo agreed, laughing weakly. "You should probably go sleep."

I looked up at him, frowning.

"Don't give me that look. You know I'm right."

I let out a puff of air through my nose.

He kissed me again. "Go, I'll be okay. They need you."

Reluctantly, I stood and brusquely wiped the tears from my face and the snot that had been threatening to start crawling down my face.

"I'll come visit tomorrow afternoon," I promised, then forced myself to walk out of the room before I lacked the conviction.

There was no one in the halls, so my walk back to my room was silent.

Chapter 22

I woke up the next morning with my hair a mess and absolutely no logical thought. I felt like a zombie.

After forcing myself to get dressed, I made my way to the ship bay, where several people were already working on the two remaining ships. The second ship was receiving final touches, and then it would be done.

I spotted Masesha standing over the blueprint table, discussing some things with the engineers. They left just as I arrived at the table.

"How's it going?" I asked, glancing at the blueprints.

"Good, we're on schedule as long as nothing goes wrong. However, I would recommend we go ahead and send off the first ship, if possible," she answered, turning to face me.

"I'll start gathering people. We'll start with friends and family of the workers, get them sent off first. They'll be the easiest," I said, nodding. "I'll broadcast a system-wide announcement. Keep it going."

Walking off, I made my way to the command room to broadcast the announcement, mentally ticking off boxes on the to-do list. After running the announcements over the base, I headed to the med bay to check in on Apollo.

Celestina was pulling out the IV just as I arrived, and Apollo grinned at me when he met my eyes.

"Hey, beautiful, how's everything going?"

"You definitely sound better," I commented, walking over to him. "Feel up to helping me build a ship?"

"Anything that will get me out of this room," he said, pushing up to standing.

With a chuckle, I grabbed his hand and pulled him out of the med bay and toward the hangar.

* * *

One week later, the third ship was finished. We hadn't sent off the first or second ship like we had planned—we all realized at about the same time that we were lacking supplies. Raven, who I had very much come to appreciate, was incredibly resourceful and had put together a small team to haul supplies back, little by little. It had been a week since they started, and now, we had pretty big stacks.

Celestina and I had taken it upon ourselves to salvage anything we could from the base. Maesha had mentioned the planetary alliance that was helping us would be providing us with resources to find a new place to live and materials and labor to build a new city. However, we wanted to grab what we could, while we could.

"This is crazy," Celestina said, packing another MRE. "I can't believe I'll have to leave my home. Everything we've built, the idea of it just… disappearing… I feel like I'm about to cry all the time now."

"Moving is not easy, and not being able to return somewhere is even harder," I replied, giving them a quick side hug. "But we can take memories and mementos with us. We've already talked with everyone about going out to get their pictures and important things from their homes."

"We have, and they're being careful about it. Marsher's got people patrolling the streets. Although their numbers have thinned—many came with family members or were swayed by Theo."

I nodded. "Theo has done a one-eighty. He's been a much better help than he was. And I was glad to see Captain Strider."

Celestina nodded and scrolled through their holo-pad. "Hey, are these the ships that your friend in your head was supposed to send?"

"His name is Muroha, and let me see," I said, leaning over their shoulder. "Yep, looks like it. Let's start packing. Send the message."

Celestina tapped a few times on their holo-pad while I continued packing. We had decided to place people on the ships in planned groups, to try and make the process as simple as possible. Elderly, children with at least one parent, and those with any mobility problem would board first, along with several medical professionals. Celestina had been doing a great job of coordinating with the staff at the SMC, who had been on board after my little stunt on camera.

"Eryn, come in. We need a hand over on Fifth Street," my communicator rang out.

I grabbed it to respond. "On my way. Hold them off."

Hooking the communicator back into my belt, I ran out of the storage room and to the hangar, where I used a car to launch myself into the air.

Pumping my wings as hard as I could, I ascended to fly toward Fifth Street. We'd had several of these attacks in the past week, and it seemed like they were getting worse.

I assumed Marsher was… unhappy with my TV interview. Although their numbers had thinned, they still had access to loads of technology that Theo and Apollo agreed were alien.

Thankfully, we hadn't lost anybody to the raids yet.

The city began coming into view, and I started maneuvering between the buildings. Soon, I could see the fight going on. A group of refugees were being protected by multiple CI agents that had defected to us, while a line of other CI agents were doing their best to get past them.

With one more flap of my wings, I shot downward, beelining for the center of the line.

Turning around at the last second, I slammed feet first into my target, who was knocked back by the force of my dive.

"She's here!" one of them yelled, until he was knocked out cold by a punch from me.

Then I heard a loud hum start to grow louder, and after knocking out another man, I looked up to see an aircraft hovering over the fight.

"Stand down and surrender, Eryn! Or they die," a voice rang out, coming from the craft.

A pair of guns descended from the bottom of the aircraft, and I silently cursed.

"You have ten seconds before we start firing!"

Without a second thought, I used the nearest enemy as a launching pad and shot up to the aircraft.

The hum got higher-pitched, until a blue blast came out of one gun.

I darted over to intercept it, hoping I wouldn't blow to pieces.

Raising my arm, it deflected off my forearm and crashed into a nearby building instead.

Stunned, I looked down at the bracers that my dad had given me.

Not a scratch on them.

I shot back up to the craft and rammed the first gun, managing to disconnect it halfway.

Hearing the high-pitched hum again, I turned and grabbed the second gun and pushed it upward, toward the aircraft.

It fired, blasting a hole through the craft and coming out the other side.

The aircraft started careening downward, and I yelled at people to get clear.

They scrambled to get away from the area, and I noticed with some satisfaction that my group had funneled into a nearby building that led out of the area underground.

However, many of the other CI agents weren't so lucky. They ran and screamed as the craft plummeted toward them.

Diving, I grabbed two of the men who were being too slow and flung them out of the way. Soon after, the craft hit the ground, cracking the pavement and making the ground shake.

"Keep moving!" I yelled, pushing the men ahead of me. "It's probably going to blow!"

They didn't need much more encouragement after that.

Seconds later, a large *boom* rang through the streets. I stared in dismay as I saw the destroyed buildings and the ash floating in the waterways that ran by the area. The plants in this sector, which was closer to the edge of the city, were already dead. Brown, black, wilted. Destroyed.

If I were to look toward the center of the city, I knew what I would see. Pristine, clean buildings and healthy plants. However, I got some satisfaction from knowing that the ash from this explosion would soon be drifting down toward the center of the city.

Taking off, I surveyed the damage, and checked for dead bodies. The wreckage of the craft was still on fire, and I could smell burnt metal and flesh from here.

I took a deep breath, then dove to glide over the mess. The smell hit me like a truck, and I had to swallow multiple times to prevent myself from throwing up.

Looking at where the cockpit likely would've been, I grimaced as I saw nothing but burnt bodies in the wreckage. Shaking my head, I angled upward, into the clouds, and flew back to the base.

Upon arrival, I immediately went to find the person who'd led the mission into the city to debrief with them. They were torn up and shaking, they were so scared. After they debriefed, I sent them off to the med bay for Celestina to look over.

"What happened?" Apollo called, wiping the grease off his hands.

I climbed up on the ship to sit with him. "Well, typical encounter, until an aircraft shows up and starts trying to fire blue lasers at everyone. I deflected the first blast into nearby buildings and used the second to take down the ship. Ship crashed, exploded, everyone inside died."

"Are you okay?"

"I'm fine," I assured him, patting his leg. "It's weird being able to take down planes though. Every time this happens, it all comes back."

I didn't have to explain any more than that, thankfully. Apollo knew I was still having flashbacks. The fighting didn't help.

"You should stay here more," he said, grabbing another tool. "You still need to recover, and this isn't helping."

"I'm the one who can get out there the quickest."

"Sure. I can still get there pretty fast in my jet though."

I punched his arm. "This is non-negotiable. You know this is what I was built for."

"No, you weren't…" Apollo started, but before he could finish, my communicator beeped at me.

"Talk," I said, pulling it off of my belt.

"Eryn, I've got news." Celestina's voice came through, strong and clear, on the communicator.

"Good or bad?"

"Yes."

"Where?"

"Med bay."

"I'm on my way," I said, clipping the communicator back on my belt. "I'll see you later, okay? I know you're not happy about this, but I don't feel like I have any kind of choice right now."

"Fine, but we're finishing this later!" Apollo called after me as I slid off the ship and started heading toward the med bay.

After walking through the ever-growing number of people in the base, I made it to the med bay, where several of the beds were filled with injured or sick people. There was a line leading outside the door for the people getting check-ups.

"Hey," I said, waving over a staff member. "Where's Celestina?"

The staffer pointed to one of the isolation rooms, and I gave them my thanks as I headed over to the door.

I knocked, then pushed the door open.

These rooms were like the other isolation rooms. Bare, white, and sterile.

Celestina was inside, tending to an old woman in a wheelchair, who I recognized instantly.

"Mom," I said, crossing my arms. "About time you showed."

"I can't exactly move that fast, my dear," she said, turning her eyes on me. When she saw the bracers on my arms, her eyes widened. "Where did you get those?"

"Dad made them for me," I said, biting my lip to keep from sending biting words her way. "And while you're here, I want to ask: when were you going to tell me I wasn't entirely human?"

"What do you mean?"

"Don't play me, Mom," I said, feeling tears start to form in my eyes. "I saw the video. You and your brother. You merged me with a metal baby."

She sighed and looked at Celestina. To my surprise, Celestina gave my mom a cold glare and left the room.

"You weren't supposed to—"

"Why was it a secret? Is that why you pushed me so hard? Was I just an experiment to you?" I shot out, approaching her.

"No, let me explain—"

"You had twenty-five years to tell me, and you *kept* it from me. I want to know why."

She sighed. "I guess I was just a terrible mother. Your uncle and I… we had the same specialties. We always wanted to see how people would bond with nanite technology. However, animal experiments proved difficult, as most of the adults died from the procedure. The young animals, however, were able to survive."

"I don't care about that," I said, strongly considering throwing the pillow across the room but deciding against it and crossing my arms instead. "Aren't you going to apologize for using me as an experiment?"

"I'm sorry. I'm a terrible mother, I know—"

"Stop guilt-tripping me, Mom. Because yeah, that was crappy of you to use me as a science experiment. Do you understand how much this has shaken me? You're my mom. I love you, but how can I trust you after a lifetime of damage?"

"I wanted something better for you." My mom placed her hands in her lap. "At the time, I thought that was the right way to go about it. I was wrong about that, and you paid the price. I'm sorry. I take responsibility for keeping this from you and for doing this in the first place. I was told it would help our city, and so I made the choice. I should've chosen you."

I stared at her, then sat on the bed nearest to her. "Mom, I love you. I understand you thought it was the right thing to do—and it still hurt me in many ways. Thanks for your apology."

"Of course," she said, tears falling from her eyes. "I should have just cared for you. But there's something you do need to know."

"What?"

"Your uncle… he was raving on at that time. Said he found a miracle that would save everyone from the fire. After what we did to… to you, I destroyed the machine. So no other child would have to go through that. Your uncle went stark raving mad after I did that, saying I had just signed our death warrant."

I bit my lip and shook my head. "And do you know anything about why I was frozen? Does that have anything to do with this?"

My mom looked at me silently, tears leaking out of her eyes.

"It does have something to do with this," I said.

She nodded.

We sat in silence for a moment, until she wiped away her tears and spoke again. "Your uncle… Like I said, he was mad. After what you did to avenge your sister, he contacted me, demanding I give you to him, as half of you was his *property*. I was terrified and knew you couldn't go to him. So, I sent you to the military. I had an old friend who was a higher-ranking member in the CI. He got you in and protected you. But then…"

She stopped as the entire base began to shake and people started screaming.

I was moving before I could form a full thought, running through the crowds of screaming people to get to the hangar. Passing Theo as I ran, I grabbed his arm and hauled him along with me.

Upon reaching the hangar, I watched as waterfalls of sand fell into the hangar.

"What's going on?" I yelled, spotting Celestina and Apollo in the chaos.

Celestina spit out some sand. "The ships are landing!"

I looked up and saw two ships that looked exactly like the ones we were building landing outside the hatch.

Chapter 23

I climbed out of the hangar, leaping off our ship to land next to theirs. Beings that looked like Muroha were soon coming out of the ships, and three of them peeled off to walk toward me.

"Eryn?" one of them asked, their voice deeper and more crackly than Maesha's or Muroha's.

"That's me. I assume you all are the rescue wagon?" I replied, nodding at the ships next to us.

"Yes. When you are ready to load, we are ready to receive."

"Then let's get this moving."

* * *

I got multiple workers to help me build a system to load people on to the ships. Ythea and Maesha were invaluable in helping to move some of the less mobile, and within a few hours, we had filled both of the ships.

"Take off now," I said, walking with the being who had originally spoken to me. Their name was Unden. "We will take care of the rest and get these ships off as soon as we can."

They nodded. "Do so quickly. Your star has begun showing signs. Muroha estimates you have three days, at most."

I let out a breath. Three days. Until my home was gone.

"I understand," I said, nodding back. "Go. We'll catch up to you. Thank you for the coordinates."

"Of course. Stay safe."

They walked away, and I stood on the floor of the hangar as the ships closed and took off into the sky.

"Your mom is on one of those ships," Celestina said from behind me.

"Good," I replied, my voice barely louder than a whisper. "I couldn't lose her, too."

Celestina patted my shoulder, then left me to it.

I busied myself with finishing up the last ship, and then loading supplies once it was finished.

We'd had a strategy meeting a few days ago discussing this, and now, the time was here.

Looking around the base, I watched as the last of the supplies were loaded onto the third ship, and then we began directing the people in the base onto the ships.

By this time, the majority of the city had moved into the base, making it cramped and more difficult to work in. So we didn't have to worry about too many more people beyond those that were already here.

Soon, the first ship was full. We situated the crew, gave them the coordinates, and had them launch.

Night had fallen, and everyone was on edge. I had spread the word about the three-day limit, firmly believing that keeping it a secret would help no one. With significantly less people in the base, we all agreed to sleep for the night and load the last two ships in the morning.

As we all went off to our separate living quarters, Apollo joined me on the walk back to ours.

"Crazy, huh? To think we'll be leaving this place forever," Apollo said, reaching out for my hand.

I held his hand and let out a breath I didn't know I had been holding. "It's terrifying. We're leaving this place. Our home. Where we grew up. And it will all be torn to pieces by that black hole."

"It's definitely terrifying."

"That's an understatement," I snorted.

"I can't think of a better word."

I didn't say anything else but just held his hand. After all, I agreed with him. There wasn't really a word to describe the feeling of leaving your whole planet behind.

That night, I slept in Apollo's arms, curled into him, and the tears I shed were absorbed by his shirt.

The next morning, we awoke and quickly got to work. We took the rest of the stuff we might need and loaded it onto the two remaining ships.

As we started loading the remaining people onto the ships, I could feel the anxiety begin to crawl into my throat. This was it. The final days.

It seemed almost easy: to watch each person walk up the ramp, into the large silver ship that had taken weeks to build. Adults, covered in grease and sand, as we had discovered the running water wasn't running anymore last night.

The second ship was full.

"Are we ready?" Celestina asked, the last few people gathering in the hangar.

I looked around, and now the base felt… empty. After the two weeks of commotion, it was quiet.

Peaceful.

"I am," I whispered.

At that, everyone began loading onto the ship. Maesha and her two friends climbed into their own ship. We had made this plan days before, since we knew there were still people left in the city. Maesha's ship and I would stay beside the larger ship, protecting it. I would escort any people left onto the ship. Once we were done, I would load myself, and we would take off past the stars.

I flew upward, matching Maesha's ship in altitude. We waited as the ship launched, piloted by Apollo and Rubi, and led the way to the city.

The city was as quiet as the base. I spotted the wreck of the craft I had taken down the other day and forced myself to look away.

Shiny buildings were more visible than they had ever been, with their foliage dead around them. The water in the canals was still, and the speed rails sat, unused. We flew toward the center of the city. If there was anyone left, that's where they would be. We had checked everywhere else.

Then I saw them. Black dots on the streets. CI agents.

I flew down to get a closer look and saw them huddled together. Being closer to the street, I could also see what they were talking about.

Around the corner of a building sat a small ship, a quarter of the size of the ones we had built. I watched as men in suits walked into the ship, and some other men in CI gear kept other people from boarding.

I landed next to a group of them, and they stopped talking to stare at me.

"We have a ship. Free. Load up. Get everyone you can," I said, motioning toward the ship, which was very carefully landing on the street.

I quickly dashed from group to group, spreading the message. They all ran to the ship and climbed on, and once a few started to move, more and more followed.

The ones next to the other ship were even starting to turn and follow.

Getting a closer look at the ship, I felt the hair on the back of my neck raise. That ship didn't look safe.

I looked on as the last man in a suit climbed onto the ship and closed the door.

There was nothing I could do.

"Eryn, get in! We're getting bad readings!"

The voice from my communicator jolted me, and I glanced around for any more people. I was the only one left on the street.

I ran to the ship and clumped up the ramp, which closed behind me.

Making my way to the front of the ship, I stood behind Apollo as he guided the ship off from the surface and toward the stars.

The city started becoming smaller and smaller, and I felt tears form at the corners of my eyes as it disappeared.

As the ship broke through the atmosphere, we could see the other ships next to us. Maesha's ship tailed close to us, and the other, less well-made ship on the other side.

"Is that...?" Apollo asked, as we watched the ship that looked like a fancy tin can fly along beside us.

"Yeah," I said, and we watched as the ship slowly puttered to a stop.

"Do you think…"

I nodded. "Probably." The aircraft didn't look like it had been made well, and I was surprised that it had made it through the atmosphere. The people inside were probably already dead.

We sat in awkward silence as the ship flew past and away from the dead ship.

"What do we do now?" Celestina asked, sitting in the navigator's seat, off to my left.

They all looked at me.

"Set a course for the coordinates Unden gave us " I put my hand on Apollo's shoulder. "We head to a new home."

Bonus Content

Lorinia City's 25th Anniversary
2055

<u>Celebration Submission</u>

In celebration of the city's 25th anniversary, we remember also the tragedy that brought us here. When a world war broke out, many countries banded together, and we watched as half the world fell to bombings, starvation, and disease amidst the war.
We remember the short period of peace before disease swept through country after country, through people, animals, and plants, leaving people sick and starving.
The deaths of so many lead our leaders to band together and create Lorinia City, the last standing city on Earth. Provided all to us by our great leaders, who made us homes, gave us jobs, and most importantly, kept us safe.
This year, as we celebrate the 25th anniversary of the city's creation, we must not forget what happened that brought us here.
Never again should we be complacent in our own demise. Never again will the government lie to our faces. And never again will we be cornered into relying on the rich for survival.

The century soldier will rise.

-Anonymous

Coming Soon

Be sure to watch out for the sequel, "Safety in the Stars," coming soon!

Follow K.R. Quill:
TikTok: @krquill
Instagram: @cozykrquill
Twitch: @KRQuill

Other books include:
A Blood Savior - A sapphic, X-rated fantasy romance between a vampire and a witch. Can be found on Amazon.

Acknowledgments

There are many people who contributed to the creation of this book - without them, this book would not be in your hands.

Much thanks to Claire, my editor, who pointed out (nicely!) all of my grammar mistakes and caught a million continuity errors (cries in ADHD).

Thanks to my parents, who encouraged my hobby of writing long before I knew it would turn into this. Special thanks to my mom, who has beta read several of my stories, and who got me into reading in the first place.

Thanks to my partner, who was a never ending source of compliments and comfort when all I wanted to do was cry and pull my hair out (their shirt has also gotten tear-soaked).

Thanks to my friends, for encouraging me and cheering me on, and giving me ideas for things to add to my book. Special thanks to Markie, who created the wonderful cover for my book and made it everything I was picturing.

Thanks to my pets, Athena and Persephone, for forcing me to take breaks from hyperfixating on my writing. Mostly to go get food.

Thanks to my friends and mutuals on TikTok who helped me to create the cover reveal video - y'all are amazing and you really warmed this indie author's heart (literally, I cannot say thank you enough!).

And thanks to my many followers on TikTok and Instagram who were so excited for this book, and really pushed me to get it out into the world. Love you all!

About the Author

K.R. Quill (they/them) is an author, therapist, content creator, and streamer, with a never ending thirst for knowledge and learning. They have spent 12 years writing, and began publishing their works in 2023. Being neurodivergent, they wanted to create characters that captured the experience of not feeling like you fit in, so they and others can see themselves represented in diverse stories. In their day job, they help individuals, partners, and families in therapy, and find great joy in seeing people grow and heal. They are currently on their third degree (a PhD), and focus their research on neurodivergence, polyamory, and video gaming. They have two pets: a dog named Athena, and a cat named Persephone (yes, there is a trend), and live with their partner. In their spare time, they like to read, garden, cook, and play video games.

And, of course, write.